Professor Vertigo
A Novel

Dyan Elliott

Copyright © 2024 Dyan Elliot

All rights reserved.

No part of this book may be reproduced, stored in a retrieval system, or transmitted, in any form or by any means, electronic, mechanical, photocopying, recording, or otherwise, without prior written permission from the publisher, except for brief quotations embodied in critical reviews and certain other noncommercial uses permitted by copyright law.

ISBN: [978-1-964513-20-1]

For Dori

Chapters

Chapter 1: Lifeboat 1

Chapter 2: Dial "D" for Department 10

Chapter 3: Notorious 24

Chapter 4: Secret Agent 38

Chapter 5: Rear Window 47

Chapter 6: The Trouble with Hanif 62

Chapter 7: Jamaica Inn 70

Chapter 8: The Wrong Man 83

Chapter 9: (Not) Young and Innocent 96

Chapter 10: Strangers on a Train 105

Chapter 11: Shadow of a Doubt 115

Chapter 12: The Lady Vanishes 129

Chapter 13: The Man Who Knew Too Much 136

Chapter 14: Saboteur 153

Chapter 15: Psycho 164

Chapter 16: Sabotage 177

Chapter 17: Woman to Woman 190

Chapter 18: It Takes A Thief 200

Chapter 19: Frenzy 209

Chapter 20: Stage Fright 219

Chapter 21: The Skin Game 229

Chapter 22: Murder! 235

Chapter 23: Suspicion 242

Chapter 24: Vertigo 248

Chapter 24: Spellbound 263

Chapter 25: Bon Voyage..275
Acknowledgements 283

Chapter 1: Lifeboat

Do you think that psychotherapy helps? Perhaps you'll say no: Freud's critics never tire of reminding us that he never cured anyone. On this point, I'm agnostic, though I have to admit that his so-called talking cure never did much for me. You shouldn't take this to mean that I've no aptitude for the process. I'm a virtuoso, in fact. I could talk for fifty minutes without prompting — revealing my foibles, analyzing my motives, second-guessing my actions, providing every indication of progress — all without receiving any benefit. Meanwhile, my audience, the pliant therapist, would be none the wiser. My stellar lack of headway in therapy is not surprising. Like most academics, I over-analyze everything, including me. I should also add that I suspect I'm smarter than most of the therapists I've encountered, as churlish as this may sound. So why assume that a therapist would necessarily have more insight into my problems than I do?

Then, one day, after a taxing and costly bout of simulated self-discovery, I called a friend who happened to be a therapist.

Me: Tell me, is Freud right? Are we basically hardwired by the age of seven and incapable of change?

Therapist Friend: I wouldn't put it like that. But I would say that certain patterns are in place that make it difficult.

Me: That sounds like hardwiring to me. Is there any therapy that works on the hardwiring?

Therapist Friend: Three years of meditation at an ashram.

Me: Seriously.

Therapist Friend: Maybe EMDR. It's supposed to mess with your subconscious.

And that's exactly what I was looking for: a mental gizmo that would slap around my id and fluff up my ego. So, I read up on EMDR: Eye Movement Desensitization and Reprogramming. The basic premise was that the REM (rapid eye movement) during the dream state helps the patient "work through" their problems. EMDR attempts to simulate the REM cycle. All the patient has to do is track the regular back-and-forth movement of a light with their eyes while focusing on their problem. EMDR was great for trauma, effecting some stunning successes with veterans suffering from post-traumatic stress. But, theoretically, its application was not restricted to capital T trauma: it could also be applied to more modest ordeals. For instance, imagine that your shitty relationship with your father was the threshold to a muted self-esteem and a broad-spectrum mistrust of men, compounded by an unfathomable desire to have a man of your very own. EMDR might be just the thing. At least, this was the hope. It began primarily as a West Coast phenomenon, and I wondered if it'd spread to the Midwest. Persistent inquiry turned up a few dabblers, but there was only one officially licensed practitioner in the entire state: Dr. Owen. And there you have it.

Every Tuesday at 2:00 p.m., I would drive twenty miles along a country road, passing the ski resort that had never gotten off the ground; an orchard that advertised not one, but two varieties of delicious apple; three flea markets in a row; and five Evangelical churches — all with parking lots the size of an office block. It was after I'd passed the church with the neon cross that I began to look for the mailbox. I'd make a left and maneuver my way up a driveway with devilish switchbacks, trying not to be distracted by the pond on my right, with its bolts of aquamarine light. I'd park, enter the house, climb a flight of stairs, and knock on the door.

"Come in," he'd say.

We'd nod at each other in a circumspect, but polite manner, before I sank into the sad leather chair that always gave out the same tired sigh. The room would dim for the light show: a green light skating along what appeared to be a giant flute. I'd stare at the light while Dr. Owen repeated what'd been my father's favorite maxim about me for as long as I can remember.

"She has a mean, malicious streak in her; I don't know where she gets it from."

Perhaps not an optimal remark for a daughter to hear. But it only morphed into a trauma-inducing utterance when it migrated from the privacy of our dining room to a public forum. I was in third grade, and it was parents' night. We were all arrayed in our very best. I remember being tired: my mother had woken me up in the middle of the night to rag-tie my hair in ringlets, which now dangled around my shoulders like a mobile of cigars. I could still smell the beer she'd used to set the curls. We sat at our desks, eyes darting like munchkin merchants purveying specimens of exemplary penmanship. Meanwhile, Miss Fiddler made the rounds. She'd stop and speak to discrete sets of parents positioned stolidly behind a son or daughter, always as if the son or daughter wasn't there. Miss Fiddler's eyes narrowed as she approached my parents with purpose. Dispensing with any pleasantries, she launched into a recital of a recent altercation that had occurred between me and one of my classmates — one that, I admit, didn't show me to advantage. My dad's response was immediate:

"She has a mean, malicious streak in her; I don't know where she gets it from."

I didn't flinch but kept looking straight ahead at some vanishing point on the blackboard.

My father pretended mystification at the origins of my mean, malicious streak, but already in the third grade, I had a theory. I had come to recognize that one of Dad's greatest pleasures was to set me up. Was he simply teasing, or were his interventions actively malicious? You'll have to decide. All I know is that he was a relentless source of misinformation and mayhem. When I was in first grade and asked him a question about amphibians for science class, he told me that all frogs were male and all toads were female — information that I duly regurgitated on the quiz. Second grade was worse, probably (I realize retrospectively) because he had a thing for my teacher, Miss Pedheary, with her long legs and very short skirts. Dad was constantly getting me to ask her questions like whether she had a boyfriend or if she knew how to do the Hustle. Then there was the sleepover at our house when he said that my girlfriend and I were behaving "like a couple of lesbians." We suspended our pillow fight long enough to ask what a lesbian was (maybe someone who engaged in pugnacious pillow fights?), but he told me to ask Miss Pedheary. My question was rewarded with an inscrutable look. When Miss Pedheary inquired how I came by this term, I referenced my father, adding that he had expressly recommended that I apply to her. *Go ask your father,* she snapped. (I did, but to no avail.) Yet, it didn't occur to me that my father's puzzling interventions in my schooling may have been spiteful until that fateful parents' night the following year when he made Miss Fiddler acquainted with my mean, malicious streak.

Dr. Owen would begin our sessions with the "mean, malicious streak" mantra while I watched the light, and we would take it from there. Sometimes, when the sessions were over, he'd give me homework, which usually amounted to raking through my past feelings of rejection and putting them in some kind of order. Such efforts helped Dr. Owen cobble together a superior trauma script for future use.

Considering the source of my lower-case trauma, you might imagine that I'd prefer a female therapist, and you'd be right. Failing that, I wouldn't have minded a stand-in for Montgomery Clift in the movie *Freud*: I could be his hysterical Susannah York and watch as he furrowed his classic brow in perplexity. But what I got was Dr. Owen — a fifty-something psychiatrist working out of his home in the woods. Although no Montgomery Clift, he had an intelligent, if jowly, face. My chief complaint was that the buttons on his shirt never seemed quite up to the task; I always had the sense that there was an unruly belly in there, struggling to get out. This gave me the impression that he was a Republican.

Are all Republicans out of shape, you might ask? No, probably not. But a lot of the ones I'd seen on TV at Trump rallies were, and they seemed to be unapologetic about it. A Democrat would probably be more self-conscious and regard an unruly gut as something of a shortcoming. Of course, Dr. Owen could be an Independent. I didn't know any Independents, so a stereotypic image of their physical type eluded me — though I did imagine most of them holding guns. Thank God he wore an undershirt. But I digress. Although Dr. Owen may not be the shrink to fulfil my transference fantasies, it did matter to me that he was a psychiatrist and not just some social worker who realized that they could get $150/hour by hanging out a shingle. OK, so I'm an academic snob. Shoot me.

As I drove away, I attempted to take stock of my progress. Not good. After almost a year, I still felt rejected, disappointed, and destined for a life of involuntary celibacy. OK, that might be a misleading self-descriptor, given the recent emergence of the "incel" movement. Let the record show that I'm not a disaffected, youthful white male with a propensity for racism, misogyny, and mass murder. Perhaps the old-fashioned word "spinster" would better describe what I am: the "surplus" woman who once dominated the textile industry without any reasonable expectation of finding a husband. Over time, the word "spinster" came to be associated with prudishness — the rationale being that a single woman with no plausible opportunity for marriage would naturally become alienated from all matters sexual. Admittedly, I'm not a good fit for the spinster stereotype. I've had bouts of promiscuity, and although I have been known to quilt, my needlework is distinctly lackluster. Even so, I seem to have unwittingly gravitated toward a profession in which middle-aged women, with no hope of a heterosexual relationship in sight, abound. If you think this is an unduly pessimistic vision of my romantic prospects, let me assure you that it has met with professional corroboration. When I told Dr. Owen that it was unlikely that I would ever have another relationship with a man at my age, he agreed.

"It's good to be realistic. Most divorced men in their forties gravitate toward younger women." He said this without looking up from whatever he was writing.

The moment Dr. Owen had seconded my angst, I realized that I'd been hoping for an encouraging contradiction. I need to stop doing that. It's like when I forgot myself and asked a certain female friend *Does this dress make me look fat?* — forgetting said friend's penchant for "honesty." Bitch. But more to the point: what's the use of entrusting myself to EMDR to resolve my vexed relations with the men of my past if there's no possibility of men in my future?

I thought about my psychological non-progress all the way to campus. It was the first day of classes for a new academic year. I'd given the introductory lecture for my course *Medieval Sex* in the morning. But the graduate student who'd initially been assigned to me as Teaching Assistant was given her own course at the last minute, and there was a scramble. I was meeting her replacement this afternoon for the first time. All I knew was that her name was Dawn Cather. I wondered if Cather could be a variant spelling of Cathar. If so, that might be a good omen: the Cathars were my favorite heretics.

There was a knock on the door. I called *Come in*, but nothing happened. When I opened the door, I discovered a tall, rather solid-looking woman with oily dark hair and bad skin, wearing a muumuu of sorts. I'd place her at somewhere around thirty-five. Clearly, a mature or returning student. She looked annoyed to be there.

"You must be Dawn. I'm Heather Bell," I said, holding out my hand.

Her hands remained stubbornly at her sides.

"I'd prefer to be called Ms. Cather, if you don't mind." It was on the tip of my tongue to say that I preferred Heather, but settled for asking her to sit down. When my door began swinging inward, as it always did, Ms. Cather jumped up in alarm.

"Just leave it," I said. "It always does that."

But Ms. Cather was not prepared to leave it. She went up and down the hallway until she located a rubber door stop and began energetically stuffing it under the miscreant door. I hoped that asking about her work would put her at ease. But she was not very forthcoming. All I got out of her was that she was a Shakespearean, writing a dissertation on the Bard's oblique references to bowel movements. There was an uncomfortable silence, by which I mean that it was uncomfortable for me. Except in the bosom of friends, my threshold for silence is low. I decided to follow up on her name, asking if she might be of French descent. She shook her head.

"The reason I ask is that there was a Cathar heresy in southern France in the twelfth century. They believed the world was created by Satan and that humans were spirits trapped in material bodies. Naturally, they were against sex in any form."

I began to tell Ms. Cather about their theology and their rituals but soon discerned a certain impatience for my narrative. Fiddling with her oversized backpack, she didn't bother to feign even a polite interest. I'm not an invariably quick study. Neither am I an idiot. After a short interval, I realized that Ms. Cather was the type of person who disdained the conventional niceties, so I got down to business. I gave her a syllabus, explained her responsibilities as Teaching Assistant, which were primarily to lead discussion groups and grade papers, and gave her a stack of desk copies. (Retrospectively, I wish I'd told her that it was part of the job to look interested during my lectures.) Ms. Cather was taking copious notes while I talked, which, considering the pedestrian information I was imparting, struck me as a little strange. By way of conclusion, I said: "Sometimes my Teaching Assistants have wanted to give lectures in the course. If any particular topic appeals to you, please let me know."

Ms. Cather only stared at me.

"Is there anything wrong?" I asked. She didn't say anything. I added, "Of course, you're under no obligation to lecture. It's just some graduate students are eager to give it a try. It's good experience, and I could write a better letter about their teaching." When there was still no response, I said, "It's totally up to you."

Silence. At this point, I asked if she had any questions.

"Yes, I was wondering about triggers," Ms. Cather said. I'd just been talking to a colleague in Charlotte, who literally dodged a bullet in the recent campus shooting and was about to reassure Ms. Cather that there was zero tolerance for guns on campus. Then I realized that she was referring to trigger warnings: alerting students ahead of time if there was any disturbing material in the course that might induce trauma.

"I wouldn't worry about that. A topic like *Medieval Sex* is probably warning enough to anyone triggered by sexual references," I said.

But Ms. Cather clearly didn't agree. "I was a part of the group of students at Wellesley College who successfully lobbied to have a statue of a nude man removed in case it triggered memories of sexual assault." The mulish look on her face implied that she had scored some major moral victory over me.

"I read about the case. The figure wasn't nude but wearing underwear. It was supposed to be a man sleepwalking." I remember being annoyed that a good school could be forced into this degree of pandering.

"Even so…"

I stopped her: "To be honest, I agree with the *AAUP* on this one. Trigger warnings are anti-intellectual and infantilizing. You could even argue that many of them are antifeminist, perpetuating the myth of female fragility."

"*AAUP*?" she queried.

"American Association of University Professors."

We stared at one another for about thirty seconds in silence. I again asked if she had any questions, and she shook her head. There was a departmental meeting at four, so I told Ms. Cather that it was a pleasure to meet her and would see her at the lecture on Thursday. She nodded and lumbered off without the usual "Nice to meet you too" or "I'm looking forward to working with you." There was something to be said for social hypocrisy.

Chapter 2: Dial "D" for Department

Most of my colleagues claim to hate departmental meetings, as do I. Yet privately, I savor these meetings for their performative elements. It was like watching a company of classically trained actors, each of whom had mastered one role: we all played ourselves to perfection.

Here's a general rundown of our average meeting. The Chair would make a few announcements (e.g., "The toilets keep backing up. Everyone is limited to two squares per visit *no matter what*" or "Does anyone want to volunteer to teach a course at the state penitentiary?"). Then came the committee reports: an *ad hoc* committee for reviewing joint appointments has rejected a candidate from Religious Studies (who specializes in the Puritan minister/theologian Wigglesworth and his struggle with nocturnal emissions) for a third year in a row; in response to cutbacks on student funding, the Director of Graduate Studies proposes that we pass out applications to needy students for lucrative part-time jobs as driving instructors and bartenders; the subcommittee on working conditions sent a memo to physical plant about the lethal level of asbestos in the building's insulation some six months ago, and have yet to hear back. Then, the floor was open, and the fun began.

A: *Any news about salaries? We haven't had a cost of living raise in over four years.*

B: *The university doesn't care about teaching. You have to churn out books at the expense of teaching to get rewarded.*

B's comment would so seamlessly overlap with A's that she never bothered to raise her hand. Their timing was perfect. But they were married and, I assume, practiced their interventions at home.

C: *What about creative writers? We teach our asses off and make a pittance.*

D: *As head of the executive committee, I should remind you that our priority is diversity — both in hiring and recruiting students — not salaries.*

E: *Let me play the devil's advocate here. Wouldn't we be able to hire better people with enhanced salaries and thus recruit a more diverse student body?*

At this point, F, who always flapped his tie rather than raising his hand, would say: *Move to adjourn.*

It was like the joke about prison after lights out when the inmates take turns shouting out numbers, which would make everyone laugh. Each number represented a joke that'd been told so many times that the number alone sufficed. If we could all just agree to using preassigned numbers, we'd save time without sacrificing any of the hilarity.

I entered the familiar classroom — a joyless battleship grey. My colleagues were seated in generic folding chairs equipped with armrests along one side, which always looked too small for adults. It was as if they'd been surprised by sudden growth spurts and gotten stuck. I nodded at the several colleagues who bothered to smile at me. The departmental Chair was standing tentatively at the front of the room, looking out of place. Poor Jan. She hadn't wanted to be Chair. Not now, not ever. But this well-known aversion anointed her as more trustworthy than the members of the department who wanted to be Chair, and I was part of the cohort that coerced her into accepting.

This was the first meeting of the academic year. The semester began in late August, before Labor Day, making August a top contender for the cruelest month. The weather was tropical, but without ocean breezes or even an ocean, Jan, who was generally immaculately groomed, was slowly coming undone. Her hair, styled in what we used to call a page boy (think Anna Wintour or, better still, Prince Valiant), hung limply around her face. Her cream-colored linen suit, crisp a few hours ago, looked like it had been worn to pilates; the seam at the back had begun to migrate toward her left side, simulating a hip replacement gone wrong. She kept clearing her throat, glancing at the clock over the door. At the stroke of four, she began to speak, beginning with a strained witticism about a "warm welcome." When nobody laughed, I offered a supportive guffaw and was rewarded with a familiar look of contempt from our former Chair. He was a sour-looking man who'd had a stick surgically inserted up his ass long ago when he was accepted at Harvard. I smiled back at him.

Jan cleared her throat again. She was one of my best friends, certainly my best friend in the department, but this nervous tick of hers always brought to mind Dora's troublesome "catarrh." Freud attributed Dora's catarrh (aka cough) to her unacknowledged masturbatory habits.

"Now, I want to take this opportunity to greet our two new assistant professors. Would they please stand up?"

Two people dutifully arose, looking impossibly young amid the sea of older faces.

"I know you don't need any reminder," but it seemed like Jan did since she began searching her pocket for notes. Ah, she found them.

"Hanif Twist works with animals and our queer connections to them." Animals. About ten years ago, a colleague confided in me that she really wanted to work with animals. From her confessional tone, I assumed she intended to leave academe to join a circus or start an animal shelter. But now I knew better. Animals were still trending upward, and Hanif's dissertation was at the forefront of animal studies. Even so, there had been some misgivings about Hanif's hire.

His talk was highly theoretical, and most of my older colleagues couldn't follow. Another faction feared that, with his degree of cool, he would only stay in the department for a couple of years. This struck me as a reasonable fear. I knew Hanif from the conference circuit. Even as a graduate student, he was something of a rock star, making timely interventions about any and all questions of gender and sexuality. I remember once at the Berkshire Conference on the History of Women when Hanif reduced a panel of eminent feminists to tears for their retrograde tendency to perceive gender in terms of binaries. In another session, he kicked around a venerable doyenne of Women's Studies for invoking the term patriarchy.

    His occasional mistreatment of seniors aside, Hanif was a captivating presence. His name reflected his interesting mixed parentage. His American father met his Palestinian mother when he was on an archaeological dig in the Middle East. Hanif was medium height — maybe five foot eight — and slender. His eyes were perhaps his most notable feature: large, green, luminescent, and fringed with long dark lashes. They did protrude slightly, however, making me wonder if he had a hyperactive thyroid. Maybe. He also had a large nose. A woman in his situation might have told everybody that she had a deviated septum and then covertly gotten a nose job. Even so, Hanif's proboscis was a shapely one. In the right light, you might call it aquiline. He obviously wasn't self-conscious about it, or why would he brush his dark hair directly back from his face? But if not exactly handsome, Hanif was most assuredly sexy. The timber of his voice clinched it — a mellifluous and sensuous baritone. He was more than a decade my junior.

    Our paths had frequently crossed at professional events, and we had often been thrown together at receptions, collective meals, or for drinks. I always felt as if he were watching me, trying to catch my eye whenever something stupid, pretentious, or covertly comical was said. It was like he considered me his co-conspirator, but the conspiracy lacked content. Shouldn't a co-conspirator be in on the conspiracy? I was teeming with ideas for promoting chaos: streaking the conference's plenary address, mixing up the banquet nametags to seat archenemies cheek by jowl, interrupting the book prize ceremony by denouncing the winner as a plagiarist and identifying myself as the true winner.

But maybe there was no conspiracy. Maybe he was singling me out (if indeed he was) because he was attracted to me. Let me state for the record that he had never made a pass at me. This was hardly surprising. He was, after all, a graduate student until fairly recently. Of course, it was always possible that he was looking at me the way you might look at a venerable dowager, like Maggie Smith in *Downton Abbey*, wondering *how does she manage to hold herself together*. Or maybe he wasn't looking at me at all: maybe those strange eyes of his followed everyone around like the *Mona Lisa*. Perhaps I only thought Hanif was looking at me because I found it difficult to look at anyone else when he was in the room, and he was simply looking back with bewilderment (and possible distaste). But then I comforted myself that, since he was probably gay, he would simply mistake me for a fag hag.

Hanif was unassailably stylish. Today he was wearing black high-tops, elegant jeans (with one artful slit above the left knee), and a black unlined jacket worn casually over a blue T-shirt with "David Bowie" written in red. His face was accented by fashionable stubble. He nodded as if to acknowledge Jan's introduction and offered a dazzling smile before sitting down. Oh, I forgot: he had beautiful teeth.

"April Fortune wrote her dissertation on Jane Austen and the supernumerary woman." A topic after my own heart, and then there's her name. *What a great name for a stripper. I'm voting for her!* Or so I said when we were discussing the finalists for the Romantic hire. The departmental Chair at the time (the same one who scowled at me at the beginning of the meeting) looked at me with disgust. I suspect it was he who reported my *bon mot* to the Dean. At least, that's what I assumed when I received an email the next day about offensive speech acts. The Bureau of Social Equity also sent me a list of *do-nots*. I hung it on my door with a dangling red pencil, taking great pleasure in ostentatiously checking off an item every time I transgressed.

But once I saw April and talked to her, it was impossible to imagine her giving anyone a lap dance. She was the epitome of professionalism: a *don't fuck with me* expression on her face that also managed to convey a certain *politesse*. Although nowhere near as stylish as Hanif, she had a certain savvy. She was what the French might term a *jolie laide* — someone with plain features who nevertheless managed to persuade the world she was attractive. Today, she was sporting an asymmetrical haircut, Fluevog shoes, and glasses with thick red frames. She gave us an airy wave, exuding an idiosyncratically hip kind of academic know-how.

An uneasy interlude followed. There were three chairs positioned side by side at the front of the classroom. Clearly, we were expecting guests. We waited, quietly engaging in desultory conversation among ourselves about what we had done over the summer recess. The minutes ticked by. Jan glanced at the clock for the umpteenth time: it was now almost a quarter past the hour. She cleared her throat again and opened her mouth as if to speak when suddenly the door flew open. Three people burst into the room exuberantly. Two were in their late twenties – one was a woman with long blonde hair and a flowing pink sundress that accented her slender elegance; the other was trans, rather stocky, with slicked-back hair. They were wearing dark trousers with a crease and scuffed Doc Martens. These two performed what can only be described as a military maneuver until they were successfully flanking the third person — a woman who was more or less my age and clearly in charge. To be frank, she was a bit scary. With her wire-frame glasses and iron-colored hair, it looked like she'd been sent by the local Politburo.

"We are representatives of the Bureau for Social Equity," she said.

So, I was close. This was the office that handled charges of sexual abuse, harassment, and gender discrimination. She spoke in resounding, plummy tones; you had to admire the way she rolled her r's.

"My name is Sally Field," she said without cracking a smile, "and these are my two

assistants, Phil," nodding toward Doc Martens, "and Wanda" smiling at the winsome sylph.

"We understand that there has been a recent incident in the department," she continued.

We all spun around to look at Joffrey — our indefatigable lech. Who the hell had he been hitting on over the summer? But rather than looking away, as one might expect, Joffrey returned our collective gaze with an indignant glare. He had recently had laser surgery and didn't wear glasses anymore. Not a good move. His eye sockets seemed uncommonly deep. Is it possible that people who have worn glasses since their youth develop regressive sockets?

"We're here to role play about boundary issues," Sally Field said.

She proceeded to clap her hands. Wanda and Phil scurried into formation, sitting down with the third chair between them.

"I am a first-year graduate student who has been assigned as a Research Assistant to the

celebrated Professor Y," said Wanda.

"And I am Professor Y, who is working on an important Lacanian reading of Edgar Allan

Poe," said Phil, speaking in gruff tones. They then took a short pipe from their shirt pocket and pretended to smoke.

Another hand clap from Sally, and the performance began.

Professor Y: *It's gratifying to know that we will be working together. I was impressed by your CV. You're very well qualified (Phil said with a leer, eying Wanda up and down).*

Grad Student: *Professor Y, this is the opportunity of a lifetime. I am enthralled by your work.*

Professor Y: *I'm afraid you'll find me a merciless taskmaster. I plan to work you very hard.*

The professor spoke through clenched teeth with the protruding pipe. The word "hard" was accompanied by the disturbing wink of a Shakespearean bawd.

Grad Student: *I'm not afraid. I'm here to learn from you.*

Another hand clap from Sally. The performers freeze. *Three weeks pass,* she says. Clap, clap. At this point, Professor Y moves over one seat so his thigh is actually touching the thigh of the graduate student.

Professor Y: *I have a very rigid deadline. You and I will have to work together late into*

the night.

Grad Student: *Your wish is my command.*

Clap, clap. And the performers freeze.

Standing to one side of her performers, the bureau chief turned to her captive audience.

"Why is this scenario unsuitable?"

No one spoke.

"Come on, there are no wrong answers!" Sally Field said in cajoling tones.[Theatrical *Beat*.]

"Well, for one thing, nobody's doing Lacanian readings of Poe anymore," someone eventually piped up. The speaker had written just such a study over a decade ago, and the subject was already past its sell-by-date then.

"Not my field," said Sally Field to some slight titters. Her eyes narrowed ever so slightly: she was beginning to perceive us as a difficult group. "Anything else?" she asked.

"We haven't been allowed to smoke in this building for fifteen years, much less smoke a pipe."

This from our resident specialist on D.H. Lawrence, whom I had once referred to as Mellors. The allusion was to the lean, well-muscled groundkeeper who was the discreet object of Lady Chatterley's desire. Our Mellors hadn't aged well, but the vintage members of the female faculty still called him that in private. Mellors, who hadn't said a word in a departmental meeting for at least a decade, was probably moved by the sight of the pipe. He carefully examined the nicotine stains on his fingers as he spoke.

Clearly, many of the senior faculty didn't understand the concept of role-playing, instead embarking on their own versions of *Where's Waldo?* Kind of sweet, really.

"True, but I was thinking more of the overall situation," replied Sally Field with a strained smile.

"Is the graduate student keeping track of her hours? It's stated very clearly in their contract that they're not supposed to work more than 20 hours a week," queried the Director of Graduate Studies. Last year, he had received several complaints from over-worked students whose teaching was interfering with their studies in bartending.

Our interlocuter was getting a little impatient.

"Good point. But I'm referring to the elephant in the room: something very obvious that we avoid talking about."

Meanwhile, the strain was showing on the frozen performers, who were beginning to twitch.

"Anything else?" she asked.

How to account for such radio silence? Easy: half of my colleagues didn't know the answer, while the rest of us found the situation so outrageously funny that we were afraid to speak.

"I'm afraid you may need to tell us," said Jan in an apologetic tone.

Sally Field looked at us derisively. Then she clapped once and barked, "At ease." The two performers gratefully scooted away from one another, leaving the third chair between them empty.

"Professor Y has no business asking *any* graduate student, especially a female one, to work late into the night with him," Sally Field said in clipped tones.

"Excuse me. Didn't he say that he had an important deadline?" objected Mellors, clearly emboldened by his first intervention.

Ignoring this, she continued: "Nor had he any business sitting so close."

"Let me play the devil's advocate," said Martin, our Spenserian — who clearly thought he knew a thing or two about the devil since he always brought him up. "What if they were attending a play together and were seated next to one another?"

Sally Field made that condescending clicking noise with her tongue. "That sounds like a date. He has no business going on a date with a graduate assistant."

"Even if she wants to go?" Silence. "OK, a lecture on Poe, then?"

At this point, I shot a furtive glance at our two new colleagues, wondering how this Q and A was going over. Hanif was having the time of his life: he had a broad grin on his face and was furiously taking notes. April, however, was looking apprehensive. She'd had more than one job offer and was doubtless wondering if she'd made the wrong choice.

Sally Field made no effort to disguise her impatience.

"What we're witnessing here is the myopia of an aging professoriate. They've never left school; they've been here forever, and they're totally unaware of the passing of time. They don't realize that they're no longer young." Then, exasperated, Sally slipped into the second person. "Graduate students aren't your peers! You're older than their parents, so stop fooling yourselves! No student would choose to accompany you anywhere were it not for the power of your position and the pressure she feels. She would be much more comfortable with an empty seat between you — maybe a row of seats!"

Sally Field wasn't the sharpest knife in the drawer, but at least she wasn't wasting our time with prevarication.

Joffrey spoke up: "I find this entire performance offensive. It seems to imply that such 'boundary issues' are restricted to male faculty. Surely, that's not invariably the case." Joffrey offended? That's funny.

The question flustered Sally Field. "Of course not. But in the spirit of the role-playing here…"

Before she could finish, Louise, who was our departmental Title IX liaison[1] with the Bureau of Social Equity, came to her commander's aid. "In the vast majority of the cases, it's a male faculty member who's at fault."

"What about the recent suit against New York University?" called out an aggrieved male voice, anxious to defend his sex. "The defendant in question was a female prof…." But Jan was too fast for him. She jumped up and exclaimed:

"Let's hear it for our spirited performers!" Tepid applause. Jan turned to Sally Field, cleared her throat and said: "Thanks so much. This was very illuminating." And then, in almost the same breath: "Meeting adjourned!"

When I bumped into Hanif on the way out, he was still chuckling to himself. He asked me whether the Bureau's performance was intended to elicit a confession — like in *Hamlet*. If so, was this strategy especially tailored to the English Department? Before I could answer, a stream of students exiting a lecture hall pressed us against the wall.

---

[1] Title IX was a law introduced in 1972 to address gender discrimination in public education. Initially it was mostly focused on funding inequities in female athletics but has expanded exponentially to accommodate anything to do with gender bias, sexual harassment, and beyond.

We were standing so close together that I could feel his breath against my cheek.

My pheromones were beginning to creep out of their mothballs when Jan interrupted, placing her hand on my arm, and said, "We have to talk." I gave Hanif my version of a fetching smile, which probably translated as randy, and left. I trailed behind Jan up multiple flights to her office. (She never takes the elevator, which is why her ass is better than mine. At least, that's one reason.) During my breathless ascent, I replayed the encounter with Hanif in my head as if I were a teenager. He was taller than me: could he see my roots growing in? Could he tell there was some grey? I wish I'd worn different pants. I'd forgotten that these ones tended to crawl up my crack when it was hot, and I'd been sitting for a while. Did he watch me walk away? Maybe I should ask him out to dinner. It would be a friendly gesture from a senior colleague, after all. But it might also look pathetic. Maybe an intimate dinner party for several colleagues, *chez moi*? That would probably mean inviting April Fortune as well, and I didn't need the competition.

My reverie ended the moment I stepped into Jan's office. She closed the door more loudly than usual and leaned against it.

"I hate you," she hissed.

"I'm sorry," I replied.

"Why couldn't you have been Chair?" she asked.

"Because the department would never have nominated me. And, if they had, the Dean would've nixed it," I replied

Jan nodded in listless agreement, pushing back her hair.

"But then why didn't you let Louise be Chair?" Jan asked. Interestingly, Louise was not just the Title IX liaison, but the only person in our department who had first-hand experience with Title IX. She was brought up on charges when she failed all the members of the female basketball team who missed her final exam, even though they were in the playoffs and had been excused by the college. What made this a classic Title IX case was not just that it involved female athletes but that it was widely known that Louise would never have taken parallel action against members of the male basketball team, of which she was an ardent fan. My point is that Louise was a moron who would've made a disastrous Chair.

"Would you really want Louise to be Chair?" The question was purely rhetorical. Gloom-encrusted silence ensued. "Come on, let me buy you a drink," I said. I'd watched *The Horse Whisperer* on cable the night before and was imitating Robert Redford's cajoling tones.

But Jan found it impossible to defer gratification for that long. She'd already opened her desk drawer and was pulling out a bottle of scotch with two Styrofoam cups, pouring liberal shots. Quickly knocking back the first drink, Jan poured herself another. Then she began to loosen up. We talked about this and that: the status of her divorce proceedings (slow), the progress of my therapy (slower), her visit to Tulsa to see her mother (bad), and my visit to Chicago to see mine (worse). Then, I cut to the chase.

"Jan, why did you invite Sally Field and her troop? Our new colleagues must feel like they're trapped in some horny geriatric hell."

"There's been an incident. The Dean insisted that I discuss it with the department right away," Jan said fretfully.

"Even so, Sally Field…,"

"Is what the Dean recommended."

I nodded. The Dean looked like someone who'd get hard watching *The Flying Nun*.

I shook my head with disgust. "I just don't see the point," I said. "Joffrey hasn't scored in years. The graduate students just ignore him."

"But it's not Joffrey. It's Sylvia!"

So, this asinine vignette had been staged for the benefit of our departmental icon, Sylvia Thourelle, who hadn't even bothered to attend the meeting.

"And it's not a graduate student, either. It's an undergraduate!" Jan continued.

I was tempted to say *I told you so* but restrained myself. All I said was, *Yikes*. As I helped myself to another scotch, Jan picked up the phone and began to order a pizza. (*Margherita*, I hissed. She shook her head, pointing at her midriff. I had forgotten that tomatoes upset her stomach. *OK, but no pepperoni!*)

We were settling in for the evening.

Chapter 3: Notorious

It turned out that Jan didn't know any of the details about the so-called incident involving Sylvia Thourelle, but, as always, the less we knew, the more we had to say, and we spent at least two hours in her office speculating. *Who is Sylvia*, you might wonder? The answer to that question takes us back three years to when our university launched a graduate program in Rhetoric designed to develop expertise in writing and communication skills. The prevailing rationale was that a degree in Rhetoric would uniquely position graduates for jobs in the public sector: government, non-profits, public relations and human resources, publishing, entrepreneurial freelance. You name it. Granted, rhetoric had worked for Cicero, but I was still skeptical. Skills in writing and communications were what the Humanities were known for, so why introduce an option that would only exacerbate dropping enrollments? Why not beef up graduate programs in traditional fields?

But everyone else seemed to have gone gaga for the new program. Because it was meant to be interdisciplinary, it did not have its own faculty — instead drawing on the strengths of other departments. In the first few years of the program's inauguration, the administration attempted to make several big splashy hires, and our department lobbied hard to ensure that at least one of these rhetorical celebrities had their home in English.

We prevailed, and the upshot was Sylvia Thourelle. In the beginning, I supported her hire, albeit with some misgivings. I supported it because she was smart. Very smart. But I'd never liked her much. My reasons were, admittedly, petty. It all started with a conference where Thourelle gave a paper on Augustine's *The Teacher* — a dialogue between Augustine and his son, Adeodatus. Thourelle made the specious claim that no one could really understand the dialogue without acknowledging its dark, incestuous subtext. Poor Augustine had a sorry enough legacy without Thourelle insisting (with no credible evidence) that he abused his son. I objected: the two of us went back and forth on the feasibility of an erotic relationship between father and son until we were shut down by the moderator. We continued arguing en route to the afternoon reception, though our point of contention mysteriously morphed into an altercation over obtaining the desirable degree of redness in one's hair.

"I've used henna since I was twenty-five. I like it because it's not a dye; it's natural," I said.

"Henna is totally a dye. It fried my hair," responded Thourelle.

"I don't believe that. It's a harmless herb!" I insisted.

"Harmless — just like tobacco," Thourelle sneeered.

It seemed like a low blow since I did, in fact, smoke back in those days. My anger mounted, and I felt that familiar spike of energy as my heroic warp spasm descended upon me.[2] I advanced on Thourelle, who cowered against the banquette. Fortunately, a group of well-wishers swooped down and separated us.

The conference was held at Thourelle's home institution, so she was hosting a potluck dinner for the speakers the next night. This was my chance to make amends, but I refused to go. Instead, I honored

---

[2] An allusion to the warrior Cúchulainn from the Irish saga, *The Táin* — in case you were wondering.

my obligation to bring a salad by sending it over in a cab, along with a package of Egyptian henna. My subsequent meetings with Thourelle were professional, if not exactly cordial.

The reason the search committee had selected Thourelle was not for her adroit taste in hair coloring. She had just written a "big book" entitled *Passionate Pedagogy: Rhetoric, Eros, and the Future of the Humanities*. It was a quasi-Freudian reading of pedagogical practices throughout the ages and was clearly influenced by the phenomena of transference and countertransference between analyst and analysand. Rather than urging repression, however, Thourelle insisted that the most effective pedagogy depended upon the erotic dynamic between teacher and student, which, she argued, was most potent when amorous feelings were frankly acknowledged.

A good portion of the book was devoted to the "healthy" sexualization of the master-student relationship from Roman culture all the way through premodern Europe, with many riffs on the master's "rod" and the eroticism of pedagogical beatings. Sadly, over the course of the Enlightenment, the West began to doubt the value of pedagogical eroticism. It resurfaced for a final victory lap in the 60s and 70s, only to be resolutely rejected by feminist ideology. The result was sublimation, which, as Freud tells us, has the potential for great art but almost certainly gives rise to neuroses. (At this point, Thourelle made a dangerous equation between the frequency of Asperger Syndrome in the Ivory Tower and the decline of academic eros.) Our job as educators was to re-eroticize the teacher-student relationship and save the Humanities.

It was a controversial thesis, especially from a notable feminist scholar writing at the crest of the #MeToo movement, and it received a lot of attention outside the academy. The *New York Times* Book Review made it the subject of a feature article entitled "Educational Eros," which concluded that any school that put Thourelle's views to the test had better begin lawyering up. Now, you might well wonder how, in present-day academia, my colleagues would consider hiring someone who propounded a thesis so apparently at odds with their professed beliefs. Frankly, I don't know. Maybe because she stressed the essential role of "erotics" versus the consummated sex act.

Thourelle was invited to campus for an interview. I doubt that many of the students bothered to read her book. Even so, she had achieved a degree of notoriety in the media, and students opposed her upcoming visit with zeal. Their resistance generated some lively slogans on protest signs like: "HANDS OFF, PROFS" or, more bluntly, "DON'T FUCK WITH ME!" Some of the slogans were more obscure. My favorite was: "PASSIONATE PEDAGOGY: A PSYCHO'S ANALISIS."

A number of faculty members pushed back against the protesters, dedicating class time to the issue of freedom of speech as well as mounting extracurricular forums. Although Thourelle's on-campus interview was scheduled for early in the new year, the protests had petered out by November. Some members of the faculty interpreted this as evidence that the measures taken to counter student protest had worked. But I think it was more a case of premature ejaculation: the student body got over-excited and shot its wad of objections. Although there were three viable candidates brought to campus, Thourelle was the clear front-runner. She alone was believed to be capable of providing the leverage that our sleepy midwestern institution needed.

None of my colleagues had met Thourelle before her arrival on campus. I don't know what they were imagining: something between a sage in a toga and a superheroine with pointy boobs and blue hair, is my guess. When Thourelle finally arrived, I doubt they were disappointed — although they admittedly had to revise their expectations. Thourelle's overall "look" was androgynous but not alarmingly so — she would still have been considered chic, albeit in a weird way, in academic circles. Her hair was short (about two inches or so) and bright red (clearly chemical), spiked with some sort of gel. Not too extreme, as far as these things go. Certainly not the full-on crested lizard look. For her lecture, she wore a loose-fitting grey suit over a lighter grey button-down shirt, open at the neck. Her trousers were cropped high at the ankles, revealing stylish scarlet booties (two-toned) with zippers on either side of her foot.

Probably the most dramatic thing about Thourelle's appearance was her jewelry. Thourelle's ear lobes had been stretched to accommodate two dark circles of hollow grey stone. Another of her trademarks was a set of brushed metal rings that she wore on every finger of both hands (including her thumbs). The rings matched a much thicker ring that she wore around her neck, which I thought evoked images of sexual bondage. Despite her commitment to haute couture (or to what passed for haute couture in academic circles), however, Thourelle was no rangy runway model. In bare feet, she was probably no more than 5 foot one or so. Although in her late thirties, she wore no makeup. Many seemed to find her attractive, but I always thought she looked like a puppet because of her oversized forehead, big mouth, and undersized chin. Does anyone remember *Fireball XL5*?

Her talk was entitled "Pure Pedagogues." The title, announced some three weeks before her arrival, engendered considerable speculation. The word "pure" was something of a double entendre. It could be interchangeable with descriptors like "just" or "only." Or it could allude to sexual purity, perhaps suggesting that she had changed her mind about the generative role of eros in academe. Perhaps she was going to perform one of those daring public self-denunciations —following in the footsteps of second-wave feminists who excoriated themselves for their white bourgeois prejudices.

Although there was no elaborate self-denunciation, it turned out that "pure" connoted sexual purity. The lecture was an extended panegyric on the Western tradition of celibacy and learning — a tradition that began with the classical philosophical tradition and was sustained by the medieval clergy but tragically ground to a halt in the twentieth century when Oxbridge dons began to marry. She ended with an impassioned plea for the value of celibacy, noting that thousands of years of intellectual tradition have demonstrated conventional relationships like marriage to be incompatible with the life of the mind. Although the erotic dynamic between teacher and student should never be underestimated, the classroom must never become the arena for any sexual acting out: all sexual impulses must be either suppressed or sublimated.

It was an impressive performance. Thourelle spoke entirely without notes, never taking her eyes off the audience. When she stopped speaking, there was silence, soon followed by thunderous applause. Yet the question period was a seething cesspool of consternation. If many in the audience had at one time found the thesis of *Passionate Pedagogy* objectionable, they were even more disturbed when it was abandoned. Although challenged repeatedly about her seeming about-face, Thourelle insisted that tensions between the two positions were illusory. The stance taken in the lecture, "Pure Pedagogues," not only complemented, but completed the position advanced in the book, *Passionate Pedagogy*. I began to see where she was going with this.

"In true scholastic form, I have chosen to argue both sides of the question — a methodology pioneered by Peter Abelard in the twelfth century. It's a kind of homage to his *Sic et Non*."

Did I mention that I was a medievalist? Well, I am, though sometimes I wish I'd gone into film studies. This might've given me a leg up professionally since every film I've ever watched in my life was still floating within conscious reach, available as an analogue for whatever emotional turds life chose to toss my way. As a medievalist, however, I felt bound and determined to defend my constituency, even though they happened to be a bunch of dead people. But they were MY dead people, so I found Thourelle's efforts to align her murky Janus-faced stance with Abelard's genius offensive. Still, her analogy wasn't entirely pointless. His *Sic et Non (Yes and No)* presented arguments in support of both sides of an academic question. Always the provocateur, Abelard posed questions like *God is good, and the opposite*. It was intended as an exercise book for his students, so it was their job to reason their way to the correct answer. We never learn what the master really thought.

And so, it was with Thourelle. Members of the audience continued to prod and probe about what she "really thought" throughout both the post-talk reception and subsequent faculty dinner, with little success. After the dinner, the search committee (of which both Jan and I were members) lingered behind in the restaurant to try and strategize how we would pin our wily candidate down the following day.

The committee met with her mid-morning in the departmental conference room over coffee and stale donuts. I know they were stale because I ate one. Doughnuts always upset my stomach, plus I knew that they had been purchased the day before. But I happen to be a nervous eater, and, yes, for some reason, I was nervous. In fact, the entire committee seemed a bit on edge. Thourelle was serene by contrast, exhibiting a degree of complacency somewhat unusual for a job candidate — even a celebrated one. She was once again dressed in grey, only this time wearing a long, loose tunic over black leggings. It would have resembled some kind of religious habit had it not been for the scarlet booties.

There were some polite preliminaries. How was her room? Did she have a nice breakfast with the graduate students? Was there time in her schedule to look around campus? It wasn't at its best in January, but we have an early spring and the campus was already greening up by March. What did she think of the library? It really was the university's treasure. Then, there was the inevitable declaration that this was a wonderful place to raise children. (My colleagues always thought this was the clincher, while I saw it as an admission of how boring it was here.) We were waiting for Martin to step up since it was agreed that he, as Chair of the search committee, should ask the first substantive question. Finally, he spoke.

"Sylvia, may I call you Sylvia?" She nodded graciously. "You've presented us with two diametrically opposed models of pedagogy. The committee is interested in which one you, as a teacher, subscribe."

"I thought I made it clear that both were viable positions."

"Even so. What do you believe?"

"I believe an argument could be made for either side."

So, it continued for some time. Her intellectual rope-a-dopes seemed to be working, and she was tiring us out. But while the rest of the search committee seemed bedazzled by her dexterous evasions, I found them profoundly annoying.

"Let me play the devil's advocate here and ask you a question that engages both of the two aspects you've presented," said Martin. "Supposing you had an extremely promising, perhaps even brilliant, student. He had a fabulous idea for his final paper, which he discussed with you at length on a number of occasions. And yet, the paper he submitted was mediocre. Would that signify that the two of you were insufficiently chaste or pure? Or that there had been an incomplete erotic exchange? Perhaps that one of you had fumbled a pass?" Martin gave his famous "twinkly" smile, confident that he had formulated the crucial question with address and wit.

Thourelle was not amused. Her diminutive lower jaw dropped, and her eyebrows shot up in aggrieved astonishment. "Your question strikes me as a crude form of entrapment," she responded. "I was making a philosophical argument about different approaches to pedagogy. These are abstract models, not tactics for getting laid." She spat out this last word contemptuously. "Perhaps we should bring this interview to a close. These questions seem to be devolving into thinly veiled insults. I feel demeaned by the process and would like to withdraw my candidacy for this position."

Martin sat there in stunned silence, trying to figure out how best to retrieve the situation. The strategy he adopted was to bray like a donkey in dismay, bleating out a string of apologies. Meanwhile, the other members of the committee were stricken dumb, alarmed at how quickly the situation had escalated. Thourelle's behavior struck me as histrionic, and my enthusiasm for her candidacy was waning. It was up to me to retake control of the interview.

"Sylvia, it's clear that our committee is genuinely impressed by your work: its scope, its theoretical rigor, and its tantalizing dialectical turns."

No response.

"You invoked Peter Abelard in your talk. He may be the dialectical forbear to your theoretical model, but I think we have to distinguish between theory and practice. He also epitomizes the practical dangers of passionate pedagogy."

No response.

"By seducing Heloise, arguably his most brilliant student, he literally destroyed her life."

No response.

"Well, not to put too fine a point on it: are you planning to screw your students?"

There was an immediate outcry. Jan, who was sitting to my left, actually hit my arm so hard that it left a bruise. When Thourelle pushed back her chair a little, I really thought she was going to walk out. In fact, I rather hoped she would. But she didn't. Instead, she leaned forward on one elbow, supporting her chin in her hand, eyes closed, like a *madonna dolorosa*. She remained in this posture of pained introspection for an entire minute, during which time I vented my spleen through silent name-calling with an alliterative bent: the secretless sphinx; sophistical siren; slippery syllogist; shallow shrew; bogus banshee.

Finally, she spoke.

"Perhaps you'd be reassured if you knew that I'm an ace," she said.

Martin, adept at kissing ass with his mouth full of humble pie, said: "Sylvia, of course, we know you're an ace; in fact, a quad. Otherwise, we wouldn't be sitting here right now."

Thourelle looked confused. But Martin explained that he was a poker player and that a quad was four of a kind. Eventually, she acknowledged Martin's gallantry with a smile (the first that I'd seen since she'd hit campus), while at the same time shaking her head. "I'm afraid that you misunderstand me. Did you know that approximately 1% of the world's population experiences little or no sex drive?"

What did that have to do with groping students?

"Such a person is referred to as an 'ace' among the asexual community. That's what I meant when I said that I was an ace."

The other three members of the committee must've practiced their surprised bewilderment in the mirror before coming to work. The external member from Classics clapped his hands to both cheeks; Jan furrowed her brow; Martin screwed up his lips like a sphincter. Me? My face remained stock still: I was focused on keeping my eyes from rolling. Nobody spoke.

"I don't like to talk about my personal life. But please believe me when I say that my knowledge of eros is entirely academic," she continued. "I have often considered my work as therapy of sorts, helping me to come to terms with my loneliness as an ace."

While the rest of the committee was compassionately cooing at her bravery in the face of sexual challenge, I was admiring the imaginative way in which she dodged my question. Cunning. The rest of the interview was more or less an intellectual love-fest, where everyone began divulging how aspects of their scholarship had helped them work through their problems and come to terms with their inner selves. (Since I'd just finished a book on medieval pedophilia, I wisely kept my mouth shut.) Thourelle's professed ace status had done the trick. The committee was even more intent on hiring her than before.

I was the only dissenting vote. To complicate matters, I was also the one whose field was closest to Thourelle's and in the best position to appraise her work. Before we made our recommendation to the department, the other two members of the committee delegated Jan to try to bring me around. Jan was not yet chair, so she didn't have any real clout. Still, everyone knew we were good friends. The evening of Thourelle's unsettling interview, Jan dropped by my house unannounced in her full-on persuasion mode, bearing a bottle of *Hors d'Age* cognac. I took it from her and silently poured us each a snifter, sat down at the kitchen table, and told her to have at it. And she did. Jan's main strategy was to use my earlier support for Thourelle against me, attempting to shame me for inconsistency.

"You were her strongest advocate: so contemptuous of the student protests and so impressed by her work," Jan said.

"The work, yes; the person, no. Remember: I knew her earlier and always suspected her of being a narcissist. Now I know she is. So, on-campus interviews have their uses after all," I replied.

"You've always said that when it comes to hiring, we should always go for the smartest," she said.

"Right, I did. But now I know better. Sometimes, you come across a person who's too smart. Slippery smart. Those people can't be trusted and make terrible colleagues." I took a sip of cognac and then looked at Jan earnestly. "There's something really off about Thourelle. Can't you feel it?"

Jan refused to take the bait.

"Isn't it ironic that you, of all people, have turned against her, especially considering how much the two of you have in common? You're the only person in the department who actually knows what rhetoric is and certainly the only one who knows anything about Abelard," said Jan, clearly trying to flatter me.

"Agreed. And it would've been great to have someone else interested in the premodern world. But I still vote no."

She tried another strategy. "You've always argued that hiring colleagues with shared interests is a plus — especially for training graduate students. But now someone comes along who does share your interests, and you change your mind. Do you suppose you could be jealous?" Jan was trying to look impish.

"That's it! Hand over her ruby slippers, and she has my vote," I cackled.

And we left it at that.

I hate to admit it, but Jan was on to something. I was rather jealous of Thourelle. We both gravitated toward similar subjects. I was at least five years older and had written more, but already her work had received much more attention than mine ever would. Of course, we had very different approaches. I always went out of my way to recreate the cultural context, which made controversial subjects seem less so; Thourelle went out of her way to fan the flames of controversy in order to turn the spotlight on herself.

Since Thourelle had the majority of the search committee's support, Martin recommended her to the department as their leading candidate. He also shared the exciting news of Thourelle's asexuality, arguing that her unique orientation contributed to the department's diversity initiative. Most of my colleagues were cooing approvingly to one another, which, not surprisingly, infuriated the only two people of color in the department. Their hands shot up simultaneously.

"Are you joking?" asked Benjamin, who specialized in Black Caribbean writers. "Are you really saying that this constitutes diversity? Does crossdressing count? Because then all I need to do is get myself a garter belt, and I'm doubly diverse."

The department's response was stunned silence. I think everyone was afraid that a straight man threatening to wear a garter belt might get them into hot water with the handful of transgender students in the department, even if he was Black.

Then Adhira, a soft-spoken woman from Calcutta who worked on post-colonialism, weighed in. "There certainly are instances when sexual orientation does represent a legitimate form of diversity, only I'm not convinced this is one of them."

The two out gay men in our department murmured among themselves, but I couldn't tell whether they were attempting to agree or disagree with Adhira and Benjamin. I suspect that they didn't know themselves but felt that it behooved them to contribute something.

The-Chair-Who-Hated-Me (doesn't that sound like a Bond film?) called on me reluctantly.

"I have to agree with Adhira. If someone who can't find anyone they're attracted to constitutes diversity, then I'm diverse," I said. This elicited some laughter but didn't drown out the Chair's grunt of impatience.

"It's not that she can't find anyone to have sex with; it's that she never wants to have sex," Martin said.

"A lot of married people never want to have sex. Is that diversity?" I asked. More laughter.

Martin had no idea how to respond. Instead, he looked over at Jan with such pathos that she came to the rescue.

"Heather is being facetious. We all know the difference between sexual disaffection and a total lack of libido. If asexuals constitute a mere 1% of the population, having someone like Thourelle in the department *would* contribute to its diversity," Jan said.

"OK, but suppose that Thourelle is choosey and just hasn't found her Mr.-Ms.-Mx. Right? And then she does. Does that mean that she wasn't asexual in the first place?" I asked.

But most of the department dismissed Benjamin and Adhira's intervention regarding diversity as territorial in nature and my skepticism as pure cynicism. Thourelle's asexuality resonated with the department as a whole, which, like most of the search committee, was carried away with empathy for her solitary plight. There were around thirty-five voting members, and thirty voted in favor of hiring Thourelle. This was far above the two-thirds necessary for the recommendation to hire Thourelle to carry. After gaining the Dean's approval, the department made the offer and held its collective breath. I had always thought that her accepting our offer would be a long shot, and at this point, I heartily hoped she would turn us down. She already had a pretty good job, and it was rumored that she was being courted by several other schools, including one of the Ivies. But she did come, at the end of all. She may have been the splashy hire we needed, but it was just as I feared. Since her arrival, Thourelle had proven to be a prima donna. She flatly refused to do any departmental service and never attended meetings. When she deigned to have contact with her colleagues, her attitude always seemed to be poised somewhere between condescension and contempt.

This is the backstory that flashed through my mind when Jan told me that Thourelle was having her way with an undergraduate.

Chapter 4: Secret Agent

Jan seemed to take Thourelle's indiscretion with an undergraduate personally and was furious. She now believed that the department had been duped and that Thourelle's claims to asexuality were entirely opportunistic. Jan wondered if there was any legal recourse for sexual misrepresentation, but I was doubtful. Meanwhile, my skepticism over Thourelle's alleged asexuality was vindicated. Why else would someone who professes to have no sex drive suddenly decide to have sex — with an undergraduate, no less?

I was no psychologist, but as someone who had at one time gone through therapists like a hooker trying to make rent, I had plenty of professional contacts. My first responder of choice was Berenice: an expert at explaining fucked up people as well as what fucks people up. She also happened to be the friend who told me about EMDR. Berenice was an art therapist, a rarefied field that she had stumbled upon by accident. Long ago, she wrote a dissertation on sixteenth-century Flemish altarpieces at this very university. When she went on the job market, however, she found little demand for her chosen area of expertise. Then she herself turned to painting and found even less demand. Berenice remained undaunted, however. Determined to support herself with a job that she found halfway gratifying, she took out a student loan and went back to school to get a degree in psychology. With degree in hand, she cornered the market in art therapy. A university town is awash with academics who pass down neuroses to their offspring as surely as Adam and Eve transmitted original sin. In other words, she never wanted for clients and paid back her loan in record time.

Berenice was a fast study. During the relatively short time that she was my therapist, she came to believe that I'd been under-parented in the extreme. My mother, originally just a nominal Episcopalian, had a visionary experience at the age of thirty-three, after which she spent most of her time at church or on religious retreats. After mother's religious turn, my father, a devout shouter who probably drove her to religion in the first place, became progressively hostile to religion, which he expressed through redoubled efforts at shouting. I and my siblings shared a phobia about answering phone calls in the late afternoon. The odds were that it would be my mother — barking out directions for making dinner to the hapless child at the end of the receiver. The house was an unholy mess, but our friends loved it: if they broke or spilt something, nobody noticed.

Berenice encouraged me to draw, paint, or sculpt my family's multi-faceted dysfunction. Here are some of my most successful assignments.

1). Draw a typical holiday.

I was using pastels. I drew a scene around a fireplace consisting of a smiling woman, wearing bright orange lipstick and a cross; a frowning man with a pipe; and four children dressed in blue, all with frowns on their faces, and looking somewhere else. On a couch, there were another four figures hunched over and dressed in black. Think Edvard Munch.

"What are these? Ghouls? Zombies?" Berenice asked, pointing at the black-clad figures.

"No. An assortment of religious personnel," I responded.

"Nuns? Monks? Priests?"

"All of the above. Whomever my mother could commandeer, which was mostly nuns," I said.

2). Draw a memorable family meal.

This time, I was using crayons. I drew a picture of the same man (you could tell by the pipe) holding a long object with a chord. He was standing beside the woman with the orange lipstick and the large cross. Her elbows were held close to the sides of the body and her hands were outstretched sideways, palms up — something art historians would recognize as the *orans* (praying) posture indicating public prayer or supplication. In front of them was an oval table surrounded by people.

"And this?" she said, indicating the entire tableau.

"That was the time I invited my best friend and her new boyfriend to dinner with the family. See, they're seated around the table with my siblings," I said, pointing.

"Why's your father holding an electric toothbrush?" asked Berenice. Her face was scrunched up in concentration.

"It's an electric carving knife," I said.

"The one with the cross is your mother, right?" I nodded. "What's she doing?"

"She's trying to tell my friends, who happened to be both confirmed atheists and zealous Marxists, about her conversion experience. My father is carving a roast. Every time she attempts to continue her narrative, my father revs up the carving knife and threatens her with it."

"So, this is a frightening memory," Berenice said sympathetically.

"No. Hilarious. One of my friends wet herself laughing."

3). Paint a picture that represents shame.

Two images immediately came to mind, but I wasn't very good with watercolors. I shakily divided the page in half: on the left, I drew a pink blob, which you could tell from its mouth was a crying baby. Above the baby was a disembodied hand.

"What's this?" asked Berenice.

"That's my little sister, and that's my hand," I responded.

"And what're you doing?" she asked.

"Pinching her when she came home from the hospital," I replied.

"How old were you?" inquired Berenice.

"About three," I responded.

"And you remember this?" Berenice asked, clearly incredulous.

"No, but it was one of my mom's favorite stories, so I knew all about it," I said.

"Did you know that it's typical for a child to respond with hostility to a newborn —especially when there is more than a two-year age difference between them?" Berenice asked.

"I know. I read about it when I was an adult," I responded.

"Did you tell your mother?" she asked.

"Yes."

"What did she say?"

"That none of the other kids ever pinched a baby."

There was a long silence.

On the right side of the paper was a green oval shape filled with circles in two different tones of green, surrounded by four lozenge shapes against splashes of red. Once again, there was a disembodied hand hovering above.

"And that?" Berenice asked, pointing.

"That's a turtle I ripped apart," I responded morosely. I looked over, expecting to see a horrified look on her face. Instead, Berenice was frowning, clearly attempting to make sense of what I had said.

"Do you remember this?" Berenice asked.

"No, I was only two. But my mother told me." I had begun to cry.

"But, if you were only two, you probably wouldn't even have known the difference between an animal and a toy," said Berenice. I was now sobbing uncontrollably, so she put her arms around me. I still feel guilty whenever I see turtles.

I became perversely attached to the pictures, perhaps because I perceived them as fruits of psychological progress. I mounted them in IKEA frames and hung them in my office. On the rare occasion anyone noticed them, I attributed them to my niece.

Berenice helped a lot. She made me realize that my father's narrative of the "mean, malicious streak" had been reinforced by, perhaps even begun by, my mother. My interest in medieval religion may even have been an attempt to hit back by annihilating the church. But that was as far as we got. It turned out that art just wasn't my idiom. When I was splashing paint around, I either felt like an unstable preschooler or a Pollock wannabe. There were no hard feelings when I packed up my brushes and left. But as the months went by, I found myself missing Berenice. Apart from Jan, I didn't have a lot of female friends. In fact, I didn't have a lot of any kind of friends. College towns operate along the same principle as Noah's Ark: the single aren't welcome. I didn't know much about Berenice's personal life, but I suspected she was single as well. Once, when I was attempting to depict my problems with men in clay, she alluded to a former husband — but did so without longing or rancor, and I found this impressive. (The artwork that came out of this session was as well: a giant prick, as menacing as it was repulsive.) Berenice was quick-witted and fun. I especially liked the fact that — despite her credentials — she wasn't an academic. So, I called her up and suggested we go out for a drink. Her answer: *Wait until I check my calendar*. Once she had ascertained that six months had elapsed since our last session, she agreed, and we had a blast.

I wanted her opinion on Thourelle, but Berenice was usually tied up during the week. She did, however, have an exercise regime that I would occasionally crash if I was in a self-punishing mode. When the weather was fine, Berenice liked to go for very fast walks in a nearby state park, circling round and round a small lake in loops, each of which was probably half a mile or so. The path was heavily wooded through terrain that alternated between crags and bog. Berenice had very long legs and easily jumped from rock to rock like a latter-day Heidi. It was a challenge to keep up with her.

"Berenice, do you mind if I bother you with a professional question?" I asked, swatting at the mosquitoes swarming my head. We were only on the second loop, and I'd already fallen several hillocks behind. I could just glimpse a mass of blonde curls bobbing around a curve.

"Sure. Where'd you go?" said Berenice, looking over her shoulder as I struggled to catch up. She stopped for a moment, watching as I tried to pull my foot out of a modest quagmire. There was a strange sucking noise when it pulled off my sneaker. I stooped to fish it out while Berenice dove into a small backpack and silently held out a fresh sock. (I always forget to bring extras.) When we were once again in motion, I asked my question: "Why would someone who professes to have no sex drive decide to have sex?"

Berenice snorted with laughter, apparently finding my question quite comical. "Are you kidding?" she said. "The vast majority of my married patients often have sex without any desire — especially women. You go to bed with someone for a number of years, and that's what happens: I call it the dumbing down of the body."

Duh! I'd made a similar argument to the department when they were advancing Thourelle's asexuality as a point of diversity. I was just remembering when I slipped on a slimy rock.

"Are you OK?" Berenice asked, patiently waiting while I wiped some of the slime off the back of my jeans. I assured her I was fine.

"Just to clarify: I don't mean couples who lose their desire for one another. I mean people who identify as asexual — people who have a distinct orientation to no one," I said, tripping over a tree root, fortuitously left on the trail to humiliate wimps.

"Some people think asexuality is an orientation; others don't. I'm with the ones who don't. But maybe we're only conditioned to think that there is such a thing as orientations," Berenice said.

"How so?" I queried, once again falling behind.

"It's not science. It's just what I've observed over the years," she replied, looking over her shoulder.

"And so, how would you define an asexual?" I said.

"Just someone who, for whatever reason, experiences a reduced libido over an extended period and finds that label appealing," she answered.

"If it's not an orientation, is it at least a stable condition?" I asked.

"Probably not. But then again, I don't think that anything that has to do with sexual desire is stable," she said.

I'd run out of breath, so our discussion ended there. The next day was Tuesday, however, which meant not only another go around with the green light but also another opportunity to raise the asexuality question with a specialist. Apart from the rarefied topic of my humiliation at the hands of men, however, Dr. Owen and I didn't talk much. I was trying to think of how to introduce the subject of asexuality casually, which must've given me a distracted air. Dr. Owen knew that something was amiss. How do I know that? Well, you might describe him as an open book. He always took abundant notes throughout my sessions in a *Mead Composition Notebook* labelled with my initials. Whenever he had to leave the room for a moment, I would steal over to his desk to see what he was writing.

Sometimes, what he wrote was interesting: *Patient remembers little about adolescence, especially the middle years. Unusual.* Was that true? I thought about it and realized that it probably was. My teenage years were something of a blank. But Dr. Owen hadn't written down what that meant. Did it mean that my teens were smooth sailing, or were the traumas coming so thick and fast that my poor psyche had chosen to suppress them? Hard to say, and I really couldn't ask without admitting that I'd been snooping. Other times, Dr. Owen's comments were more cryptic: *Patient arrived five minutes late, clutching yesterday's New York Times* (yesterday was underlined), or *Patient wore a black dress with green tights. Crossed her legs at the ankles again.* What? Gloss, please!

Today, just when the session with the green light was ending, the doorbell rang. He apologized, saying he was expecting a package, and headed for the staircase. I jumped up to have a look at his notes. *Didn't do her homework. Seems distracted.* When he returned, Dr. Owen resumed his scribbling. As I was handing him the check, I said:

"Dr. Owen?"

"Hmmm." He was still writing. I'm wondering how he could wax so prolific about my apparent distraction.

"I have a question," I said.

He looked up politely.

"Do you know what an ace is?"

"We aren't talking cards, I presume."

I shook my head.

"Then perhaps you're referring to a self-identified asexual."

I nodded.

"I say self-identified because it's not an orientation that physicians or psychologists recognize," he added.

"So, anyone could just decide that they're an ace?"

Dr. Owen gave me an odd look that seemed to be positioned somewhere between amusement and impatience. "I'm not sure what exactly is behind your interest in aces. But if you're imagining that you might be an ace yourself, I can only say that I doubt it very much. Of course, there are always gradations in orientation. Still, you strike me as more unequivocally heterosexual than most women." He started writing again and then looked up: "You even have a touch of old-fashioned female masochism."

In this day and age, when queering was all the rage, I was a tad deflated that my own psycho/sexual profile was so unnuanced. But I hastily reassured him that I wasn't asking on my own behalf. I was wondering how likely it would be for someone who identifies as asexual to still engage in sexual relationships. Apparently, the answer was far from straightforward. There was an asexual spectrum that made the Kinsey scale look like *Sexual Orientation for Dummies*. A classic asexual, that is, someone with no sexual libido, could still have romantic attractions. By the same token, someone could feel sexual desire but have no romantic impulses. Individuals such as these represented the Split Attraction Model, abbreviated as SAM.

"And such individuals would consider themselves asexual?" I asked

"I believe so. But even a classic asexual, who associates with neither part of the SAM dichotomy, might choose to engage in sexual relations," he said.

"Why?" I asked.

"Well, for the benefits that come with them: companionship, children, economic support — the usual stuff," he said.

In fact, it now seemed obvious — so obvious that it made me feel like a dullard for asking the question in the first place. The fact that Thourelle was having an affair with an undergraduate didn't necessarily mean that she'd lied about her asexual identity. Not lied, perhaps, but nevertheless perpetrated a deception. Hadn't she brought up her alleged asexuality in order to reassure us that she would never be interested in putting *Passionate Pedagogy* into practice?

Chapter 5: Rear Window

Hanif Twist <Twisted@gmale.com> Fri 9/4/20 11:30 p.m.
To: Heather Bell
Subject: Fetish

Hey Heather!
I was looking at the program for the "Fetishization of the Fetish," and I see we're both on it. Wouldn't it be cool to drive there together? H

***

Heather Bell <Heathcliff@fmale.com> Sat 9/5/20 9:45 a.m.
To: Hanif Twist
Subject: Re: Fetish

Dear Hanif:
Very cool — especially if you drive. I hate driving. H

This was true. I was one of those anomalies who hadn't learned to drive until my mid-thirties. Of course, I'd tried to learn in my teens like everyone else. But my in-car instructor was a dyspeptic Swede who would shout at me to speed up on the highways and to quit burning rubber in the parking lot. The whole experience was unnerving, so I gave up and settled for public transport. This solution only worked as long as I was living in a real city, not a college town. I eventually was forced to learn to drive but would never be an Easy Rider.

Nor was I a sanguine conferee. The conference was in two weeks. I was giving one of the keynotes, which I had yet to write. It was an exploration of how the general flaccidity of knightly culture was epitomized by a self-defeating fetishization of the dominant vaginal Grail at the expense of the servile phallic lance. This was realized in court culture where Guinevere, as phallic mother, gained ascendancy, precipitating the demise of Camelot. The entire enterprise had me on edge. Although I was in an English Department, I really saw myself as a cultural historian and felt out of my depth with literary analyses. So why did I propose this topic? It must be the phallic ascendancy of pen over the vaginal swamp of brain.

The conference was held at a neighboring institution that was an easy two-hour drive. It began on Friday afternoon and concluded Saturday evening with a banquet. The two keynotes were at the opening and the close of the conference. I got the latter spot, scheduled just before the banquet. I suppose that most scholars would be gratified by this singular position in the program since it implied that I was being entrusted with transporting the conference to its consummate level of fetishization. But this prominent placement only amplified my insecurities.

When Hanif picked me up Friday morning, I'd been up most of the night and almost had a completed draft of the paper. He drove considerably faster than I do, but who doesn't? I was also struck by his quasi-adolescent habit of gratuitous passing, clearly relishing the weaving in and out among the cars. I, for my part, have always been a nervous passenger but registered my dismay by falling asleep. When I awoke, we were almost there. I apologized: after all, what's the point of carting around an extra passenger who neither entertains the driver nor offers to drive? But Hanif just laughed, saying that having me in the car was entertainment enough. I was afraid that this might be an allusion to my snoring.

We arrived with just enough time to register and get settled in our rooms before the first keynote, which would be delivered before lunch in the same banquet hall in which lunch would later be served. Because I was an invited speaker, the fee for both my registration and my room were waived. But I would've happily paid an inordinate amount had I realized that the room in question was in the college dorms. "So much more convenient for the attendees," the woman at registration said in a chipper tone. Hanif and I accordingly set out to find our convenient lodgings, which required carrying our luggage for at least half a mile, only to discover that the entrance to our dorm had been cordoned off by yellow tape with a hazard sign that read: **Danger. Construction Site. Hard Hats Only.**

"I have two back in the car," said Hanif.

"Really?"

"OK, I'm lying. I only have one," Hanif replied.

I can't believe I fell for that one.

"I'd better call registration," he continued.

Hanif's phone was on speaker, so I could hear the same upbeat gal answer, saying: "Fetish Meeting. How can I help you?" When Hanif explained that our rooms seemed to be part of a construction site, she assured us that the signs didn't mean anything. That particular dorm was for "overflow" accommodation. They hadn't expected so big a turnout for the conference, however, so they hadn't bothered to remove the signs. Though the building was scheduled to be demolished in a couple of weeks, she assured us that it was perfectly safe. We entered the sepia-toned lobby and tried the lights. The electricity had been turned off. Both of our rooms were on the second floor, however, and there were windows in the stairwell. We decided to drop off our luggage before contending with the lighting situation.

The corridors leading to the rooms were entirely without light, so we used the flashlights on our cell phones to locate the rooms.

My phone died the instant that I got into my room. The windows gave off enough light to allow for some sort of unpacking. My bladder was bursting. I could see the yawning door of the adjoining bathroom, but the interior was like a black hole. I entered tentatively, arms stretched in front of me like some silent film somnambulist. I was edging toward what seemed to be the middle of the bathroom when I collided with a soft mass. I screamed at the top of my voice, and a blinding light appeared before my eyes.

"It's me," said Hanif. He was holding up his cell phone.

"What the hell are you doing in here?" I asked in feral tones.

"Brushing my teeth," he said.

"Why here?" I insisted.

"We share a bathroom. I'm in the room next door," he said.

"Why?" I asked.

"Because the registration form required you to put someone else's name down in case you had to share accommodations, and I didn't know anyone else," he said, rather plaintively. I started to laugh. Hanif apologized for having forgotten his dorm manners: when using the bathroom, you're supposed to lock the door that leads to your roommate's room so they won't barge in. He showed me the lock on the inside of each bathroom door, which was designed to keep the rival roomie in their respective chamber like a caged beast.

"I'll leave you to yourself. Just remember to lock the door that leads to my room." As he was closing the door, I remembered to ask for his phone so I could see. He gave it to me, and told me he would be waiting in his room.

By the time we had apprised registration of our residential outage and managed to locate the banquet room, the lecture was just beginning. The speaker was Philippe Lepew, a prominent academic from a trendy East Coast university. Lewpew was a prolific publisher with a well-earned reputation for looking down upon just about everyone he encountered. We had met on numerous occasions, but I always felt like I needed to reintroduce myself to him. He had a battered but handsome face and the kind of receding hairline that one associates with dictators like Nero and Napoleon.

But his girth had increased considerably since I last saw him. He had a reputation for being a "ladies' man" (i.e., someone who slept with his students), but I'd heard that he'd recently remarried. Domestic bliss was rarely kind to the physique. His talk was entitled "The Victorians' Deadly Fetish," which sounded like a spinoff from his recent book *Sick of Disease.* The beginning of the lecture was rather hackneyed: the nineteenth-century aestheticization of the consumptive female. He referenced authors like Keats and Edgar Allan Poe, displayed paintings by the Pre-Raphaelite Brotherhood, and played clips from Puccini and Verdi. This overview of artistic fetishization was but an envoy for the main focus of the paper: the medical advances of René Laënnec and his own struggle with the tubercular death drive. Lepew approached Laënnec's *On the Diseases of the Heart and Mediate Auscultation,* with its lexicon of the sounds discerned in a consumptive's chest, as the consummate feminization of disease: the aqueous gurgling, burbling, and sloshing epitomized the dangers of the female genitalia.

"With the invention of his phallic stethoscope, Laënnec fought the disease like a conquistador." (Lepew's PowerPoint presentation showed Laënnec's drawings for the original monaural instrument, which were, indeed, quite phallic.) "But the maternal embrace of tuberculosis overwhelmed him." At this point, the audience was bombarded by a quick succession of images alternating between tubercular lungs and liquid refuse coughed up by those suffering from the disease. The montage concluded with a clip from Alain Cavalier's 1986 film *Thérèse,* in which a nun attending the tubercular saint on her deathbed drinks the bowl of blood, pus, and sputum that the saint has coughed up. Lepew froze the scene precisely where the nun was about to quaff the fetid liquid.

"In the end, Laënnec succumbed to the death drive and drank deeply of the very female effluvia that had been the obsession of a lifetime."

A luncheon of polenta and tomato sauce was served immediately after the talk. I had been allotted the position of honor to the right of speaker. But when the waiter placed the roiling bowl of effluvia in front of me, my stomach embarked on a series of acrobatics, and I barely made it to the bathroom in time. When I got out, there was Hanif, smiling. He handed me a breath mint.

"I'm beginning to think that you're one of those weirdos who hangs out around women's restrooms," I said.

"No, just your usual castrated male afraid of female effluvia," he answered. "Actually, I wanted to make sure you were alright."

I returned to the table once the polenta course had been removed. When I sat down, Professor Lepew shot me a contemptuous look, either for interrupting him or for missing part of his discourse, and continued talking. He was holding forth about the doctor in Freud's *Psychopathology of Every Day Life* who always kept a wooden stethoscope between himself and his patients during his consultations. The other auditors, either transfixed or anaesthetized by this dazzling show of pedantry, neither moved nor said a word. I made sure that my attentive mask was securely in place before gratefully tuning out. Lepew had written an article on this very subject that had appeared in *Re-Presentations* several years earlier. He was quoting himself almost verbatim.

After lunch, I went to Hanif's session, which was called *Animal Crossings*. His paper examined Marian Engel's controversial novel *Bear*, in which a lonely female librarian in Northern Ontario has a sexual relationship with a bear, and its meaning in the context of Canada's First Nations. I hadn't read the book. Even so, I could tell that Hanif's paper (entitled "Bear Naked") was a class act: eloquent and witty with a confident delivery. He was wearing a shirt in that lapis blue color that Renaissance artists reserved for the Virgin Mary, and the color made his green eyes deepen in color. Then came a rather strident woman with purple streaks in her hair who was an assistant professor from somewhere near Seattle. Her paper, entitled "God and the Animals," was an impassioned attack upon a literal reading of Genesis, focusing on Adam's God-given dominion over animals. She argued that fundamentalist farmers interpreted Adam's dominion as a divine license for animal abuse, concluding with some disturbing photos of Amish puppy mills.

The first two papers were good, but the last one, entitled "We Are What We Eat," was batshit crazy. (This, of course, meant that Hanif was writing profusely.) The speaker, a bearded graduate student who was a dead ringer for Rasputin, gave a reading of *Moby Dick*, interspersed with his own observations of fishing communities in Maine. His basic argument was that the more fish people ate, the better swimmers they became. As one might predict, it was this lunatic who got the most questions in the Q and A. Here are some of the highlights.

Q: Why would ingesting fish make people swim better?

A: Because the fish-eater's body begins to change.

Q: Can you prove this? Did you examine the bodies of people in the fishing community before and after ingesting a controlled quantity of fish?

A: I slept with three different girls while I was there. They all smelled like fish and had protruding bones in their back that were rather scaly. All of them were good swimmers. Furthermore, I have noticed on my own body…

When the speaker began to take off his shirt, the moderator precipitously ended the session.

That night, Hanif tried to get me to go out to dinner with a group of his friends. I still had work to do on my paper, however, so I begged off. At about half past nine, I heard a knock on my door. It was Hanif, bringing me a bag of take-out fish and chips. I was starving and thanked him with genuine ardor, but he brushed my thanks aside, claiming it was an experiment to see if I'd grow fins. I'd almost finished my paper, so I invited him in for a drink. I never left home without a bottle of scotch. Sadly, there was no ice.

Hanif and I chatted about his session, drinking scotch while I nibbled on the fish and chips. It was unfortunate that Hanif hadn't gotten any questions, but he didn't mind because he had enjoyed Rasputin's talk so much. But Hanif wanted my feedback. His paper was good, but I did have some criticism. Still, I reminded myself to go easy. If he was anything like me, when he asked for a critique, what he really wanted was for me to tell him that it was perfect and not to change a thing. In fact, if an academic friend dared to proffer some helpful suggestions, I would almost certainly go into attack mode — even if I was the one who had solicited their opinion. That was, of course, why I rarely showed my work to other scholars before publication. It was a risk, but otherwise, I wouldn't have any friends. So, I gently brought up his use of de Certeau and whether he needed him at all.

"I thought you liked theory," he said.

"Sometimes. But sometimes, it gets in the way if it's unnecessary. Imagine an Armani dress with a bizarre baroque broach stuck on it. It undercuts the dress's elegance," I said.

Hanif mulled this over, nodding.

"I'd also like to see the importance of the First Nations developed. Do you know their legend of the Bear Mother?"

"No, I don't. Do tell!" said Hanif eagerly.

"A woman, picking berries in the forest, drops her basket, and a man in fur robes rushes forward to help. He invites her back to his house (which looks suspiciously like a cave), where there are a bunch of other people in fur coats. Eventually, the woman and the man who helped her with the berries get married and have children, who turn out to be half bear and half human."

"This is fabulous stuff," Hanif said, eagerly scribbling.

I was seated on the bed with my back to the window. It made a strange, crinkly sound whenever I moved. This was the protective plastic sheet over the mattress, placed there to minimize the damage done by menstruators, bedwetters, ejaculators, and drunken vomiters. I wondered momentarily if I should remove the plastic sheet before going to sleep but then decided that what lay beneath could be considerably worse. Oh well. I would sleep regardless now that I had a draft of my paper. Meanwhile, Hanif read me some of the notes he had taken in his session, feeding me choice tidbits from the paper "We Are What We Eat," when something outside caught his eye.

"You're not going to believe this," he said, rising from his chair and going to the window.

I got up and followed him. There in the next block of dorms on the second floor was Professor Lepew in his underwear with an unlit cigar in his mouth, struggling to take the screen out of his window. The removal of the screen would allow him to blow smoke directly outside, thwarting the dorm's ubiquitous smoke detectors. The sashes on the window were thick – probably to forestall the removal of the screens in the first place. Hanif and I watched transfixed as the professor wrestled with the recalcitrant screen. His undershirt, which had initially been tucked into his boxers, came loose in the course of the mêlée, and his hairy paunch appeared like a full moon.

Suddenly, he lunged forward with a strangled yelp. (There was no air-conditioning and my windows were open, so we heard his *cri de coeur* very clearly.) Lepew had succeeded in removing the screen; we could see its ghostly contours on the ground. But in the course of its removal, he had over-balanced and was now hanging out the window, stuck at his midriff. The opening of the window was narrow in order to prohibit precisely this sort of undergrad shenanigans. We could see that his feet were no longer in contact with the floor. In other words, apart from the extremely circumscribed rocking horse moves he was attempting, he had no leverage for getting out.

"What should we do?" I asked in alarm.

Hanif was doubled over laughing, however, so it was hard to get his attention. Eventually, his laughter subsided.

"I don't see what we can do," he said. "He's one of those great men who also happens to be proud, petty, and vengeful. He'd never forgive anyone who'd witnessed this. You're a full professor: at the most, you'd get a bad review for your next book. For me, it could be a career-breaker."

Hanif was right. We decided to call 911 and were connected with the campus police. We made our report under assumed names. (Peter Abelard and Heloise Abelard.) Then, we waited. The police were surprisingly prompt and had the foresight to bring a ladder, which they set up outside the window. One officer climbed the ladder and, taking one of those oversized flashlights from his belt, began to examine the window frame surrounding its suspended victim. He seemed to have determined that the windows would be very difficult to remove, at which point Plan B was immediately put into effect. The officer on the ladder began to push, and the two other officers, who had, in the meantime, entered the room, began to pull on each of Professor Lepew's legs. It took so long that I was certain that they would have to return to Plan A, perhaps dismantling the entire window. But eventually, something popped, and his eminence flopped back into the room on his stomach.

After the officers left, Lepew stood there for a time, rubbing his stomach, which I am sure was quite sore, while he looked outside. Unfortunately, he looked directly at our window and locked eyes with me. Hanif clearly hadn't seen *Rear Window* because he just sat there staring back at Lepew in fascination. I jumped up and turned out the light, though I feared it was too late. We were the only ones in the over-flow building, after all.

"Hanif, he saw us! We have to sleep in your room," I exclaimed.

"A dream come true," he was gallant enough to say.

I seized my nightgown, my scotch, and what was left of the fish and chips, and we both fled through the bathroom. And sure enough — ten minutes later, we could hear Raymond Burr's avatar stalking down the hall. In the movie, the rancorous Burr's apartment was directly across from the voyeuristic Jimmy Stewart's abode, so the would-be murderer was in no doubt as to the location of his adversary. Fortunately, our building was at an angle from Lepew's dorm, which meant that it was probably difficult for Professor Lepew to fathom which door concealed his secret liberators. We sat petrified on Hanif's bed, unconsciously holding hands, as we listened to Lepew's relentless progression down the hall, banging on all the doors and twisting the doorknobs. He was almost at my door.

"I don't think I locked my door," I murmured, feeling panicked.

"Maybe it's not too late," said Hanif, shaking off his paralysis. He ran through the bathroom into my room. The door wasn't locked, and Hanif turned the bolt just in time. Lepew must've heard something because he seemed to remain outside my door longer than any of the others. Eventually, after having tried all the doors on the floor, we could hear his heavy tread retreating down the corridor. I was about to get up when Hanif's arm went around my shoulders, and he leaned his head against my cheek.

"Don't go," he whispered.

"I've got to go. Otherwise, I'll be a wreck for my paper," I said.

"Alright, but this night has been so much fun. I don't want it to end," he said.

I leaned over and kissed him on the cheek.

"So much fun! Now, don't turn on your light no matter what," I said, and with that, I left.

The next morning was relatively uneventful. I did, however, see Professor Lepew harassing the woman at registration, trying to find out which rooms were occupied in our building and by whom. She stoutly resisted. I was also relieved to see that Lepew was carrying his suitcase, apparently on his way home. This was pro forma at these conferences: the big shots never stay around.

Having skipped lunch, I took my thumb drive to a copy center to print a hard copy of my paper before going back to dress. The results of my toilette were so-so. I was wearing a dress with two vertical panels, one black and one white, both front and back, with two long strands of white pearls. It looked like a variant of the Dominican habit with its white chasuble and black scapular. Too late to worry about that. I got to the auditorium a little ahead of time to make sure that the mic worked and that there was water at the lectern. Cicero wrote that he was always terrified before he had to make a speech. I was of his school. I've no problem in the classroom; I'm only anxious about formal lectures. I also hate flowery introductions. They're so inflated that I feel compelled to contradict them and have to force myself to remain quiet. Worst of all, I'm an easy target for the noonday demon whose depressive capacity causes me to disinvest in my paper while I'm in the midst of delivering it, suddenly thinking: *Who cares about this shit anyway? I must be boring them to tears.*

For my keynote, entitled "Feudalism, Erectile Disfunction, and the Holy Grail," however, I was determined to sidestep the usual pitfalls. I graciously thanked the moderator for the overly generous introduction; I also remembered to recognize the organizers and thanked them for inviting me. Perhaps most importantly, I remembered to sip water at regular intervals so that my throat wouldn't contract involuntarily and make that embarrassing belching sound. When the noonday demon started to disparage me, I told it to get lost.

In other words, things were going well. The audience seemed receptive and laughed uproariously at my observation that "Guinevere's phallus was too big for the palace." I was on the final lap, metaphorically holding my breath, when the worst thing imaginable happened. The last two pages of my talk were missing — every academic's nightmare. Betrayed by Kinkos! Still, I didn't panic. I shuffled through my papers in case my conclusion had gotten stuck somewhere, all the while giving the audience a mawkish smile. I got my satchel out from under the lectern and poked around inside. Nothing. Then I said "fuck" very distinctly, and everybody heard me. I'd forgotten that the mic was not affixed to the lectern but attached to me as securely as a lascivious incubus. It picked up every word I said.

My inadvertent obscenity must have triggered temporary amnesia. I had no idea what the last two pages of my talk contained, so I was forced to stay the course. I didn't retract; I didn't apologize. Instead, after my initial *fuck*, I doubled down.

"Yes, indeed, *fuck*. That's the one noble feat that the knights of Latin Christendom feared they could no longer perform. The population decline among military aristocracy suggests that their fears were valid. They were *fucked*, and the golden age of feudalism was no more. Thank you very much."

I can't remember whether the audience clapped or booed. My blissful oblivion persisted throughout the Q and A and into the post-lecture reception. I do not recall any of the various people who attempted to engage me. The first thing that I do remember was seeing Hanif, standing to one side with two glasses of wine in his hands: one white and one red. I broke free and went up to him, and we both burst out laughing.

"I love it when you talk dirty," Hanif said as I accepted the glass of white wine. "Let's skip the banquet."

I was tempted. I felt that I had disgraced myself enough, and the food at these events was always terrible. Besides, Hanif was much more fun than any of the other participants. But I felt guilty.

"I can't. I just gave a keynote address," I said.

"Professor Bell, you just said 'fuck' into the mic — three times, by my count. I think you can do anything you want," Hanif replied.

"OK, then. Let's get out of here." I said.

We had dinner at an Italian restaurant. The waitress, covered in tattoos with her long blonde hair fashionably sheered on one side, looked like she knew her way around town. When she brought us after dinner grappa, Hanif asked if there was anywhere to dance. My God, every woman's dream: a guy who wants to dance. Our waitress said, regretfully, that there was no place with a live band that night, at least not one that lent itself to dancing. There was a bar with a dance floor, however, although the dance sets usually alternated with karaoke.

"That's great," said Hanif. "My friend here loves to sing."

So Hanif and I went dancing. He was fabulous — one of those rare men who could not only move well on his own but was an adept at the lost art of partnered dancing. Hanif was a terrific lead. It took me back to my graduate school days when there was only one boy, Eddy, who knew how to jive. All the women would queue up to dance with him, while the other male graduate students looked on sullenly. Not only did I have Hanif all to myself, but he was much better looking than Eddy. I felt like Emma Stone in *La La Land*.

While we sat out a karaoke set, Hanif turned to me and said: "I'm such a lucky guy. I'm in the same department as Heather Bell, so I've found my dream job. I mean it."

Had he really said that? And was this just an expression of professional admiration or could Hanif possibly be hitting on me?

Nah!

"And you're even more fun than I'd ever imagined," he continued. "I love dancing with you."

It was getting late, but Hanif insisted that we each sing one karaoke song before we left. I sang Gary Puckett and the Union Gap's "Young Girl"; he sang the Beatles' "If I Fell."

I was glad Hanif was driving the next day. While it had occurred to me over dinner that this night might end in passionate abandon, it so happened that there was a Margarita special at the karaoke bar, and I had the bright idea of getting a pitcher. In short, I was bombed, and nothing happened. It could be that Hanif was: a) indifferent to my charms; or b) like Jimmy Stewart in *Philadelphia Story,* too much of a gentleman to take advantage of me; or c) didn't want me to throw up on him. Your guess is as good as mine.

Chapter 6: The Trouble with Hanif

On the drive home from the conference, I made a special effort not to fall asleep. What with Professor Lepew, Rasputin, karaoke, and all, the conference had been memorable enough to give us something like a unique personal history together, and we chatted like old friends.

"Lepew was gross. I refuse to believe all those stories about his sexual conquests," Hanif said.

"Maybe he's like his namesake, who was always striking out," I said.

"What do you mean?"

"Pepe Lepew."

"Who's that?"

"A cartoon character. The amorous skunk. He speaks with a French accent and is modeled after Maurice Chevalier," I responded.

"Maurice who?"

"Oh, come on! The old lech in *Gigi*? The song 'Thank Heavens for Little Girls'?" I prompted.

"Sounds like kiddy porn," Hanif said.

"Chevalier was supposed to be the epitome of a classy ladies' man. So, to make him into a cartoon skunk was funny — at least in the 40s. But when *The Sorrow and the Pity* came out in the 70s, it turned out that Chevalier really was a skunk."

"What's *The Sorrow and the Pity*?" Hanif asked.

"A documentary about Vichy France. There are all these clips of Chevalier, singing merrily away to German troops — just like the turncoats in *Casablanca*. You have seen *Casablanca*?" I asked, suddenly apprehensive.

"What do you take me for?" said Hanif with a smile.

Is that a yes? Had he seen *Casablanca*? I didn't want to know if he hadn't, so I let it drop. Instead, I turned the subject to graphic novels. This was an area in which Hanif was an expert that I knew nothing about. I wanted to give him the opportunity to shine. How strategically womanly of me! Yet, while he was talking, it occurred to me that both my in-depth knowledge of Pepe Lepew, coupled with my total ignorance of graphic novels, must make me seem like a dinosaur in Hanif's eyes.

We had a delightful drive home, replete with lively conversation and a lunch stop at a roadside greasy spoon. Yet this sense of camaraderie seemed to dissipate as we approached campus. We were not, in fact, old friends — just two people from the same institution who had fallen under the inevitable leveling spell exerted by the conference milieu. Everybody knows that academia is all about hierarchy, not just in terms of the movement from Assistant to Associate to Full Professor but also in terms of institutions. These hierarchies never entirely disappear at conferences: they are, after all, printed on the very nametags we wear. Yet, somehow, the conference setting manages to suspend hierarchies. Instead, the conferees enter what anthropologists refer to as a liminal state in which individual achievement and identity give way to a strange sense of *communitas*: *we are all in this together*, we tell ourselves. This sense of group solidarity rarely outlasts the conference, however. On more than one occasion, I've arrived at airports at the end of a conference only to be ignored by (or to ignore) fellow academics with whom I'd been laughing, drinking, and even exchanging intimate confidences the day before. That Hanif and I had immediately relaxed into conference familiarity at the Fetish Conference was not surprising: prior to his arrival in the department, the conference was the only context in which we'd ever encountered one another. Yet once Hanif and I returned to campus, our differences in age and rank began to reassert themselves.

The next few times I ran into Hanif, it felt awkward. Yet, I have no way of knowing if Hanif felt the same distance that I did or if he was merely responding to my aloof behavior. Either way, Hanif must've been determined to break down whatever barriers were in place, real or imagined, because after two weeks of my reflexive coolness, he invited me to dinner. Of course, I was pleased. I wanted to have good working relations with my younger colleagues. OK, I know what you're thinking. But I was trying to put any inappropriate attraction I might feel behind me. Besides, Hanif's invitation seemed purely collegial, and I told myself that was a good thing.

Although very much looking forward to dinner, I was almost fifteen minutes late. Believe me when I say that I was not trying to be mysteriously aloof. I was late because it took me at least two hours to get dressed. My body seemed intent on waging war with everything I tried on. Initially, I was going to wear a dark green dress, very plain, with a boat neck collar -- easily one of my favorite outfits. But today, it would not cooperate. It had been hanging wrong; the shoulders looked like they were sprouting wings. The dress looked shapeless. Well, not exactly shapeless. More like Joan Rivers' description of Elizabeth Taylor's dress as: *two boy scouts struggling in a tent*. When I tried a belt on to rein in some of the turbulent zones, it looked like I was packing heat.

I thought maybe jeans: vernacular, comfortable, hip. But not this pair. Speaking of hips, mine seemed to have grown since the last time I wore jeans. I pulled them off, threw them on the bed with the other discards, and stalked toward the closet, swearing out loud. I took down a simple dress with an empire waist. It was flattering, but the black velvet seemed too dressy and too wintery. My herringbone pantsuit made me look like Hillary Clinton. But exactly! So, I finally went back to the fail-safe green dress; if I steam the shoulders… No time! The thick black belt had already betrayed me; try it with a light chain belt hanging loosely. Shit, forget the loosely part. Where the hell are my boots? And so on.

My boots got their four-inch heels entangled in the heap of rejected garments, and I almost broke my neck exiting the bedroom. Still, I realized as I was parking that there was a golden lining in that depressing show of disarray I'd left behind. My bedroom was so trashed that there'd be no danger of me inviting Hanif home. But when I walked into the restaurant and saw him stand up and smile, I instantly changed my mind. The living room looked OK. If the timing seemed right, I could always invite him back so long as we stayed on the couch. I instantly told myself not to be so ridiculous.

Hanif was drinking a martini, and I desperately wanted one as well. But we were close to campus, and the campus police were always trolling for student drunks: I was afraid I might get pulled over. So, I settled for a glass of Pinot Grigio. Neither of us made any reference to the conference, as if that was some lost domain to which we couldn't allude, let alone reenter. Instead, we talked about teaching, and different degrees of student disaffection.

"What do you do if someone routinely falls asleep during your lecture?" Hanif asked.

"I used to empathize. I figured that nobody sets out to fall asleep in class, so I just felt sorry for them and kept quiet. But I think my MO has to change. In my *Medieval Sex* class, every time I look over at my Teaching Assistant, she seems to be in a deep sleep." In my mind's eye, I could see the hulking form of Ms. Cather slumped over the desk, her oily hair hanging over her face like the evil drowned girl from the horror flick *The Ring*.

"Are you kidding me? Your Teaching Assistant will be grading the students' papers, and they know that. How're they going to react when they see her out like a light?" asked Hanif, clearly outraged.

"I know I should've said something by now, but I'm afraid it would backfire," I said apologetically.

"Backfire how?" Hanif asked, incredulous.

"Supposing she has narcolepsy. She'd file a complaint against me for discriminating against someone with a handicap," I replied.

"If she had a legitimate handicap, you'd have been notified by Student Services."

"But maybe she didn't register her handicap for fear she wouldn't be assigned as a Teaching Assistant."

"Then tough luck. If she can't stay awake, she shouldn't be anyone's Teaching Assistant. You can't let her get away with this. You've to call her on her shit," Hanif insisted.

I knew he was right and felt embarrassed by my pusillanimity (a word I hardly ever get to use: Google it!). I was impressed at his degree of assurance. Even though I had been teaching much longer, Hanif seemed more confident and commanding. Why this difference in pedagogical approaches? It's all about gender, compounded by age differential. Young men always get the highest points in student rankings: the female students find them sexy; the males want to emulate them. Men also do well at the other end of the age spectrum when they fit into the type of the *eminence grise*. By comparison, women never get a break. A young woman is not authoritative by definition; if the male students find her sexy, worse still. Older women are despised crones. But arguably the worst off are the women my age, who were about the age of the mothers that students have left behind.

"What if you think someone is searching the web while you're lecturing?" Hanif asked.

I was hardly guiltless in this area myself. I remember when the Chair-Who-Hated-Me punitively stuck me on Faculty Senate for five consecutive years. The only thing that saved me was searching the web for underwear during the meetings.

"Well, unless you have a Teaching Assistant trained to creep up behind them and spy, it's hard to be sure what they're doing on their computers. So I just give them the benefit of the doubt. Let's call it *Compassionate Pedagogy*," I said.

Hanif laughed. But the play on Thourelle's title either jolted something in his memory or provided an opportunity that he'd been looking for because he segued into the topic of Sylvia Thourelle. What'd she done? He'd heard rumors but nothing substantive.

"Let me guess. She was caught sleeping her way through the wrestling team. No? She charged her PornHub Live Cams to the department. Am I getting warm? I know! She was discovered pleasuring an inflatable doll in the parking lot. Is that it?" Hanif asked.

"Sorry, but I don't know any more than you do," I replied.

"Come on. The Chair is your bestie," he said.

"She doesn't know anything either. But why're you so interested?" I asked.

"Well, as an Assistant Professor, I figure that I'm vulnerable to predatory older profs, so I've a right to know." He took a sip of his drink. "Or should I apply to Sally Field for information?"

He may've been joking, but Freud said a joke was always at someone's expense – mine, in this instance, though I doubt that Hanif intended it as such. Even so, the reference to predatory older profs was de-libidinizing in the extreme. Good. I should be de-libidinized. I kept telling myself: *You're an old bag, and nothing sexual is going to happen. Not now; not ever.*

"There was, as you probably heard, an incident with a student, but it could be that it's only a rumor that's totally unfounded," I responded.

"I doubt that. I know Sylvia Thourelle, and I know what she's like."

I must've looked confused because he added: "Don't you remember that I did an MA at Peitho U.?"

Now I remembered: the English department that was especially savvy in rhetoric.

"Well, she was there as a Visiting Professor," Hanif continued. "The position would've become a permanent position the following year, and she was the one who was being groomed for the job, but she mysteriously left."

"Why?" I asked. This was prior to her new-found eminence, and tenure-track jobs were rare.

He didn't answer right away. Instead, he bought time by removing one of the olives off his swizzle stick and popping it into his mouth. He offered me the stick of olives, but I shook my head, waiting for his answer.

"She was doing research for *Passionate Pedagogy* and encountered some difficulties. Student complaints, to be exact."

"How do you know?"

"Because I was one of the plaintiffs."

Although tantalizing in the extreme, Hanif would provide few details. There was ultimately a lawsuit brought against the university because of Thourelle, but the university had settled out of court. Hanif, along with the other plaintiffs, had signed a document promising not to reveal any of the details of the suit. From the little he said, I gleaned that some kind of sexual transgression led to an overall breakdown in trust between Thourelle and her students. But the nature of the transgression remained unclear. It could've been a verbal offense: for instance, Thourelle could've inadvertently outed somebody or snubbed a transgendered student in some manner.

Even so, the fact that there was such a suit served as a warning to me. Hanif had experience with charging his professors with sexual harassment for whatever reason. Perhaps similar charges might be leveled by an Assistant Professor against "predatory older profs," as he had so charmingly put it. I protectively crossed my legs under the table, now determined that they should stay crossed. The rest of the evening was uneventful. The waiter came to take our order. We both ordered gumbo, which I barely touched. No appetizer, no dessert, no suggestive lingering. In fact, no suggestive anything. Somehow, the specter of Thourelle had managed to cast a pall over our dinner.

I didn't ask Hanif to come home with me, nor did I get any indication that he wanted me to.

Chapter 7: Jamaica Inn

I could think of several reasons why it was for the best that I hadn't invited Hanif home with me.

    a) I didn't want to get brought up on Title IX charges

    b) he probably wouldn't have come unless I hog-tied him, and I couldn't stand the rejection (I'm sure Dr. Owen would agree)

    c) did I mention that I didn't want to get brought up on Title IX charges?

    d) the Gender Studies Program was having a dumb retreat the next day, and I had to be up early

I said "dumb" retreat — but what I meant was "useless" because the retreats didn't accomplish much of anything and were a waste of money. Even so, I didn't mind going. In fact, I rather liked them. The basic premise was that the disparate faculty members affiliated with the Gender Studies Program, scattered throughout the Humanities, should have the opportunity to relax, bond, assess and critique the status quo, and brainstorm about future directions. However lofty its purposes, however, the retreat reminded me of the hallowed slumber parties of my youth, where we would sit around in shorty pajamas talking about boys and eating gummy bears, toffee, and SweetTarts until our tongues turned white and felt like pincushions — all without gaining any weight.

Of course, there were differences. With something in the vicinity of thirty or so attendees, the retreat was many times bigger than the slumber party. Also, in contrast to the uni-sex slumber party, our retreats had a degree of gender diversity: there was a handful of transgender and/ or queer faculty members who showed up. But on the rare occasion that a straight male faculty member got up the nerve to put in an appearance, he didn't usually make it through lunch.

The exception to the rule was Daniel Eisenerz. Daniel was the former President of the Faculty Senate, forced to resign after he managed to finagle a tour of the university's experimental medical facility only to expose the heinous exploitation of animals in an interview on public radio. I remember particularly the segment about cats: their backs were surgically broken for a study on chronic pain. The researchers were vague about what happened to the animals: all Daniel could get out of them was that none of the survivors were ever put up for adoption.

The response to Daniel's interview was immediate. The powers that be at the medical school, who had lucrative contracts with pharmaceutical companies, were incensed, as was the administration at large. But the Gender Studies Program was impressed and asked Daniel to give a talk at a retreat several years ago. Ever since then, he'd been a regular at our retreats. He was from the Design Department, which meant that he was sufficiently well-dressed and demonstrated an unusual sensitivity to matters of gender that we initially assumed he was gay. When it turned out that he wasn't, the heterosexual women, who were still the majority, were delighted: it meant he was available for serious flirtation.

The retreat routinely took place in a town about an hour's drive from the university, graced with the suggestive name French Tickle. The town was home to an inn that was supposed to have been quite luxurious during prohibition but, having failed to modernize, had since fallen on hard times. The rooms only had window box air conditioners, and most of them didn't work. This usually wasn't an issue in late September, but this year, it was still uncomfortably warm. The participants had done their best to prepare for the unexpected heat wave, sporting their own version of hip relaxation garb: pastel-colored jeans, capri pants, handkerchief dresses, and a bizarre range of sunhats.

We gathered in the conference room for the keynote address, resembling nothing so much as the phantasmagoric meeting of the Women's Hydrangea Club at the opening of *The Manchurian Candidate*. That is everyone, except for my new colleague, April Fortune, who clearly hadn't gotten the memo. Rather than looking unassailably dopey like the rest of us, she looked cool and relaxed in a short-sleeved tunic and leggings. The speaker was to be Dr. Carlson — a cheerful sixty-something sociologist from one of our regional campuses who looked a lot like Claude Rains' scary Nazi mother in *Notorious*. But then the woman who was supposed to introduce her stepped forward, announcing that Dr. Carlson had an accident with a lightbulb that had resulted in a broken ankle — a compound fracture, in fact.

"But fortunately, Sylvia Thourelle has agreed to step in at the last moment. Although Professor Thourelle needs no introduction…," the commentator went on to list her numerous publications and awards at length.

"Her lecture today is entitled 'I Walk the Line.'"

Many of us were surprised that Thourelle had been tapped as substitute speaker; everyone was confused. But as the good Pavlovian academics we were, we managed a credible show of applause as Thourelle, who must have been lurking at the back of the conference room, strode down the center aisle. The palette of her clothing remained the same, with an amplified degree of panache, perhaps reflecting an enhanced salary. She was dressed in a dark grey silk kimono-like dress lined with a wine-colored fabric and a multi-colored brocade obi belt. A remarkable pair of off-white cowboy boots completed her ensemble, the laser-cut kind for warm weather. I'd always wanted a pair of those: Lucchese, I thought. The outfit looked like it cost a modest fortune. Once she reached the mic, there were no preliminaries; she immediately started speaking.

"Every day across America, students are being subjected to the invidious sexual advances of their faculty mentors, the very people they're conditioned to trust. Yet the rising numbers of abusive situations do not correspond to rising student enrollments, but rather reflect one of the sad bi-products of affirmative action in academe: the female professor run amok." She went on to excoriate the middle-aged academic who had sacrificed everything for her scramble to the top, including husband and family, and now decided that she was lonely and deserved compensation in the form of "the student body." The proverbial line that Thourelle herself walked ensured a perfect balance of compassion (not passion) for her students without stumbling into intimacy.

I used to hate the expression "gob-smacked": what the hell is a gob, and who in heaven's name is smacking it? But once I made the connection between gob and the Old English word for beak, I warmed to it. Gob-smacked is the only way to describe the response to Thourelle's keynote from both a theoretical and practical perspective. Theoretically, Thourelle's censorious position once again conflicted with *Passionate Pedagogy*, and its emphasis on the erotic exchange between teacher and student. Many, if not most, of the attendees had already heard rumors of Thourelle's involvement with an undergraduate. Nor did her assault on the collective gob end there. Because she had spoken some fifteen minutes over the allotted time, and lunch was imminent, there was no Q and A. Thourelle strode out of the conference room faster than you could say gender equity. She seemed to have made a clean getaway. At least she did not appear again during our retreat.

The rest of the day dragged on interminably. After lunch, we had an exercise in "trust" where we divided into groups and were required to fall backward into one another's arms. (I was having hot flashes and was annoyed that we couldn't do this in the pool. Some women pleaded that they had their periods and were out of sorts, however. Fecundity always wins out.) After a short break, we were then presented with a series of obstacles that the Gender Studies Program had encountered over the course of the past yearand were divided into groups to role-play the various "solutions." I was pleasantly surprised by April Fortune, who proved to be something of a virtuoso in this regard. The job our group was assigned was to eke more money out of the Dean. April role-played a hunger strike outside his office, marking the supposed passing days by the number of fingers she held up and an ever-greater show of hunger-induced decrepitude, all the time singing "We Shall Overcome."

Then there was an interminable tour of the hotel's museum by one of the female desk clerks with over-whitened teeth. Apparently, the hotel had once been a favorite haunt of midwestern outlaws. The chief exhibit was a gun that Dillinger had managed to fire accidentally into his own foot during a raid on the hotel, along with the perforated shoe that he was wearing, and the slug extracted from said foot. Finally, there was dinner. It was a buffet offering three overcooked entrees: vegetarian lasagna, meat lasagna, and cheese manicotti. Since three quarters of the participants seemed to have been gluten-intolerant, and the rest were lactose intolerant, they made the most of the salad bar. I had the manicotti all to myself.

After dinner, all I wanted to do was drink and gossip. Instead, I dutifully sat through a documentary called *The Seven Year Bitch*, which consisted of a series of interviews with recently tenured Associate Professors who bitched about working their butts off for six years, finally achieving tenure, and then experiencing a numbing sense of fatigue and letdown. Even so, the seventh year was their sabbatical year, and they were expected to generate a new project. But how could they possibly when they were feeling so burned out and disaffected? The film, which ended on this equivocal note, garnered only tepid applause. The director, a woman in her thirties who had recently been promoted to Associate Professor, was there to take questions. (Please don't tell me that this film won her tenure.) There were no questions. She just stood there waiting, perhaps imagining that the weightiness of the theme had silenced us.

Whether because of my celebrated low threshold for awkward silences or out of sheer perversity, I stuck my hand up. The director called upon me with a pathetically eager look on her face.

"I have more of a comment than a question. I was struck for the first time by the biblical rhythm of the whole tenure clock. Like God himself who worked for six days and then rested on the seventh, the Assistant Professor toils for six years and is given the seventh year off."

"Interesting," the director said in a voice that was anything but interested. This wasn't the kind of response she was hoping for, apparently. "But I'm not sure I get your point."

"Well, my point is simple. These people are bitching when they have been given an entire year to do nothing — just like God resting on the seventh day. They now have tenure, no one checks up on them, they can just relax." I looked over at April Fortune, the only untenured person there as far as I knew. She was nodding as if she alone understood my intervention. I smiled at her, and she smiled back and held up her thumb in approval. But the director looked pissed off.

"Yes, but if they want to be promoted to Full Professor …," the director stammered, turning a little red.

"Ah, but no one says they are required to be promoted to Full. They can stay in rank as Associate Professors forever, if they like; they can retire as Associates. They may not receive the same salary or level of esteem in the profession as they would, had they been promoted to Full, but they would certainly experience less pressure and have less to bitch about. They wouldn't have to write another book or (in your case) direct another movie. No one can take their tenure away."

The director had moved beyond flustered to annoyed. "I'm afraid that I still can't see where you're going with this."

Now it was my turn to get annoyed. "OK, it turns out that I do have a question after all: why are these Associate Professors bitching? The people who should be bitching are the graduate students who work for six years on a dissertation; defend it; then find out that there are no jobs; and who, rather than resting in their seventh year, end up waiting tables."

I was perfectly serious, thinking of several of my own students, brilliant but unlucky, who were forced to follow versions of the path I outlined. What I couldn't figure out was why everyone (apart from the director) was laughing. Jan, who was sitting beside me, had started kicking the backs of my calves to get me to sit down. So, I chirped, *Great film,* and sat down.

When we were finally dismissed, Jan, April Fortune, and I ran to get our bathing suits. I was already beginning to like April for her spirited pantomime, but she won me over completely by "getting" my comment to the director. Apparently, several game colleagues from other departments were of like minds and also hustled to the pool. But now it was my turn to bitch: I'd been looking forward to a swim all day, but the pool had closed at 9:30 p.m. The other would-be bathers were about to give up, but I refused to be defeated. It was an outdoor pool, surrounded by a stucco wall, that was generally accessed from inside the hotel through the exercise room. But on the outside, there was a metal gate that was locked from the inside. My plan was to scale the fence and open the door. I found a stainless-steel cart outside what I assume was the kitchen door – the type they use for delivering room service. Two of my colleagues held the cart steady while I attempted to clamber up.

"What if someone sees us and asks what we're doing?" Jan asked nervously.

"That's the easy part. We tell them that we had to do this because the gate was locked," I said from aloft my wobbly mount.

There was a loud clank of metal on metal and then a thump, which caused my startled handlers to jerk the cart so that I almost fell off. Someone gave a little shriek. I told them to calm down: it was only my flask. Would one of them please pick it up? I was sitting on the top of the wall at this point. I carefully turned myself around and began easing down the other side of the wall so the drop would be as short as possible. I could feel the skin being scraped off my thighs. I dropped to the ground and, feeling valiant, opened the gate. The others poured in, and we were soon in the pool, circulating flasks. (It turned out practically everybody brought one.) It was a fine night: the sky was clear and, every once in a while, someone caught sight of a falling star. The smell of wisteria hovered in the air. Initially, we just floated around contentedly until I remarked on what I assumed everybody was thinking: that Thourelle's talk was a bizarre exercise in self-righteousness.

"I don't think you should prejudice April against one of her senior colleagues before she's had a chance to make up her own mind," Jan said. There were certain things we weren't supposed to say around junior colleagues.

Then someone quipped: "Yes, it's important to 'Walk the Line' by not attacking senior feminist scholars in her presence."

"April, are you offended by my indiscretion?" I asked.

"We just broke into the hotel's pool. Haven't we left discretion in the dust by now?" April replied.

This seemed to be the consensus: most of us were itching to talk about that flaming hypocrite, Thourelle. The unfortunate "incident" involving Thourelle may have been widely bruited about, but we were still low on details. The Dean had led Jan to believe that Thourelle had been caught diddling one of her undergraduates. But there were no formal charges brought, as far as we knew. And then suddenly, Dr. Carlson breaks her ankle, and Thourelle gets the opportunity to protest her innocence to the Gender Studies Faculty. She emerges as the paradigm of pedagogical propriety.

"Brilliant rearguard action, really," someone said with admiration. There were no lights in the pool, but I thought it was the senior classicist, who decades ago had written a very controversial book on the Vestal Virgins, arguing that they were really eunuchs in drag. Ahead of her time, really. She was long past retirement age, but still plucky, and her linguistic edge was as sharp as ever.

"Well, she'd better stop identifying herself as a *feminist* scholar of rhetoric," someone else added with indignation.

Most of the older feminists snorted agreement, but I was uncertain. Despite my antipathy for Thourelle, there was at least a part of me that took issue with this last remark. Didn't most of the world meet their future partners at work? If we defined feminism in terms of gender equity, one could make the case that female academics should be entitled to the same prerogatives that our male colleagues had enjoyed for centuries: a student body that could double as a romantic body. Yet, once women entered the profession *en masse*, the situation changed, and it was the women who changed it. I understood why: most of us knew what it was like to be chased around the desk by faculty mentors, not only as graduate students but even as undergraduates, and did not relish the experience. (Those who did often married the louts and did not bother to complete their degrees.)

I probably should've shut up, but I didn't. "I think most of us agree that feminists, by definition, do not sleep with the students who're in their classes. Even so, now we're censuring sexual relations with students altogether. This means not only current students, but former students, undergraduate and graduate students alike; even students we've never taught. Doesn't it seem like feminists are shooting themselves in the collective foot — especially those of us who're unfortunate enough to be heterosexual?" I asked.

"Heather, be careful. You sound like a chauvinist pig," Jan said testily.

"Give me a break! When I was a grad student, more than half of the men in the department married their students, and nobody thought anything about it. It was OK with the administration too: every year, they sent around a memo reminding faculty members to resign from dissertation committees if they were 'in a relationship' with the dissertator," I responded.

"But those were the bad old days when women were being sexually harassed constantly," Jan contended.

"Great. And now at least half of our demographic is divorced or perpetually single women with no hope of ever getting laid again, let alone having a relationship," I retorted.

"But younger men don't want middle-aged women," someone said.

"How do you know that? Rank and seniority translate into power, and power's sexy," I responded.

"Not according to Sally Field," April said wryly.

"Fuck Sally Field. She's an idiot. Power has the capacity to transform our sagging contours into Foucauldian aphrodisiacs. It worked for the male professors," I countered.

This prompted a professor from biology to weigh in. "But it won't work for women. Lab experiments demonstrate that male rats only want to mount the female rats with greater reproductive potential," she said.

This gloomy factoid seemed to have thrown our group at large for a loop. For a while, all you could hear was some gentle paddling.

But I'd finished most of my flask and was now prepared to throw caution to the wind.

"OK, I promise not to hit on any students. But even relations with junior faculty are becoming taboo," I complained.

"Ah, how like the parched Tantalus: doomed to live by a fountain but unable to drink," said the classicist with feeling.

As the reader well knows, this was hardly the first time that I'd entertained such heretical thoughts about junior colleagues, but any specifics had, up until now, remained part of an inner monologue. This night I'd been drinking, however, and what was better left inside must've slipped out. At least, I assume this was the case because someone asked: "Who in God's name is Hanif?"

"He's a recent hire in English who queers animals." I recognized Jan's voice.

"What the hell!" said the putative classicist. "Is that legal now?"

I was quick to reassure her that this was the way that scholars who worked in hot areas like animal studies tended to describe their work, presumably so that no one thought they were vets.

"But, speaking of queer, isn't Hanif gay?" someone asked.

"I heard that he was bi," said April.

I did not want Hanif to be either of these things. I suppose bi was OK. Yet when it came to men who were allegedly bi, it seemed to me that they almost invariably preferred males to females.

"I think he must be straight. If he were gay or bi, wouldn't he be here?" I asked.

Before the other bathers had a chance to appreciate the acuity of my deduction, the flood lights came on, and several policemen burst out of the hotel's health center, guns drawn, bellowing, "Freeze."

The lead officer had a bull horn through which he shouted, "Drop your weapons," mistaking the glint of our flasks. When they saw the flasks bobbing harmlessly in the water, they must've realized that we were not weaponized. Even so, they clearly regarded the flasks as essential evidence because we weren't allowed to retrieve them ourselves; the police fished them out of the pool with a long-handled net. Then they made each of us get out of the pool, *Slowly! One at a time*, as they sized up the threat we presented to public safety.

"Officer, I am Jan Westlock, Chair of the English Department, and I can explain all this."

"You can explain down at the station."

Two of the police officers had their guns drawn, while the third, a female officer, patted each of us down and then bound our wrists behind our backs with zip-cuffs. When it was my turn, she whispered, "I'm so sorry, Professor Bell."

I recognized her. Debbie. I'd directed her honors thesis about five years ago: "The Theme of Exile in Anglo-Saxon Poetry." Always a very polite, attentive student. She didn't tie my hands very tightly; maybe she thought that I should make a run for it.

We never learned who called the police. There had always been some town-gown tensions in the area, but this was ridiculous. We were, after all, the guests of the hotel. Be that as it may, the charges were breaking and entering and possession of illegal drugs (meaning drinking in an unlicensed area). Before we were finger-printed and booked, Jan was allowed to call campus security, where someone had the presence of mind to go to the Dean's residence and wake him up. (It was after midnight.) The Dean sent one of his lackey's down, who attested to our basic probity.

In short, we got lucky, but not too lucky. Just as we issued out of the station and were on the verge of getting into the campus security van, a couple of flashes went off. Our well-wishers at the hotel seemed to have alerted the local press. And, sure enough, there in the morning paper was an unforgettable picture of a disparate group of female faculty members, disheveled and in their bathing suits. Renoir's bathers we were not. I shouldn't generalize: April Fortune looked pretty good, but I looked like hell. Maybe it was because of the incipient scabs forming after my slide down the stucco, but my goddam thighs looked even worse than I'd ever imagined.

Chapter 8: The Wrong Man

Move over Thourelle: the denizens of the pool break-in were the new scandals of the department. When anyone asked what prompted our so-called break-in, I blamed it on the provocative Dillinger display in the hotel museum. Hanif regarded our escapade as the stuff of legend and secured five copies of the newspaper for me in case I didn't have the presence of mind to buy extras. Daniel sent me a cookie-o-gram, both congratulating me for my bold undertaking and rebuking me for not inviting him to the pool party. Jan was deeply mortified, however, and I was afraid she'd never forgive me. Apart from that, I didn't mind much. This wasn't my first run-in with the police. My ex-husband once called them on me.

Yes, gentle reader, I was once married. So, I don't fit perfectly into the sorry pattern of the surplus female academic that I sketched above. Or perhaps I should say that there was a time when I didn't fit, though Marcel, my ex-husband, fit into the category of privileged male to perfection. We met as colleagues but in different departments. Marcel was in the French Department and something of a luminary. It was my first job. I was thirty, nervous, and grateful to be employed. Marcel was fifteen years older, handsome, with a sexy accent and gracious continental manners. (In fact, I later learned he was French Canadian, but that only seemed to make him try harder.)

Marcel and I met in a Medieval Studies Committee meeting sometime in early November of my first year. After the meeting, he asked me to go for coffee: *We're colleagues and medievalists. We really should get to know one another.* He was urbane and suave, and that made me nervous. I'd never met a man who consistently wore silk shirts before. I poured some scalding coffee down the front of my sweater, but he was polite enough to pretend not to notice.

When he learned that I had no plans for Thanksgiving, he immediately invited me to his home, and I accepted. I asked what I could bring, but he said *Only your delightful self.* Long years of insecurity had turned me into a gift giver, however (*please like me*). So, as a matter of course, I arrived with an expensive bottle of Bordeaux, a large bouquet of flowers, and a tasteful assortment of chocolates. At the time, he was married to a woman his own age who had, indeed, as I later learned, supported him and cooked his meals while he was in graduate school. They had two children: Mimi and Fidelio (Marcel was an opera buff). Mimi was just finishing high school, while Fidelio had already begun university. Marcel's wife, Evelyn, was beautiful and gracious; his children were bilingual and smart; as a family, their collective degree of charm and accomplishment was astonishing. So, I was, of course, surprised, but oh so gratified, when Marcel began to court me. And court me he did. Champagne, flowers, and first-class flights to his speaking engagements all around the world, where we stayed in sumptuous hotels. He taught me to waltz in Vienna, eat snails in Paris, and pretend to like carp in Prague. (I never quite took to it.) In no time, I was head over heels in love.

I guess you could say that I broke up his marriage. But does anyone really break up a marriage that isn't already in trouble? Evelyn had made him a wonderful home where they'd raised two superior children. Even so, there were problems, but Marcel was always strangely vague about what they were. At the most, he'd just shake his head and say things like *Ah, she's just not an intellectual. She's always resented my work,* or *It's only the children that matter to her; Evelyn no longer loves me.* Retrospectively, I see that Marcel was one of those feckless gentlemen rats who preferred to mount the more fertile lady rats, and for a while, I was that lady rat — ripe for mounting.

I didn't know this at the time, even though I had early warning. After the divorce proceedings were in motion, I spotted his wife in the grocery store. Coward that I was, I pretended not to see her. But she came over to me and asked how I was doing. I've no idea what we spoke about at first. I was too overwhelmed by fear and shame. But eventually, her words began to penetrate:

"I knew that I'd eventually leave; I just didn't know when."

But that was wrong! Marcel had told me that he'd wanted to leave his wife for a long time but that she was a Catholic who didn't believe in divorce. Then he fell in love with me, and this gave him the strength to leave. Surely, this was the correct narrative. Marcel left Evelyn, not the other way around. I wasn't about to contradict her, however.

"At first, I was convinced you'd eventually disappear, like the others. But I still resented — even hated you. My confessor told me to pray for you, but I just couldn't." (*So, she was religious.*) "Then one day, I woke up, and it was gone. All my hatred. You could've been anyone. I was finally able to tell him that I was leaving."

She must've realized that her narrative was potentially hurtful because she immediately put her hand on my sleeve and said gently, "I don't mean to insult you. I hope for your sake that Marcel has changed, and you'll have better luck than I did."

And so, Evelyn thought I would disappear "like the others," implying that she was veteran to a succession of infidelities. She also implied that Marcel only proposed to me after she'd left him. Of course, I didn't believe any of this. Plus, how could she possibly be sincere in her hope that Marcel would remain true to me? In her situation, I would've cursed any rival; my jealousy would've made Medea look like a Quaker. At first, I assumed that Evelyn's seeming empathy was just an act to conceal her seething rage. Eventually, however, I came to believe not only that Evelyn was sincere but that the petty duplicities that became reflexive behavior for many of us just weren't available to her. Her sincerity surrounded her like a second skin. Before continuing with her shopping, she leaned over and kissed my cheek, murmuring: "I will pray for you." When she turned away, I actually thought that I might faint. I abandoned my grocery cart and fled the store.

I didn't tell Marcel about this encounter. I don't know why I didn't because I was desperately in need of reassurance. Of course, I accepted his version of the divorce and believed it when he said that it was only when he met me that he knew love for the first time. *Love is precious and not to be wasted,* he'd said. Marcel was handsome and had an enchanting way about him. That didn't necessarily make him a womanizer, did it?

But, of course, he was. Only three years into our marriage, I became suspicious. When someone possessed the kind of romantic genius that Marcel had — with a constant flow of caresses, gifts, and compliments — it is impossible not to notice when the well is beginning to dry up. He no longer wanted me to travel with him to his various speaking engagements. (*My darling, you must get on with your own work. You're still untenured!*) He spent more and more time at the office. When he was home, we spoke less and less. A numbing dread spread over me like moss on damp rock. Even so, I worked hard. I had to get tenure; I couldn't be a failed academic; I had to prove and keep proving to Marcel that I was not like Evelyn; I was a real intellectual.

When I did get tenure, Marcel threw me the most marvelous party to celebrate. He reserved a local restaurant and ordered a special dinner with all my favorite foods. There was a string quartet, dancing, and a steady stream of friends and colleagues congratulating me. I wore a beautiful dress of black taffeta — off the shoulder with a full skirt. I was so happy, reassured by what I perceived as incontrovertible proof of Marcel's love. Only it wasn't. The party was really a farewell gift. He left me three days later with no explanation except to say that he wasn't happy. Evelyn had held onto him much longer because of the children.

And then I went off my head. You hear about spurned females sending the men who rejected them pizzas in the middle of the night. That's nothing by comparison. I sent bloated emails, which alternated between blandishments and threats, begging him to come back. I phoned and texted unceasingly, but met with chilling silence. And then, through low cunning that I won't expand upon here, I found out where he was temporarily leasing an apartment.

After hitting a series of buzzers in the lobby, someone eventually buzzed me up. I knew his apartment was on the fourth floor but didn't know the apartment number. I checked the mailboxes for his name, but it wasn't there — presumably because the apartment was a sublet, though it could be a precaution in case I took to sleuthing. Still, I was prepared for that. It had already occurred to me that I could identify the apartment by the ringing of his cell phone. I knew that if he recognized my number, he wouldn't answer, so I'd purchased a burner phone expressly for the purpose. The fourth floor had about twenty units, but it was ten in the evening, and there was very little noise coming from the different apartments. When I dialed Marcel's number, I could hear the telltale ringing about halfway down the corridor. He answered on the third ring.

"Marcel, it's me. Can we meet for a drink and talk?"

"There's nothing to talk about."

"What about the house?"

"My lawyer will be in touch with you," Marcel said and abruptly hung up. I wasn't really surprised by his response. If I'd thought he was willing to meet with me, after all, there would've been no need for all my subterfuge. I went to his door and tried it to see if it was unlocked. It wasn't. Then I knocked. There was a moment's hesitation, and then I heard him moving toward the door. I put my hand over the peephole so he couldn't see it was me, but, of course, he knew.

"Heather, you're behaving like a child. Don't you have any pride?" he asked through the door.

With this allusion to my undignified behavior, I totally lost it. I began beating on the door, screaming: *Open up, you coward!* Marcel never opened the door, but he did call the police. Fortunately, he wasn't interested in pressing charges. He just wanted me gone. The officer who came to get me asked where I wanted to go. I was crying hysterically, incapable of answering, so he took me down to the station. Eventually, I calmed down enough to call Jan. Thank God she was there. She came at once and put her arms around me, whispering, "Heather, you're scaring me. You have to stop."

I was scaring myself as well. So, I did stop.

It made things easier that Marcel had accepted an offer at a university that would also provide a tenure-stream position for his lover and bride-to-be. She'd been his graduate student, who'd almost finished her degree (although her progress was slowed down by the requisite changing of dissertation directors). Once our divorce was finalized, they immediately married. I was thirty-seven then and haven't had a real relationship since. Oh, there have been several interludes during which I got involved with some sort of reprobate, almost instantly over-invested in an illusory relationship that was never really on offer, and then got dumped. Admittedly, a couple of times the dumping was mutual. There was, for example, the guy who would "borrow" my credit card to shop maniacally at Sam's Club, stocking up on huge quantities of peanut butter and toilet paper. I also remember that he never closed the bathroom door, no matter what he was doing. It wasn't hard to let go of that one. But it was this string of failures that drew me into therapy and, finally, to Dr. Owen.

Right after Marcel left, Jan insisted that I stay with her and her husband, Marty, for a few days. I didn't want to, but I knew I was a mess and was afraid to be left on my own. All the time I was there, I couldn't eat or sleep. Yet Jan was so sweet. She'd tip-toe into my room every night at 11:00 p.m. and stand there, waiting in the dark. I eventually realized that she was listening to ensure that I was breathing. Did she really think I was going to off myself? I wasn't that far gone — honestly. Besides, I already knew from reading *The Bell Jar* at the tender age of thirteen that suicide didn't always turn out as one expected. I refused to be one of those incompetents who takes pills, passes out, vomits, and ends up with brain damage.

But maybe Jan didn't think I was going to kill myself: maybe she was afraid I'd die from an adult version of SIDS. I say this because, once I'd fallen asleep, Jan seemed apprehensive that I'd never wake up. Not on her watch! If I slept past 9:00 a.m., she'd tap on the door, still on tippy toe. Our conversations would go something like this.

"Morning in bed?" she'd ask lightly.

"Yes, mourning in bed," I'd answer. Shallow irony and deep melancholy seemed to complement one another.

"It's a beautiful day," she'd say.

"I don't care. I'm mourning in bed," I'd respond, stressing the gerund.

"Oh," she'd say, followed by a long pause. "Do you feel at all better?" she'd ask.

"Yes, because I feel even number." Then I'd laugh. I meant that I felt even more numb than usual. But once I said this, for some reason I could see the words spelled out in my head (the effect of too much proof reading). It looked like I was claiming to be an even number; maybe tomorrow I'd be an odd number.

"I'm glad," Jan would say — unable to fathom my laughter but cheered by it, nonetheless.

"Do you want to go for a walk?" she'd ask.

"No."

"I'm going to make you breakfast then," she'd respond in a firm voice.

"I won't eat it," I'd answer — equally firm.

I won that round, I'd think with smug satisfaction. But I soon realized that I must be regressing. Not since I was ten years old would I have regarded such an exchange a triumph. I didn't want to read either, which was unusual for me. The one exception was the poetry of Emily Dickinson. I could read it because she understood: she was the mistress of the numb at heart.

Even through my numbness, however, I knew that all was not well between Jan and Marty. And my presence was not helping. Early one morning, a week into my retreat, I heard the following:

"What the fuck is going on?" Marty said.

"What do you mean?" Jan replied.

"What do you think? With the lump upstairs," he sneered (I couldn't see his face but I could hear the sneer). "Why is she still here?"

"She's my best friend."

"So, why would she want to destroy her best friend's marriage?" he responded.

"You hardly ever see her. So, what's the big deal?" Jan said.

"I feel her presence," he snapped.

Wow! Marty felt my presence: it was like being the malevolent spirit at a séance. But Marty was lacking the kind of sensitivity one would expect in a medium: his inner self didn't extend beyond functions like circulation and digestion. Even so, it was time – time to leave. And I wasn't drawing any comfort from being there. After I left Jan and Marty, I discovered that it was good to be home. It was mid-

May; teaching was over, and the flowers in my garden were unfurling like a prolonged beauty pageant. I could cry with impunity, drink as much as I wanted (which was a lot), and keep the TV on all night.

My only visitors were Jan and Daniel. Jan had told Daniel about my plight after I left her house — presumably so he could check up on me. She knew that Daniel would empathize with my situation because his own heart had been broken when his wife left him several years earlier. Daniel and I were both rather competitive types, however, so his condolences often morphed into contests.

"Betty dumped me for another woman. At least Marcel didn't leave you for another man," Daniel would say.

"A woman being left by her husband for another woman is more insulting. When the old and the new objects of desire happen to be of the same sex, the new one is somehow superior," I said.

"Or perhaps Marcel is just one of those immature individuals who needs constant variety. That wouldn't reflect on you one way or the other. But if he'd gone for another man, that would mean that his relations with you were so bad that he jumped the tracks," Daniel said.

"What do you mean by 'jumped the tracks'?" I asked.

"That the defector becomes so disaffected that they give up on the opposite sex altogether," said Daniel.

"So that's how you interpret Betty's departure?" I asked.

"That's right," he replied.

"It could be worse. What if Betty were bi? That would mean that she wasn't necessarily rejecting all men — just you," I said.

"Oh, thanks. That helps a lot," he would respond.

And so on.

I have to confess to an irascible disposition that resents people who don't agree with me. So, these conversations were always strong medicine: I'd get so annoyed with Daniel that, for a few blessed moments, I'd forget about Marcel. Plus, Daniel was an ardent and gifted vegan, so our arguments generally occurred over his delicious soups and stews. A born proselytizer, Daniel rarely showed up without a book or a documentary about the suffering of farm animals. Since I already refused red meat and chicken, he spared me the horrors of the abattoir or the deplorable treatment of poultry. The materials he presented me with were honed on the suffering of dairy cattle or new evidence about the piscine nervous system and the degree to which fish and other aquatic creatures suffer.

Jan continued to be attentive for those first few months. She would drop in unannounced to check up on me, insist that I accompany her to the gym, and even force me to fly to a conference in San Francisco with her. She knew that American literature didn't do it for me, but she'd splurged to get a hotel with "amenities." I spent most of my time in the posh hotel's pool and sauna. In short, she got me on my feet again. Who could possibly know that I would very soon be called upon to return the favor?

Jan's marriage to Marty had begun as something of a compromise formation and hadn't evolved much beyond that. Jan was in her late thirties when they married — a classic case of a woman who desperately wanted kids, and took whatever husband-material was at hand. Sadly, no children were forthcoming, and it became clearer every day that Jan had married beneath her. Even though such a statement is despicably classist, not to mention antiquated, that didn't make it any less true. Jan was superior to Marty in every way: educated, intelligent, sensitive, and loyal. She also happened to be a striking beauty, with thick chestnut hair and large hazel eyes. Admittedly, Marty wasn't bad looking; in fact, he was rather attractive — provided you like that kind of sloe-eyed guy in a leather jacket who stares at women in elevators.

After five years of marriage and several heart-rending miscarriages, they had pretty much given up on having kids. Then, a year before my relationship with Marcel ended, Marty lost his job and showed no interest in getting another one. I never quite figured out what he did. It was definitely white collar: he was some kind of executive, I suppose. But whatever Marty's job may've been, it seemed to have conditioned him to perceive every subsequent employment opportunity that presented itself as beneath him. I knew from my father's unfortunate employment record that an unemployed man is an unstable element and that his self-pity had the capacity to jeopardize any relationship. One would think that having lost his job, any husband would feel grateful that his wife was still gainfully employed, but that was often not the case. The male sense of self seems to be coextensive with his professional life. That means that many unemployed men stand in danger of losing themselves. They often feel emasculated and resentful — especially if their wives are successful at what they do.

About six months after Marcel left, Jan called me one evening, absolutely frantic. She was having trouble breathing but refused to call 911. She begged me not to call but wanted me to come over. When I got there, I could see that something terrible must've happened between Jan and Marty. It looked like a cyclone had gone through the house: practically everything breakable was lying around in smithereens. I insisted on driving Jan to Emergency.

It turned out that Jan had experienced a panic attack which had succeeded in triggering her asthma — an affliction that hadn't bothered her in years. She was put in an oxygen tent, kept there overnight, and discharged the next afternoon with, what I can only assume, were powerful antidepressants. I was glad they hadn't discharged her sooner because it gave me the opportunity to clean up her house.

That evening, while we were watching television on her bed, I broached the question of Marty and his whereabouts. That's when I learned about Marty's gambling problem. Jan hadn't known how dire the situation was until the incident that had precipitated her panic attack. Someone had called from the bank to say that they needed to come up with 300K or move out of their house, leaving behind most of the furniture. Sadly, Jan and Marty's finances were not separate, so Jan's credit rating was destroyed.

"Marty had taken out a bunch of liens on the house and never told me. At first, he wouldn't admit it. Then, he finally came clean. We fought, and I threw him out. I have no idea where he is and I don't care," Jan said.

"And he trashed the house before he left?" I asked.

"No. That was me. I was so angry that I needed to break things," Jan responded.

Jan had always been the epitome of rationality and calm. It was difficult to imagine her running riot like that. Even so, her rampage contained a degree of selectivity. I was touched to see that one of the few ornaments that remained intact was a ceramic dragon from Nepal, which I'd given her long ago.

We managed to find a furnished condo the very next day. It wasn't great, but it would have to do for the time being. Since the bank owned the house and practically everything in it, Jan only needed to move her personal effects — clothes, dishes (what was left of them), books, linens, and the like. Fortunately, it was a weekend so I called Berenice, and she came over to help. Berenice and Jan had never met before, but they'd heard a lot about each other. Initially, the atmosphere was strained: Jan's formidable defense mechanisms were activated by the presence of a stranger, especially one who happened to be a therapist. And so, the three of us wordlessly moved boxes for several hours. Once everything had been moved into the condo, and we were about to begin unpacking the kitchen, Berenice couldn't take it anymore.

"One of you had better tell me what the asshole did. Otherwise, I'm out of here."

As inelegant as it might've seemed, Berenice's comment was the perfect icebreaker. Jan unerringly went to the right box and pulled out a bottle of single malt. So, while drinking and unpacking, Berenice and I learned just how much of a loser Jan's estranged husband really was.

Afterward, Berenice called Jan up periodically to see how she was doing. They shared a mutual passion for exercise and began working out together. Jan frequently joined Berenice on her walks around the lake: she was more athletic than I was and found the repetitive loops very therapeutic. Although Jan was much too resistant to ever go into therapy herself, there couldn't have been a better time for Jan to befriend a shrink. Very soon, they'd become fast friends in their own right.

Chapter 9: (Not) Young and Innocent

The conversation at the pool the night we were busted had ramifications I should've anticipated but hadn't. Later that week, April asked me out for a drink and ambushed me as soon as we sat down.

"So, tell me about you and Hanif," she said with a suggestive smile.

Me and my big mouth.

"I'm ashamed to admit that I can't remember what I said. But I'm pretty sure I was speaking in hypotheticals. If I mentioned Hanif, he was just an example that came to mind." Even as I was speaking, I was aware of how unconvincing I was.

"Listen, you can trust me. I'm on your side."

"Meaning?"

"You and Hanif clearly have a connection. And I resent the way Big Brother's always watching us. The university's efforts to regulate interpersonal relations have gone way too far," April said.

"Well, I can't argue with you there," I responded.

"Anyway, I'm here to help," she said.

This flummoxed me. What sort of help could April provide?

"Hanif and I are only a year apart in age. I can probably read him better," she continued.

I thanked her, but said I was certain I would not be needing her services and then proceeded to change the subject.

I kicked myself all the way home, feeling like an idiot. April's probes, her offers to translate, and her overall coy demeanor reminded me once again just how risible it was for an older woman to be interested in a younger man. My mind flashed to all those misogynist stories about rich widows marrying doughty young men and how the men came to despise them. In *The Widow,* a medieval yarn, the woman's second, much younger husband complained that "Goliath gapes too often." This was the gender-bending name he'd assigned to her over-needy vagina. Men could be cruel. Based on how children treat animals, little boys in particular, I'd always assumed that the younger the male, the more vicious. If this was true, then a fling with a younger man was the last thing I needed.

But maybe I was wrong. Maybe it was just that younger men were more transparent, which could be a good thing. Marcel was the only "older" man I'd ever been involved with, yet I always found him inscrutable. I never knew what drove him: why he was attracted to me in the first place and why he stopped. Was he ever deliberately cruel? Maybe. In our final days, he reminded me of Charles Boyer in *Gaslight,* who not only tortured Ingrid Bergman but seemed to enjoy it. But perhaps this was because they both had French accents.

Whether Marcel was sadistic or not, why shouldn't the same basic game plan of finding a younger mate work for me as well? It seemed only fair. I estimated that there was about the same age difference with Hanif as there had been with Marcel. If not a superstar like Marcel, I was at least quite successful in my field. Wouldn't this surround me with at least a modicum of the glamor that drew me to Marcel? When I raised this question with Jan, her response was:

"I don't know about glamor. But the younger colleague might see the senior woman as a vehicle for furthering his career."

"Gee, tell me what you really think," I replied. It struck me as far-fetched that Hanif would be either cynical or self-deprecating enough to hit on a middle-aged woman as a career move. I assumed Jan was trying to deter me so I wouldn't get hurt or perhaps so I wouldn't disgrace the department.

It was Saturday night, and we were at Berenice's house. This is where the three of us usually congregated — not only because Berenice had the best house but also because she was a fabulous cook. Tonight, she had made mussels à la Marcella Hazan with just the right amount of garlic.

"Women in their mid-forties just aren't glamorous — unless you mean glamor like the witches in *Macbeth*," said Jan.

"Why not?" I asked.

"Because aging women aren't seen as sexy," Jan responded.

"What about Meryl Streep?" I shot back.

"The last time I looked, she was playing a balding New York socialite who couldn't sing," Jan said (on a sour note).

"Hey, I like that movie," Berenice chimed in.

At this point, Jan told me to stop compulsively eating the bread, or I'd hate myself in the morning.

"Oh, leave her alone," said Berenice, who was daintily digging paint out from under her cuticles. "If you're right, and her sex life is over, what does it matter if she puts on a pound or two?" she said, smiling at me.

It was all very well for Berenice to say: she could eat like a pride of lions and never gain a pound. I put the bread down, not prepared to retreat into my middle-aged body without a fight.

"What about Edith Piaf?" I asked. "She had a younger man."

"Piaf was an icon, and her young man was a loser. More a caretaker than a lover," said Jan.

"But there are plenty of other examples," I said, flailing around to think of one.

"Like *The Roman Spring of Mrs. Stone?*" Jan said with a smirk. She knew that I loved that movie.

"I don't know that one," said Berenice.

"It's a total downer," said Jan. "Mrs. Stone is a retired American actress whose husband dies of a heart attack on a plane to Rome."

"It's one of Warren Beatty's earliest films," I said.

"He plays the dead husband?" Berenice asked, confused.

"No. The husband was age-appropriate. Warren Beatty is the young Italian gigolo who gloms onto the widow Stone," I said.

"I can guess where this is going. He dumps her, right?" Berenice asked.

"Not only that. Feeling desperate, she throws her key over the balcony to some creep who's been stalking her. You just know he's going to kill her," responded Jan.

"Who plays Mrs. Stone?" Berenice wanted to know.

"Vivien Leigh, who is, of course, still breathtakingly beautiful. The only sign of aging is her over-sized sunglasses," I said.

"Even so, if Leigh is credible as a pathetic aging widow, what chance do the rest of us have with younger men?" was Jan's retort.

"Come on! Vivien Leigh is a great actress, and this was hardly a documentary," I said.

There was a lull in the conversation, but before they could change the subject, I couldn't help but ask: "Well, if Hanif isn't attracted to older women, why does he flirt with me?"

"Because he flirts with everyone! Haven't you noticed? He's like Browning's *Last Duchess,*" Jan said.

Berenice was wrinkling her brow, clearly befuddled by the reference, so Jan added: "Like Johnny Depp: someone who seems to be coming on to the world."

I don't know about Johnny Depp, but Jan was right about Hanif. He did flirt with everyone.

"If you factor in Hanif's flirtatious behavior, that could put the Title IX suit he brought against Thourelle in an entirely different light. Maybe she thought he'd been coming on to her for months," Jan continued.

"We don't know that his complaint was about sex per se. And that would hardly explain the complaints of the other plaintiffs," I responded.

"What Title IX suit?" Berenice asked.

I explained to her what I'd already told Jan: that Hanif was one of the alleged plaintiffs in a sexual harassment case that had been brought against Thourelle when she was a Visiting Professor at Peitho University. Berenice, however, was struck by the very existence of such a case.

"And you weren't told about the Title IX complaint against Thourelle before you hired her?" Berenice asked.

We both shook our heads.

"How is that legal?" Berenice persisted.

"Apparently, there was a settlement out of court, and the case was sealed," I responded.

"But supposing the charges were true: doesn't that make Thourelle something of a sex criminal? And shouldn't this information be made public? You do know that sexual predators are almost always repeat offenders, right?" Berenice's therapist voice had kicked in.

Jan nodded gloomily. "I agree with you, but it happens all the time with men. A male professor causes a scandal with a student — or students, plural. The university agrees not to press charges provided that the offender leaves. He goes on the job market, gets another job, and the whole thing is hushed up. But the pattern continues. It happened here in the Journalism Department a few years ago. The female students filed a class action suit against the jerk. It turned out that he'd already been bounced from two institutions for sexual harassment," Jan said with disgust.

"Well, if Thourelle is getting away with similar behavior, it proves that affirmative action works, doesn't it? Women are now just as predatory as their male colleagues." My off-color thinking was always more in evidence when I've been drinking.

Jan took this opportunity to warn me that I should be careful who's listening because *that night at the pool, you were totally out of control*. When Berenice looked over quizzically, Jan simply told her that I'd been talking *just like this*. Berenice nodded in comprehension.

"But supposing Hanif and Thourelle were in a relationship. Hanif was in his twenties then, so well past the age of consent," I said. Was I actually defending Thourelle?

"You're assuming it was a consensual relationship," Jan responded. "But what if it wasn't?"

"Do you mean what if Thourelle pinned Hanif up against a wall and stuck her tongue down his throat?" Given Thourelle's diminutive stature, the image was ludicrous.

"Don't be an idiot," said Jan. "Think about Reitman vs Ronell."

The ultimate example of the abusive potential of teacher-student relations. Avital Ronell was a celebrated feminist philosopher at New York University who relentlessly harassed her graduate student, Nimrod Reitman — the object of the sixty-something professor's unwanted affections. And the poor guy was gay! Even so, the feminist scholars rallied around Ronell: in the age of #MeToo, they were reluctant to see the genders of predator and victim reversed.

"But Ronell was clearly delusional and forced herself on Reitman," I responded.

"The point is that a professor has an immense amount of power over her students. Any advance she makes could be interpreted as an abuse of power," Jan said.

Meanwhile, Berenice had produced a bottle of Calvados and poured some for each of us. *Na zdrav* (I cried); *Lechyd da* (shouted Jan); *Gesondheid* (bawled Berenice) — all at the same time. Somewhere along the line, we'd decided that knocking back shots was classier with multicultural toasts and that no one would mistake us for three middle-aged lushes.

Then Berenice spoke up. "Jan, I followed Reitman vs Ronell. It was in all the papers. And I agree with everything you say, in principle. But what about the other side of the equation: the immense power of the student should the relationship go wrong? Supposing Thourelle did get involved with a student but developed qualms and broke it off? A rejected student could change their mind and decide that they'd been abused — if not physically, then emotionally. Brow-beaten into a relationship by a senior scholar."

She was right. The weapons of the weak; or not so weak, in fact. There was a recent case at Northwestern where that was precisely what happened. A philosophy professor had a night on the town with an undergraduate who'd taken one of his classes the previous quarter. She'd asked him out. But apparently, she got drunk and, according to him, hit on him. He claimed to have resisted. Yet (according to his account) she was in no shape to go home, and that's why she wound up in his bed. Although they hadn't had sex, she still pressed charges. It's unclear how the case would've been resolved on its own merits because two former graduate students, with whom he'd had consensual relationships at his previous job, joined in. He was run out of the profession. Northwestern took the position that, even in a relationship between two consenting adults, the more powerful party was not protected from claims of sexual harassment. This also pertained if the plaintiffs had decided that they were harassed in retrospect, as was the case with these graduate students. The professor, now jobless with no prospects, moved to Mexico, where the cost of living was low.

"Well, the guy was obtuse: at most institutions, it's illegal for a faculty member to get involved with an undergraduate," Jan insisted.

"But a senior faculty member with a junior colleague?" I asked.

"Risky as well," Jan responded. "A recent university task force maintained that relationships between junior and senior faculty members have the same asymmetrical power dynamic that you find with teacher-student relations. That makes them almost as suspect."

"But I don't have any supervisory or evaluative authority over Hanif," I objected.

"Yes, you do. You'll vote on his tenure. Supposing Hanif didn't get tenure. He could always hold you accountable. If he does get tenure and wants to dump you, he can always claim that he had to sleep with you in order to get tenure," Jan responded. Berenice was nodding in agreement.

But as Emily Dickenson would say: "The heart wants what it wants, or else it doesn't care." And I clearly did care.

That night, I took the long way home just in case I was pulled over: I hadn't had that much to drink, but I was afraid that the Calvados was potent enough to set off the police breathalyzer. When I'd first learned to drive and was uncertain about the legal limit of alcohol, I used to keep my own breathalyzer in the glove compartment. Daniel, who was often my "date" to academic dinners and receptions, called it my drunk-o-meter, claiming that I used it to make sure that I was getting sufficiently loaded. Sadly, it broke — hence, the long way home. I had plenty of time to replay the dinner conversation with Jan and Berenice and think about how it might pertain to Hanif. Jan was right: he was not only younger; he was untenured. Any parallels to my relationship with Marcel were limited because Marcel had been in a different department than I was. He wouldn't have been voting on my tenure and promotion. Of course, if I were to get involved with Hanif, I could always recuse myself when he came up for tenure, which is what spouses in the same department did.

But what if the relationship between Hanif and me was kept secret, and we broke up before he came up for tenure? And what if I were unhappy about the breakup? I thought about Avital Ronell with her vindictive efforts to destroy Nimrod Reitman and shuddered. If truth be told, for a crazy week or so after Marcel left me, I would have done anything I could to harm him.

Chapter 10: Strangers on a Train

It was late October, and I was sitting by myself in the faculty club, gazing at the turning leaves. The faculty had lobbied hard for this — place of respite until finally, three years ago, there was an anonymous donation designated for precisely this purpose. The result was an airy and cheerful zone which wore its institutional affiliation lightly. There were five or six discreet seating arrangements punctuated by some brightly colored area rugs. The floor was parquet, and the furnishings were mid-century modern. Kind of. No, the lounge chairs were not real Eames, and the two couches were Florence Knoll knockoffs. The only thing that was authentic was the Noguchi coffee table, which was on permanent loan from me. Marcel had bought it for one of my birthdays, and it was too big for my now pocket-sized living room.

Wednesday was a non-teaching day for me, but I was sitting in the club feeling sorry for myself because of all the grading I had to do. I always hated grading, but the worst was re-grading something because of student complaints — especially complaints over a grade assigned by a Teaching Assistant. The problem was, I couldn't just regrade it on my own because I didn't want to undermine the Teaching Assistant's authority. So, I had to send the grieving student back to the Teaching Assistant who'd assigned the grade in the first place. It was their responsibility either to reconcile the student to their disappointing grade (kindly showing the way to how they could do better on the next assignment) or, when appropriate, to acknowledge that they'd been too harsh (or made an error) and assign a new grade. If the student did not receive satisfaction, then they could come back to me as a last resort, and I would regrade it. Ever since Ms. Cather had been assigned as my Teaching Assistant for *Medieval Sex*, complaints were legion and I needed to add extra office hours to field the grievances. Part of the problem was her graceless comments, which tended to be as insulting as they were unilluminating. I always told my Teaching Assistants that their final comments on any paper should lead with some positive remark, and the ensuing critique should provide sufficient detail that, were the student to rewrite the paper, they'd be able to raise their score by at least half a grade (i.e., from a B to a B+). But Ms. Cather either didn't understand my directives, chose to ignore them, or applied a novel interpretation. The following comment on a student paper on medieval crossdressing is a case in point.

This paper is the right length. Good. But you do not write well and your argument is week. Its not my fault you can't read directions.

Did I mention that Ms. Cather was grammatically and orthographically challenged? I should also add that, although Ms. Cather was not very adept at assessing the work of others, once she had given a grade, she was implacable. This meant that every one of the grieving students I sent back to her were returned to me, and I was forced to change the grade without her corroboration. There were only forty students, so I would have infinitely preferred to have done all the grading on my own. But to be a Teaching Assistant is to be an apprentice of sorts. It counted as one of their courses, and at the end of the semester, they received a Pass/Fail grade.

I also had fifteen papers to grade on "The Wife of Bath's Tale" for my freshman seminar the next day. I was hoping it would help if I got out of my office and came up to the faculty club, but it didn't. All I was doing was staring out the window. *Make a start*, I said to myself, trying to channel my inner schoolmarm, and plunged in. In four hours, I'd managed to plow through all of Ms. Cather's latest victims and two-thirds of the Chaucer papers. I was just beginning a paper that seemed to be missing a page (about a third of the students don't bother to staple their papers together) when a shadow fell across my table. I looked up and saw Hanif. He was wearing jeans, the midnight blue kind, and a dark navy jacket over a green paisley shirt, looking very stylish.

"I've been watching you for fifteen minutes, and you've barely moved," he said, grinning his co-conspirator grin. "Very impressive focus."

I laughed. He was right: I didn't move. But I'd not always been like this. Long ago, I'd discovered that whenever I had a good idea, I would unwittingly get up and wander around and walk the idea off. So, I began tying my foot to my desk whenever I was writing. The practice was inspired by a colophon in a medieval manuscript in which the monkish scribe complained that he'd copied the manuscript while chained to his desk by his abbot for fourteen days. A fellow wanderer. I explained this to Hanif, concluding:

"I once recommended this method to one of my graduate students who had trouble writing, and he promptly changed thesis advisers."

"It does sound nuts," Hanif admitted.

"But it works," I said.

Hanif sat down beside me and started to flip through my papers. He put them back on the table and said: "Did you know that there's a drive-in twenty miles out of town?"

I nodded.

"Don't you think we need a mid-week break?" he said.

"What's playing?" I asked.

"Who cares? It's an opportunity to slack off and eat junk food," he said.

It was an offer that I couldn't refuse. Suddenly elated, I ran to my office to ditch my papers. (I'd wake up early and finish them in the morning.) I grabbed my jacket and galloped downstairs to meet Hanif. (The elevators were either stuck, which was not unusual, or moving too slowly for my heightened degree of excitement.) Hanif was waiting in the parking lot with his car.

When we arrived at the drive-in just before sundown, it turned out we were in luck. It was a Hitchcock double feature: *Strangers on a Train* and *Suspicion* — arguably two of my favorite movies. Hanif hadn't seen either of them, so he was, in his own words, *psyched*. We went to the consignment booth and loaded up with hamburgers, fries, and soft drinks.

"Maybe we should come back for some soft ice cream during intermission," Hanif said, and I nodded enthusiastically. This struck me as a festive occasion, so forget the battle of the bulge.

We were watching the tennis match scene in *Strangers on a Train*, the one in which the heads of the spectators were bobbing, following the ball — back and forth, back and forth. Everyone was watching the ball except the psychopath, Bruno, whose gaze never left the beleaguered player, Guy. Poor Guy was desperately trying to finish the game early and get to the amusement park before Bruno (who had killed Guy's estranged wife and was planning to frame him for the murder) had time to plant Guy's lighter there. The whole movie turned on smoking and cigarettes. It brought back the days when smoking was sexy, and when I used to exhale through my nostrils just like a diminutive dragon. It was easier to keep the weight off when I smoked. I also had a better personality.

And then I felt Hanif groping for my hand. Once he had found it, he gave it a squeeze before raising it gently to his lips, palm inwards. When I felt his lips on my palm and then his tongue, it flashed through my mind that he couldn't possibly be enjoying the movie, or he wouldn't have picked this moment. As I watched Guy grab his trousers from his fiancée, and charge up the stairs, little tremors were beginning to run up and down my spine. Meanwhile, the fiancée's sister was flirting with the policeman, who had been tailing Guy, to divert his attention. The problem with this scene was that the flirtatious sister was played by Hitchcock's daughter, who was, well… funny-looking.

All these thoughts were running through my head as Hanif's lips began to move up my wrist. And then he stopped and turned to me.

"Have you been avoiding me?" he asked softly.

At this point, I turned away from the screen. Guy would have to face his trials alone.

"Of course, I haven't been avoiding you."

This wasn't exactly true. Since our dinner, I'd encountered Hanif in any number of venues: at a reception for a visiting lecturer; during two departmental meetings; at a performance of *Lieder* in the music school, where he sat only a few rows away (with April Fortune, of all people). In short, although I'd told myself repeatedly that we were just colleagues and that nothing *was going to happen*, I'd consistently acted like a schoolgirl with a crush. I was all too aware when my be-crushed was in the room and determined not to look his way.

"In fact, I was wondering what you were up to," I added. This, at least, was true.

"Waiting for you to notice me. In fact, ever since I first met you, I've been waiting for you to notice me. We had such a good time at the conference. I thought maybe it would change things, but it didn't," he said.

Was Hanif being sincere? Was he, in fact, forlornly yearning for my attention? It seemed as implausible as Hitchcock's funny-looking daughter enticing the cute cop. *Stop it*, I said to my libidinous persona. *Nobody has wanted to touch you in years. Maybe no one ever will again, and this is all you can think about?*

Hanif leaned over to kiss me. We were at the tense scene where Bruno drops Guy's lighter in the gutter by mistake — a psychological tour de force. The audience is on Guy's side, of course, and yet when you watch Bruno's hand, see it straining within the grate to grasp the lighter, you find yourself rooting for Bruno. When Bruno finally managed to regain the lighter, I closed my eyes.

Hanif had thrown off the shackles of his stylish stubble and was clean-shaven. I could smell the fragrance of sandalwood soap on his skin. But I will spare you the other details. Who could possibly be interested in how, when Hanif put his hand under my blouse, all I could think was that the elastic underneath my bra was conspiring against me, making the roll of flab on my upper abdomen seem bigger than my breast? Nor how, when Hanif's other hand crept under my skirt, I was thinking that I hadn't had a shower since 6:30 a.m. and wondered what I smelled like. And I'm certain that nobody cares about my awkward encounter with the stick shift.

This latter incident should've constituted what medieval theologians refer to as a *felix culpa*: a happy mistake — like how the Fall of Adam and Eve brought about Christ's Incarnation. In other words, when Hanif murmured, *Let's get in the back seat,* and I was still feeling the depredations of the stick shift, one might suppose that I wouldn't risk devolving any further into this adolescent scenario. After all, fulfilling your fantasies had its attendant dangers, especially in cars. Think of the actor Hugh Grant who, in the course of fulfilling a lifelong desire to have sex with a black woman, was arrested in his car while receiving head from a prostitute. Was the handsome, successful, Hugh Grant one of those people who never got away with anything?

If so, I was a lot like Hugh Grant: I got caught for everything I did, as well as blamed for things I didn't do. If this pattern persisted, this could be my most mortifying arrest to date.

But supposing I got lucky: Hanif and I had sex in the backseat, and no one was ever the wiser?

Yet consider the plight of Hugh Grant's erstwhile long-term partner, the exquisite model and actress, Elizabeth Hurley. How mortified she must've felt when the news of Hugh's criminal indiscretion was splashed all over the tabloids! Perhaps it was Elizabeth's inevitable lot to be forever humiliated in love, in which case I might have even more in common with Elizabeth than with Hugh. Hanif would dump me after having had his way with me in the course of the cheapest date possible (I paid for the burgers) and in, arguably, the most degrading of venues. (The upside would be that I was spared the still more degrading walk of shame back from Hanif's house the next morning.)

I never resolved whether I had more in common with Hugh, Elizabeth, or was something of a hybrid of both members of that most glamorous of hapless couples. Instead, I clambered after Hanif into the back seat as if this was my last possible chance to have sex, because it probably was. Admittedly, the circumstances weren't ideal. It wasn't the most satisfying act of coitus; nor was it a total disaster. Besides, I was distracted by the thought of the heavy hand of the law landing squarely on my shoulder, not to mention the movie. I couldn't help glancing at the screen for the climax. (I didn't, by the way.) The carousel operator had been shot in the crossfire, and the carousel was out of control, its wooden horses looking crazed and dangerous. It collapsed on Bruno and, as he lay dying, his hand sprang open, revealing Guy's lighter.

As I watched Guy and his fiancée's ecstatic reunion, I knew it was time to leave. True, I would've dearly loved to see *Suspicion* on a big screen. Maybe I could come back later in the week with Jan or Berenice.

"We should go," I said. We were still in the back seat, intertwined but only semi-recumbent, so I could watch the end of the film. Hanif didn't seem to be watching, preferring to tease my nipples and nibble my neck. I was, of course, delighted at this show of post-coital attention but was nervous about the neck-nibbling, trying to reassure myself that he was too old to think that giving a hickey was cool. I also worried that Hitchcock's magnificence eluded Hanif.

Hanif smiled at me amorously. "Will you come back to my place?"

I shook my head. "No. I have to teach tomorrow and return those damn papers. Another time?"

Hanif acquiesced, showing just enough disappointment to make me feel desirable.

Once we were back in the university lot where my car was parked and I was about to clamber out, Hanif put his hand on my arm, leaned over, and gave me a lingering kiss.

"Do you promise this won't be the last time?" he asked with touching earnestness.

"I promise."

God, he's hot.

I knew I wouldn't be able to sleep. So, instead of going home, I went up to my office to grade the rest of the papers. When I finally did make it home, I just lay on my bed, simultaneously reliving and regretting my interlude in the backseat with Hanif. Just because we hadn't been arrested didn't mean that I hadn't made a mistake. I resolved not to tell anyone.

When I did finally fall asleep, my dreamscape was troubled. I dreamed about my younger self, sometime in my teens. I was at a coffee house where a young man with long hair was playing folk songs on the guitar. I remember hearing: *Let the midnight special, Shine a light on me*. It was a cool environment, in a countercultural kind of way; an environment that most teenagers would savor. But I couldn't enjoy it. I was in a panic because it was late, I didn't know how to get home, and my parents would kill me. It was after 11:00 p.m., and I was afraid to phone them. I woke up in a cold sweat.

The next day, I stalked around school, totally exhausted, like a zombie in heat. I snapped at a student in my seminar who was poking fun at the Wife of Bath's libidinous banter: the Wife was about my age, and I took it personally. (I later emailed him an apology; he wrote back that he hadn't noticed.) I fell down half a flight of stairs and landed painfully on my tailbone, fortunately without witnesses, but, in so doing, broke a heel on my favorite pair of boots. Although I had office hours from 3:00-4:00 p.m., I decided to pack it in. As I limped to my car, I reasoned that any student who did show up for office hours would only be there to complain about the paper that I'd just returned. This would contravene my twenty-four-hour gag rule: no griping about a grade for at least twenty-four hours after the assignment was returned and my comments were properly digested. Given my present state of mind, there was a good chance that I'd strangle any precipitous plaintiff.

Yet, once I got home, I was restless and wished that I'd stayed at school. If I'd gone up to the faculty club for a drink, I might've run into Hanif. But to do what? To pretend I didn't see him? To make it clear that I did see him and had decided to ignore him? To give him a curt, professional: *Hello. How're you doing?* Or to go up to him with a knowing smile that seemed to say: *I had a great time last night. We should do it again, and much more!*

Get a grip! How old did you say you were?

I poured myself some scotch, wondering why, since I was the one who wouldn't go home with him last night, I still felt as if I was the one being rejected. OK, I knew the answer to that one: because I always feel rejected — whether, in fact, I am or not. That was why I was in EMDR, after all. Besides, doesn't every woman want to hear from the person with whom they were intimate the night before? Unless she was intoxicated and accidentally slept with a leper, I would say yes. Maybe this situation was different because I was his superior in rank, not to mention age. Maybe I was the one who should call. No, the age difference made me more vulnerable. But supposing he did call, what did I expect him to say anyway? That I'm steaming hot? Or that he still respected me?

I was sitting in the kitchen, nervously chewing on my cheek — a bad habit I'd tried to overcome with hypnotherapy, but it didn't work. I was listening to the dishwasher. Just like the hapless Selma in Von Trier's *Dancer in the Dark,* I had a strange relationship with mechanized sounds. Usually, the dishwasher sounded as if it were saying *Borgia, Borgia, Borgia, Borgia.* Today, however, it sounded like it was saying *Told ya, Told ya, Told ya, Told* ya. Told me what, oh spirit of the dishwasher? Told me that if I succumbed to my attraction to Hanif that I'd feel like shit? I wasn't going to take that from an appliance, so I yanked its door open before the cycle had finished and was blasted by steam. I was swearing to myself when the doorbell rang, and I jumped. It wasn't him. It was a delivery man with a big bouquet of flowers. The card said simply: *With love from Hanif,* and I was elated. I put my nose into the bouquet and took a deep breath: how did he know that lilies make me swoon?

Yet the afterglow of this timeless gesture was all too brief. I relentlessly moved forward to the next uncomfortable issue: what did it mean?

Chapter 11: Shadow of a Doubt

I had to acknowledge the flowers. The question was, how? The possibilities were:
- a) the direct way: pick up the phone
- b) the oblique way: send a text
- c) the even more oblique way: send an email
- d) the still more oblique way: leave a thank you note in his faculty mailbox
- e) possibly the most oblique way: mail a thank you note to his home
- f) the casual (quasi-rude) way: wait until you run into him and say *Oh, by the way*....

Of course, I chose option c: the email. After deleting a series of cloying messages — some anticipating a future rendezvous, some not — I settled for the following: *Hanif: You are so thoughtful. Thank you, XXOO, H.*

I didn't always go into school on Fridays, sometimes preferring to work at home. Maybe I should stay home today because I felt apprehensive about running into Hanif. I wasn't straight on the source of my apprehension, however. Was I afraid that the incident at the drive-in had somehow changed our relationship, or was I afraid that it hadn't? Were the flowers a celebration of a burgeoning something or a gesture of farewell?

Then I remembered that I didn't have the luxury of staying home because today was the day when I'd finally managed to insinuate myself into one of Ms. Cather's discussion sections. She didn't take me up on the offer to give a lecture (thank God), but every semester, I would routinely visit a section just to see how the Teaching Assistant was making out. Usually, I saw the classroom visit as an opportunity to cull plaudits about the graduate student's teaching in case they ever asked me to write a letter of recommendation. When I tried to schedule a visit to one of Ms. Cather's sections (I would never have popped in), however, she seemed resentful and highly suspicious. She told me that none of the other faculty members had ever come to observe her classes. I didn't doubt her. I always thought that my colleagues were rather slack in this regard.

When I persisted, she begrudgingly agreed to a date. I got to the room early in order to seem as discreet and undisruptive as possible, but there was little to disrupt. Although these discussion groups usually have somewhere between ten and fifteen students, only three showed up: Amos, Darlene, and Aria. I knew all three of them relatively well. Amos and Darlene (who were always together, but may or may not have been a couple), had both taken at least one course with me before. This was the first time I'd taught Aria, but I'd gotten to know her because she frequently dropped by my office hours to chat. All three were good students: engaged and animated in lectures, asking questions and laughing at my jokes. Since Ms. Cather had yet to arrive, we chatted casually about the course.

"I like your hair, Aria," I said. She'd just dyed it green and looked like Billie Eilish.

Aria looked shy and pleased at the same time. "Professor, you're the only one of my profs who ever notices things like clothes or hair," she said.

Oh God, I keep forgetting. No personal comments!

"It's great," she continued. "You make me feel seen."

I just smiled, relieved. She wasn't about to turn me in.

"Is Ms. Cather sick? Are you taking the seminar this week?" Amos asked. The other two looked toward me eagerly.

I shook my head. "I'm only here to observe." They all nodded solemnly. For some reason, they reminded me of prisoners presented with the tantalizing possibility of reprieve, only to see it suddenly whisked away.

"Are you the only ones in the class?" I asked.

"No, there are about ten others?" one of them said.

"Where are they?" I asked.

The three of them exchanged looks.

"We met with some of them last night," Darlene said.

"That's nice, but why?" I asked.

"We were really excited about this week's reading and wanted to discuss it," Darlene responded.

The reading up for discussion was the eleventh-century Peter Damian's attack on sexual relations between the clergy entitled *The Book of Gomorrah*. The book was a polemical rant, which I knew from experience prompted some interesting responses — especially from the LGBTQ community.

"That's great. So, you'll really be on top of the discussion today," I said brightly. The three of them were silent.

At that point, Ms. Cather trundled in. Rather than joining the informal circle, Ms. Cather stood at the lectern at the front of the room. From there, she proceeded to grill them.

"Who was Peter Damian?"

"When was the first secular legislation against same-sex relations in the High Middle Ages?"

"What date was the Third Lateran Council?"

"What year did Richard the Lion Heart go on crusade?"

This went on for 50 minutes. It was an ordeal for me; for the students, it must've been cruel and unusual punishment. Admittedly, all these questions were in some way related to same-sex relations. But they were hardly open-ended questions that would foster discussion, and none of them had anything to do with analyzing *The Book of Gomorrah*.

I'd scheduled a meeting with Ms. Cather in my office to discuss the seminar immediately after the class. As I sat there waiting for her, I was unaccountably nervous; the longer I waited, the more anxious I felt. Ms. Cather eventually showed up half an hour late with no apologies. As I observed the door roll shut, I said, with malice of forethought: *Just leave it.* I watched in silence as she wandered away to secure a rubber stopper from somewhere or other and meticulously worked it under the door.

"Well, Ms. Cather. It's always interesting to visit a class. How do you think it went?" I asked.

"Fine," was all she said.

"Didn't you think the attendance was rather low?" I asked.

"Not really," she said. "They're all studying for midterms."

"I was interested in some of the decisions you made for the discussion. Why the emphasis on dates?"

"Because students are very lazy about learning dates. You said yourself that a certain grasp of dates is important for understanding change over time," she responded.

"But weren't they supposed to be prepared to discuss the *Book of Gomorrah*?" I asked.

"That's what's on the syllabus. But when I went to the Title IX office and showed certain passages to Sally Field, she agreed that teaching such obscene material was infringing on my own and the students' rights," Ms. Cather.

"Sally Field is, of course, entitled to her opinion. But it is, after all, my course," I said.

"But it's me who might get sued if I taught that kind of filth in a seminar," she shot back.

I was so shaken by her truculent, low-mindedness that I ended the discussion right there. I thanked her for letting me attend her class and stood up to indicate that our meeting was over. I even said *have a nice weekend*, or something to that effect. She left without a word.

My encounter with Ms. Cather left me feeling depressed, demoralized, and powerless. And infuriated. It was my course, and she was censoring the readings. Ms. Cather had made that moron, Sally Field, the ultimate arbiter for course materials. Meanwhile, the students, eager for real discussion, were holding informal seminars in the evenings. At this point, my ambivalence about running into Hanif vanished. In fact, I would've liked nothing better than a few words of reassurance — possibly some of his confident millennial-style advice. I knocked on his door, but there was no answer. I thought I saw him walking a block ahead of me toward the parking lot, but he was with someone else (a woman, but I couldn't see who it was), so I just trailed behind at a discreet distance.

I knew I was bound to see Hanif on Saturday because we were having our inaugural departmental party, the express purpose of which was to welcome new faculty members. The party was at Jan's house. It was a catered event at which the caterers would set up, pass trays of food, and clean up. Even so, she asked that I come early, if only for moral support. When I arrived at 3:30 p.m., I was surprised to see Berenice's car in the driveway as well. The two of them met me at the door and whisked me inside.

"Look what Berenice bought!" Jan said, waving a bottle of Oban, her favorite single malt. "Let's drink some quickly so we can get a head start, and then hide the bottle."

Jan poured: the pleasant sound of clinking glasses was drowned out by the clamorous shouts of *L'chaim, Salute, Skål*.

"So, Berenice, to what do we owe your presence? It's usually impossible to get you to any event with our colleagues," I said.

In fact, Berenice had a pronounced aversion to academic conversation, so it was probably something of a blessing that she never got a job as an art historian. I wasn't quite sure why she made an exception for me — or Jan, for that matter. I can assume that, in my case, my puerile behavior undercut my potential for gravitas.

Berenice shrugged. "Listen, business is slow, and I know that you both work with some pretty sick folk. I was going to make the rounds, introduce myself, hand out a few business cards. No big deal," she said.

"Ha, ha. Not very convincing. You may as well come clean," I said.

"Alright, Jan invited me over so I could see your toy boy," she said.

I looked over at Jan reproachfully. "I knew it!" I said. I shudder to think what they would say if they knew about the incident at the drive-in.

"Come on, he's cute. You should be happy to show him off," Jan responded.

Both Jan and Berenice laughed while I looked around to make sure that we were still alone and that no one had come in.

"Don't embarrass me," I pleaded, just as I used to beg my parents decades ago. I was every bit as serious now.

Then suddenly, the room was full. It may sound like I passed out temporarily or have fast-forwarded to when the party was in full swing, but I haven't. In my experience, academics tend to arrive early but hate to be the first to arrive. In order to avoid the ignominy of arriving solo, they arrange themselves in clumps of three or four, and sometimes more. To the casual observer, this simultaneity might seem like a pattern imposed by drive-sharing or Uber-ing. Yet, on more than one occasion, I have seen a colleague standing at the end of a driveway in freezing weather, waiting for a group to which to attach themselves rather than coming to the door alone. It was but another instance of the *longue durée* of adolescent behavior. But who was I to point fingers? Look at my speedy relapse into teenage behavior when it came to sexual relationships. Sometimes, it felt as if adolescence was my reflexive norm and adulthood but a theatrical scrim.

I was, of course, watching out for Hanif, who arrived about half past the hour. He was not alone, however. Rather, he was accompanied by an extravagantly good-looking man, perhaps five years younger, whom I instantly pegged as Italian. How else would one account for the head of Dionysian black curls that, in a welter of expensive pomade, evoked satyrs and grapes; the flawless olive skin; the chiseled nose; and the magnificently tailored clothes? The drape of his microfiber trousers said it all.

I was not wrong. Hanif introduced him around as Paolo. They'd met during Hanif's undergraduate exchange year, which Hanif spent with Paolo's family in Milan. It was rare to see two such striking and sartorially splendid male specimens at the same time — especially rare in an academic context. Not surprisingly, everyone in the room congregated around them. It was evident that the two men were close: they projected an emotional ease, especially manifested in their physical interaction. They stood inches apart, speaking directly into one another's face while reminiscing about the past. Their stroll down memory lane was a tactile one: a hand on the arm, a make-believe slap across the face, an arm across the shoulders, a modicum of grooming (Paolo did up a button on Hanif's shirt that had come undone). We all looked on in fascination. But there was one exchange that was especially memorable. Paolo was recounting a time when Hanif chased down the thief who'd stolen Paolo's wallet and exclaimed:

"That's when I first knew that I was in love!" Paolo held open his arms; Hanif laughed and moved in for the embrace. They kissed each other on both cheeks for good measure. Then Paolo slapped Hanif on the butt.

Hanif added, "Just to clarify, this was no macho act of bravery. The thief was a little Romani girl who couldn't have been more than twelve."

Both men laughed and gave one another a hug for good measure.

I have to admit that I was rather taken aback by this ardent display of homosocial camaraderie. Maybe Hanif was gay after all but wasn't happy about it. A gay friend of mine maintained that an infallible way to distinguish a closeted male was if he were relatively attractive, but his wife was a dog (his words). This indicated that the husband in question was either not very discerning of female pulchritude or altogether indifferent to it. (Whenever I attended a conference with said friend, I would come away with bruised ribs because he insisted on elbowing me every time he saw a decent-looking man with an ill-favored woman.) If Hanif had randomly selected me to be his heterosexual beard, chances were that I was a pooch and an old one at that.

This line of thought caused me to reflect upon the innumerable times that I'd heard Hanif make queer interventions at conferences. Were they prompted by personal gay pride, or were they predictable Queer Theory moves? The same question might be asked of his article in a recent Modern Language Association forum entitled " 'Straight Up Your Ass: The Hypocritical Hypochondria of Heteronormativity." And then there was Hanif's unfailing adherence to what the Italians called the *bella figura:* dressing well to make a good impression. The ideology of the *bella figura* was so deeply engrained in Italian society that even their public officials had to be well turned out: Armani had designed the uniforms for the Polizia, as had Valentino for the paramilitary Carabinieri. So, while I could understand that it was a point of national pride for Paolo to be impeccably groomed no matter what his orientation, I was doubtful that any male in American academe would make that kind of effort unless he were gay.

There was one final Machiavellian factor that could explain the opacity of Hanif's sexual orientation, one that I hadn't yet considered. While being gay or queer was still a liability in many academic fields, with the advent of Queer Theory, it was arguably an advantage in English Departments.

Question: What is the difference between the Modern Language Association and the American Historical Association meetings?

Answer: At the American Historical Association, all the gay men try to act straight, while at the Modern Language Association, all the straight men try to act gay.

OK, it's a terrible joke, and I shouldn't have repeated it. My bad. Freud said jokes either expressed aggression or unconscious sexual desire, but I don't think either category described my current iteration. How about perplexity? Can jokes be an expression of perplexity? Because I was perplexed as to whether someone ambitious (say, Hanif, for example) would be craven enough to attempt passing as gay in order to advance themselves in certain literary circles. It was a disturbing, but fascinating question. I could even get teaching credit for addressing the problem if I were to launch a graduate seminar entitled *Cynical Sexualities.*

My disconcerting thoughts were suddenly interrupted when the crowd parted, and Thourelle was in our midst. She was wearing yet another comely grey costume, but one with a difference: rather than her usual quasi-monastic robes, she was sporting a shiny grey sheath with high black patent boots. The material must've had a generous amount of spandex because the dress hugged her every contour. It turned out that she had a lovely figure. Who knew (damn it)? We hadn't seen our diva at a departmental function since at least last spring, so everyone was surprised that she'd bothered to come.

More surprising still was her apparent date: a young man with tousled blonde hair who, barely out of his teens, was dressed simply in black jeans and a white shirt. He had large sea-green eyes and a flawless complexion with a hint of a tan. I was reminded of Tadzio in Visconti's *Death in Venice*. But perhaps I made this association because this was the first time that I'd ever seen Thourelle wear makeup. (OK, she didn't look as bad as Dirk Bogarde melting on the beach, but she did have her foundation on pretty thick, and I swear she was wearing false eyelashes.) It was also the first time I'd seen Thourelle without her strange set of silver rings. They seem to have been ousted by what looked like an engagement ring — a striking band of white and black diamonds. The couple slowly processed, arm-in-arm, past the various members of the department, now conveniently divided into two columns on either side. Eventually, they reached Jan. It seemed that Thourelle intended a formal presentation. The room had fallen strangely silent, and everyone could hear Thourelle say,

"Jan, I would like you to meet my fiancé, Tommy. Tommy, this is the Chair of my department, Jan."

Jan offered him her hand, and he shook it. "Very happy to meet you," the two of them said simultaneously.

A caterer emerged from the kitchen with another tray of drinks, and the spell was broken. Now, everybody seemed to be speaking at once. I bumped into Mellors, who was looking jittery, presumably because he wasn't allowed to smoke inside.

"Where's Emily?" I asked

"Visiting her sister in Maine," he said glumly. "I've been on my own for almost two weeks." He looked it. Long hairs were protruding from his ears; dandruff dappled the shoulders of his tweed jacket; dirty white cuffs stuck out of its sleeves.

I made sympathetic noises. He was one of the few men who was still with the woman who'd put him through grad school, all the while cooking his meals and ironing his shirts. I respected him for his loyalty to Emily. Her absence had seemingly left him bereft. So, you can imagine my surprise when he leaned in and said:

"Come home with me tonight, Lady Chatterley. We're both on our own, and no one would be the wiser. We've waited a long time."

The bourbon and tobacco on his breath did not have the same aphrodisiac-effect as they do in film noir. Even so, I had to let him down easily because I may've been at fault here. Someone must've told him, probably long ago, that I'd nicknamed him Mellors, and so over the years, he assumed that I was lusting after him (not unlike *Far from the Madding Crowd*, when Bathsheba Everdene [Julie Christie] thoughtlessly sent that Valentine to Farmer Boldwood [Peter Finch]). And Mellors may've mistaken my sympathetic noises for expressions of lust. So, I told him that up until now, we had done nothing that he would have to conceal from Emily. (That's more or less what Lara [again, Julie Christie] said when she spurns the initial advances of the good doctor [Omar Sharif] in *Dr. Zhivago*.) He nodded, muttering, "You're right; you're right," gave me a sloppy kiss on the cheek, and wandered off.

Is there anything sadder than a man who's a shambling ruin of his earlier sexy self, I asked myself. But I already knew the answer: a woman who's a shambling ruin of her earlier sexy self. That's just the way it is.

The encounter with Mellors was sufficiently unnerving that I was on the verge of leaving. Yet I realized that I was much too old to play the shrinking violet, so I deliberately went over to Hanif and Paolo, who were standing in the bay window talking to April Fortune. I joined them, and Hanif introduced me to Paolo, who gave me a warm smile and kissed my hand. They were talking about Italy. Apparently, April had never been, and Paolo was urging her to come to Milan, offering to show her around. I told them about my time last year at the Humanities Center at Bogliasco, a gracious villa right on the Mediterranean, and encouraged April and Hanif to apply. *And Bogliasco's right near Genoa, which is a wonderful city,* Paolo added. There now, I've approached Hanif, taken part in a conversation, and acted perfectly normal. I was congratulating myself and about to drift away when Hanif caught my arm.

"Paolo's leaving on Wednesday. Will you have dinner with me on Thursday?"

When I said yes, he squeezed my arm. I felt reassured: maybe he's bi after all.

The party was supposed to begin at 4:00 p.m. and end at 8:00 p.m. By 8:30, the last stragglers had left, and Jan, Berenice, and I were sitting in the living room. We poured ourselves another round of single malt (*Noroc, Na zdrowie, Sei gesund*) and settled in while the caterers cleaned up around us.

"What a performance," Jan said.

"Which one?" asked Berenice. "Thourelle and her fiancé or Heather's fella and his fella?"

"Hanif is not my fella," I said defensively.

"Which is probably a good thing," Jan responded. "That Paolo was pretty cute, and they both seemed pretty gay."

I sighed. "Listen, in Italy, that's the way young men act."

"That could be," said Berenice. "Sexual practices are more fluid there. I've read that many, if not most, Italian men have had sexual experiences with other males, especially when they were young. And very few of them identify as gay. Maybe Hanif's like that."

"Maybe," I replied, making an effort to keep my tone light.

But we all agreed that Thourelle was the main attraction: it was thoughtful of her to bring her "incident" to the departmental party so we could all examine him up close.

"Is he an undergraduate here?" I asked.

Jan nodded. "Yes. He's a senior majoring in history and seems very nice, for what it's worth."

"Is he one of Thourelle's current students?" I persisted

"No. He's never even taken a course from her," Jan said. "He told me they met at Darby's playing pool."

Darby's was a local dive, dominated by a couple of pool tables with a string of pinball machines along the back wall. We were all silent for a moment, trying to imagine that austerely elegant couple playing pool at Darby's.

"The university's position is zero tolerance for teacher-student relations if the student is enrolled in one of the teacher's classes. A former student might be something of a grey area. But if Tommy was never Thourelle's student, he's probably fair game — provided he's above the age of consent," Jan continued.

"That makes sense," Berenice responded. "She isn't grading him; won't be asked to write recommendations. She has no power over him."

"Maybe not formal power. But one could argue that her position gives her power. Tommy's probably heard Thourelle lecture, seen her books, and is convinced she's one of a kind," I said.

I was conscious of assuming the opposite position to the one I'd expressed the other night. Could my dislike of Thourelle have something to do with it?

Berenice just shrugged. "You're making it sound like power's an unfair advantage. That would mean that professionals like lawyers, CEOs, and politicians shouldn't marry anyone who's not as successful."

"Making society a closed set of hierarchies," added Jan.

"Welcome to planet earth," I responded. "Like not only marry like but produce like. Especially academics. It's amazing how many of my colleagues come from academic families. But I doubt teacher-student sex is the great equalizer."

"You forget. Thourelle's not just having sex with Tommy: he's her fiancé." Berenice pronounced the last word with a dramatic prolongation. "Marriage sanitizes things."

"You're right about that," said Jan. "As soon as the administrators found out that they were engaged, any potential Title IX inquiry folded."

"So, it's all OK, then? Even though Thourelle is almost twice Tommy's age?" I asked.

"It could be worse. You can get married at fifteen in this state, with parental permission. Still, if the gender roles were reversed, I doubt anyone would even think twice," said Berenice.

"True. But that doesn't make it a good thing," I responded.

"What's the age difference between you and Hanif?" Jan asked.

That shut me up. Sometimes, I felt as if Jan and Berenice liked to gang up on me.

Chapter 12: The Lady Vanishes

Dr. Owen was fiddling with his green light. The on-off switch seemed to have broken, and he was installing a new one. He was wearing a pair of reading glasses at the end of his nose and holding a very small screw driver. I told him how impressed I was that he knew how to do that kind of repair, and I meant it. My father invariably broke everything he tried to fix.

"Oh, my dad was an electrician and used to drag me along from job to job so that I would learn the trade."

It was always interesting to be reminded that someone like Dr. Owen had a life outside of this room, peopled with real parents and, perhaps, even real problems.

"Didn't your dad want you to go to medical school?" I asked.

"Not really," he responded. He flicked the switch, and the light began its hypnotic pole dance. "He wanted me to be like him. But so long as I paid for school, he couldn't really object." His glasses were collapsible. He twisted the arms so they ran parallel to the lenses and stuck them in his shirt pocket. I wondered where he got them; I needed a pair of those.

"Of course, when Dad found out that I was going to become a psychiatrist, that was another matter," Dr. Owen said, frowning in a simulation of paternal indignation.

"Why didn't he want you to be a psychiatrist?" I asked.

Dr. Owen just shook his head dismissively. We were here to talk about my father, not his.

"Did you do your homework?" he asked.

I nodded, pulling a folded piece of foolscap out of my purse that detailed the slings and arrows of the past week, and handed it to him.

"But before we begin, would it be alright if we talk about something that I have on my mind?" I asked. He didn't answer right away. "It's related to the work we do here," I added.

"Alright then."

He didn't sound enthusiastic, and I could guess why. Dr. Owen was not an ordinary therapist but a psychiatrist. His work was (I imagined) primarily concerned with EMDR or assessing the nature of a patient's suffering and doling out the appropriate medication. (The white coffee cup that held his pencils was emblazoned with *Lexapro* in bright orange letters; the blue cup, which contained an assortment of pens, had *Zoloft* stamped in white lettering.) In other words, Dr. Owen did not really engage in talk therapy. It could be that, like myself, he was only interested in therapeutic interventions that had the capacity to mess with the hardwiring. Even so, I felt that the situation with Hanif had the potential to undermine any progress I might be making in EMDR. Besides, I couldn't bring myself to discuss Hanif with Jan or Berenice, who seemed so set against the possibility of a relationship that I doubted they'd hear me out.

I told Dr. Owen about my attraction to Hanif, the complications of him being a junior colleague in my department, and even gave him an expurgated account of the night at the drive-in. I couldn't bring myself to tell him how far it went.

"Dr. Owen?" I said tentatively.

"Hmmm?"

"What do you think?" I asked.

Long pause.

"Do you think that it'd be safe for me to pursue this relationship?"

He was giving me an inscrutable look, probably suspecting that I'd already slept with Hanif, damn it! Why was he so suspicious? Maybe because I was lying. Why was I lying? Why didn't I just tell him?

Eventually, Dr. Owen shook his head and smiled. "You're an intelligent woman. You don't need me to tell you that romantic relationships are never safe."

"Of course. But you probably have a better sense of my history with men than anyone else. You're bound to be aware of certain patterns or pitfalls."

Dr. Owen sighed. "It's probably occurred to you that this could be something of a do-over of your relationship with your ex-husband."

Yes, this had occurred to me. I guess I shouldn't have been surprised that it would occur to him as well, yet I was.

"How old was your husband when you first met?" asked Dr. Owen.

"Forty-five," I responded.

"And you are?"

"Forty-five."

This wasn't looking good, but I persisted.

"If this is, as you say, a do-over, could I be trying to get it right — like that movie *Groundhog Day*? Or do you think it's more like Freud's view of repetition?" I asked. Freud had argued that it was easier for a person to repeat an experience, even a painful experience, than to change their underlying patterns. I may've been mixing my points of reference, but who hadn't seen *Groundhog Day*?

Dr. Owen shifted uneasily in his chair, apparently not relishing this doctor-patient dialogue. The room seemed abnormally quiet. There was a large clock behind his desk (with *Wellbutrin* stamped across its face), but this was the first time that I'd ever noticed its pronounced tick-tock.

Eventually, he spoke. "The *Groundhog Day* kind of do-over implied that the Bill Murray character had evolved and grown in the course of the relationship with… with…"

"Andie McDowell," I said. He nodded and continued.

"You, on the other hand, are not working this through in the context of the relationship with your former husband."

"Is it a case of Freudian repetition then?" I asked.

"The age difference is, of course, suggestive," he responded.

Damn it. I knew this, but it wasn't what I wanted to hear from Dr. Owen.

"I also want to caution you that chances of failure are, arguably, even greater than with your former spouse — greater because, in this case, a younger man has an inevitable advantage over a middle-aged woman and in many, if not most, cases will eventually leave her for someone younger," he said.

"But I could be the exception," I said, realizing that I sounded just like that desperate woman in *He's Just Not Into You*. Even so, I persisted.

"Maybe I already am an exception. You yourself said that the chances of a woman my age meeting…." But he held up his hand.

"Let's stay with the question of repetition for a bit longer, if you don't mind. Supposing that you are, in fact, drawn to this younger colleague because a relationship with him would repeat the dynamics between you and your former husband. This could mean that you're anticipating, or even ensuring, the demise of this new relationship. Your choice of a younger partner may be fulfilling an unconscious desire to be rejected by men," he said.

That was a shocker. Of course, I was afraid of being rejected by Hanif. I never thought of myself as choreographing this rejection, however.

Dr. Owen looked at me for a long time as if he were trying to decide something. Finally, he said:

"When you first came to me, you were in a lot of pain. I hope that this treatment has benefited you."

I suddenly saw where this was going. "Dr. Owen, are you firing me?" I laughed nervously.

"Not firing. Certainly not. I only 'fire' patients who refuse to do the work. That's not you. Right from the beginning, I've admired your work ethic," he said.

I was dismayed, but I was also annoyed. Why fire me now? Was it because of my expurgated account of my relations with Hanif? Maybe this chair was rigged with some built-in lie detector. I felt like I was being rejected. Was I? My throat was contracting the way it does when I'm about to cry. A relationship with a psychiatrist isn't like a normal relationship, is it? Isn't it more of a commercial transaction, paying to have my neuroses removed like a wart?

"Even so, I feel that we've gone as far as we can go for the present. There are certain obstacles that're important for you to work through," he said.

Obstacles? Was he describing my attraction to Hanif as an obstacle?

"I'm not saying that you can't come back at some point in the future, but right now, I think it's time for you to take a break and assess your progress," he continued.

"But I still hurt," I said plaintively.

"Everybody hurts. But there are also some things that can help you sort through the pain." He handed me a set of papers labeled *For Professor Bell,* which was stapled in the corner. It described how a person could do EMDR on themselves in case of emergency without the green light. I looked up in confusion.

"For instance, you run into your ex-husband at a conference and feel panicked. You could slip into the restroom, take a seat in the stall, and let your eyes move back and forth along the parameters of the door. It's just about the same length as the light fixture," he said.

I eyed him suspiciously. He must've known ahead of time that this would be my last session.

Dr. Owen walked me to my car for the first time and shook my hand.

"Do you have any parting words of advice?" I asked.

His response was immediate. "Yes, you need to think more about your father," he replied.

"About my father? Really?" I exclaimed.

Hadn't I already spent too much time thinking about my father? From our first appointment, Dr. Owen knew that the relationship between me and my father had been steeped in hostility. I'd told him that my father didn't like me — perhaps even hated me. Dad's classic utterance was, after all, number one on my EMDR hit parade. Rather than trying to reassure me that all parents loved their children, however, Dr. Owen took me at my word. He nodded and said that it was a difficult thing for a child to come to that realization. Sometimes parents don't like their children. Dr. Owen never tried to sugar-coat harsh truths. I valued his honesty.

"Yes, your father. I know you've been struggling with this issue most of your life, but there's still work to do. Don't try and repress your thoughts about him. It's never worth it," he said.

I was about to open my car door when I remembered that I hadn't paid him.

"I'm sorry, Dr. Owen. I forgot," I said, fumbling with my purse.

"No, no. This one's on me," he responded.

He stood in front of his house and waved as I drove off. I maneuvered my car down the convoluted driveway for the last time, glancing briefly at the pond with its little dock. I'd always meant to ask him if you could swim in that pond and was sorry that I never had.

That night, I had the same dream about the coffee house, again terrified that I couldn't get home. But then the scene changed, and I was in a cab approaching my parents' house. When the cab stopped at the curb outside the house and the driver turned around, I saw it was Dr. Owen. *Everybody hurts,* he said. I woke up in a panic, with those words echoing through my head. He seemed to be, in his own way, articulating Freud's pragmatic view that a treatment was a success if the patient had managed to exchange their neurotic misery for everyday unhappiness. Maybe Dr. Owen believed that I'd succeeded in making that transition.

Chapter 13: The Man Who Knew Too Much

When I was an undergraduate, and everyone was experimenting with the occult, I bought a Ouija board. One disappointing evening, my roommate and I wasted hours trying to conjure up Geoffrey Chaucer. My roommate quit, alleging that there was a 50% chance that she knew her future already. When I asked her to explain, she said:

"I know that if I die first, all your messages will begin with: 'What should I wear to….?'"

She wasn't wrong. You've probably figured out by now that getting an outfit that suits the occasion was not simply important to me: the right outfit imbued me with paranormal capabilities, or at least it felt like it did. Whenever I attempted to share this arcane insight with a shabby graduate student interviewing for a job, it sounded something like *the only thing about the interview that you can control is what you wear*. In fact, I believe this piece of wisdom pertains to practically everything that life can throw at you.

I was having dinner with Hanif. We'd already had sex, and yet I was convinced that a special effort was in order if I ever wanted to repeat the experience. I couldn't compete with Paolo, but still, I had to do my best to achieve that smart, sexy, casual persona. The *thanks,*

I just threw this on kind of look. Possibly, I was too old. But then there's Isabelle Adjani: she still manages to look hot when she's in her 60s. She's French, however. It's too bad I hadn't settled on something in the morning because soon I was wading through the familiar pile of detritus — still in my underwear. *The end of all our exploring will be to arrive at where we started and know the place for the first time,* which is to say that I ended up wearing what I'd tried on in my first attempt: jeans, cowboy boots, and a long black V-necked sweater (which conveniently covered my ass). I made sure to throw the heap of clothes in the closet — just in case.

The restaurant didn't take reservations, so Hanif had volunteered to get there before me to secure a booth. Once again, he stood up when I entered the door. Someone had taught that boy good manners. We kissed each other on both cheeks. "Shades of Paolo," I said coyly, and we both laughed. I asked if it was a good visit, and he said that it had been.

"But I have to admit he exhausts me. I hardly got any sleep while he was here."

Could this be a reference to Paolo's taxing sexual stamina? That's ridiculous. If Hanif was attempting to present himself to me in a courtship mode, alluding to gay romps with gorgeous Italians would hardly serve the purpose. It occurred to me that I hadn't told Dr. Owen about another wrinkle in Hanif's romantic candidacy: his possible gay/bi persona. I don't know how this additional information may have factored into Dr. Owen's assessment, but I doubt very much that it would, in his eyes, enhance my prospects for happiness. But rather than plumbing the depths of Hanif's relationship with Paolo, I changed the subject. Right now, I really didn't want to know.

Instead, I asked Hanif about his family — which it turned out was, of course, picture perfect. He was from Columbus, Ohio. His father was a professor of archeology at the university; his mother was a lawyer who worked for the city. He had two sisters, both younger, and a giant schnauzer named Jerry which he really missed. The whole family seemed close-knit and enjoyed spending time together.

"We have a beach house in Maine that's awesome. You'd love it," he said.

I was reminded of Emily, Mellors' wife, visiting her sister in Maine. I hope she got home soon enough to rein him in.

When Hanif returned the volley by asking about my family, I didn't know how to respond. I never do. I didn't have the typical academic background. My father never finished high school; my mother did, but only managed to get a university degree after the four children were mostly grown. My family had always been a source of embarrassment to me. We were a rowdy brood, everybody shouting at one another all at once, and my father shouting most of all. We lived in a middle-class neighborhood, but there was never enough money, so utilities tended to flicker on and off. The first time I brought a boyfriend home for dinner, there was no dinner, and the house was a mess. My younger brother decided to pitch in and help by setting the table, but because he was riding his new unicycle, he kept dropping dishes here and there. Meanwhile, said boyfriend was enchanted, saying with a sense of awe: *This is exactly like the Glass family!* I hadn't read much Salinger at this point — only *Catcher in the Rye*. So, I thought he was complimenting us. I didn't realize he was comparing us to a deeply dysfunctional family.

I wasn't going to tell Hanif any of this. So, I settled for the anecdotal: I told him about my older brother who, as he was approaching forty, decided he hated working a normal 9:00 to 5:00 job, sold all his things, and bought a thirty-seven-foot sailing boat. He'd been sailing around the world for some seven years, picking up odd jobs (and the occasional hottie) along the way. *Last time I heard, he was in Panama working in a tuna cannery,* I said cheerily, as if I admired his antic choices. In fact, I didn't. What I did admire, however, was the extraordinary measures that my brother had been prepared to take in order to put some distance between himself and his family.

The service at the restaurant seemed very slow that night, or maybe I really wanted that martini. (This time, I did order one.) We put in our dinner order at the same time as our drinks, just in case the waitress went missing again. Hanif promptly ordered a cheeseburger with fries. I suddenly wasn't hungry, even though I remember being quite hungry on the drive to the restaurant. Why does this always seem to happen to me? Why is it that whenever I'm with a man that I find attractive, I lose my appetite? (Case in point: I never touched my burger at the drive-in — just as well since it was loaded with onions.) Did I think there was a fat-goddess who, in return for a couple of hours of abstention, would reward me with a miraculous weight loss? Or perhaps, overthrown by the heady combination of sexual desire and awe over the beauty of my beloved, I suddenly become afflicted with lovesickness. Medieval physicians affirmed the existence of such a disease but claimed it only afflicted noble and high-minded souls, which meant that all the sufferers were male. Well, I had news for them: no guy that I'd ever gone out with had lost his appetite in my presence. I settled for a salad Niçoise, which was a safe bet. If my appetite had rallied, I might've been tempted to get clams linguine, which was a challenge to eat with grace and had derailed more than one date.

I poked around at my salad while Hanif told me about an article he was writing on shapeshifting bear-lovers.

"So, I really got into the Bear Mother myth. Great stuff. And there are so many different versions. I'm using them to argue how Engel's *Bear* is a modern-day variant of the legend. Thanks so much for turning me on to the indigenous Mama Bear," he said.

"You're very welcome. It sounds like you are doing great things with her," I said. "Do you know that I've never read *Bear*?" I added.

"Oh, you must! It's so erotic," he said. His eyes were sparkling.

"Erotic for whom? The protagonist? Or is the reader supposed to find it a turn-on?"

"Both. It's all about female desire."

Really. I was wondering if I would find it sexy. Maybe not. There was that story about the Desert Father who was supposed to be so holy and chaste but came to grief when he was put in charge of the monastery's donkeys. I never found that particularly sexy. I frowned.

The waitress came to clear the table. We both ordered coffee. I wanted to order decaf, but realized that this was something only people over forty tend to do. But who was I kidding? I looked around to amend my order, but the waitress had disappeared.

Hanif reached across the table and took my hand. "I can't stop thinking about the other night," he said.

"The backseat: so regressive," I replied.

"Well, you said no at the conference, where at least there was a single bed. So, I thought maybe Hitchcock was your thing," he said, smiling. But the smile faded. "Retrospectively, the drive-in might seem funny. But I don't want us to be funny. I want you to take me seriously."

I nodded but didn't say anything.

"But you seem so reluctant. Is it that you don't want a relationship, or is it just that you don't want one with me?"

"Frankly, I'm worried about the age difference," I said in a rare burst of honesty.

"Why?"

"Because I don't want to do a remake of *The Roman Spring of Mrs. Stone*, no matter how tempting."

"Heather, I don't know what you're talking about."

Exactly. He was too young to get any of my film references. But rather than saying that or explaining who Mrs. Stone might be, I told him about my apprehensions about the age difference as well as about my final conversation with Dr. Owen.

"He doesn't even know me!" Hanif said indignantly. "What right does he have to warn you away?"

"He didn't say to stay away from you. And although he may not know you, he does know me. Or at least, he's gotten to know the kind of patterns I repeat in relationships," I said.

Hanif refused to be reduced to just part of a pattern.

"It sounds to me as if he's just some weird ageist who's determined that everybody stay within their own generational demographic." Hanif looked petulant.

"No, he just wants me to be apprised of the risks of a January-May relationship." *For instance, if I ever got up the courage to take my clothes off in front of you, I'm afraid you might run screaming from the room*, I added mentally.

"Your Dr. Owen's clearly an illiterate," responded Hanif. "In the Merchant's Tale, it's the male — the geriatric knight, January, who gets cuckolded, while his younger wife, May, screws the squire in the pear tree."

I hastened to assure him that it was I who'd introduced the January-May analogy — not Dr. Owen — all the time, wondering if there could be a greater turn-on than a man who knows his Chaucer.

Still, my apprehension about getting involved with Hanif went beyond the question of age or the perversity of my past choices. There were a number of things about him that set off alarm bells in my head. His nebulous sexual orientation, for one, even though I was prepared to put that issue on hold. I wanted to know, of course. But if he was serious about pursuing a relationship with me, and by that, I meant an exclusive relationship, did it really matter if he were bisexual? OK, twice as much competition, granted. I get that.

But I was also very conscious of his part in the action against Thourelle. Hanif must've gleaned my concern since he said, without any prompting: "I wish I'd never raised the matter of Thourelle. It was stupid. But I was curious. I'm new to the department and wanted to know what she'd been up to."

"Well, I have to admit that the way you raised the question was anxiety-inducing," I responded. He looked quizzical, clearly not recalling, so I continued: "You presented yourself as an Assistant Professor who needed to protect himself against predatory older professors. I might also point out that Thourelle is my junior by at least five years." I said this last part with a nervous laugh.

He hit his forehead with the heel of his hand in frustration.

"I was kidding! Please tell me you know that. Doesn't the fact that I would say anything that dumb indicate that I don't see your age?" Hanif said.

He had a point.

"OK, I believe you. Even so, you did tell me that you were a plaintiff in a lawsuit against Thourelle. That's an unnerving factoid," I said.

Hanif frowned, resting his chin in his hand. He was quiet for about a minute or so. I knew he was trying to figure out what he should say — or rather, what he could say. Or, more to the point, he was trying to figure out if he could trust me. I'd try and make it easier for him.

"Hanif, I don't want you to tell me anything that you feel uncomfortable about. But if you do choose to tell me about what happened, I swear to keep it a secret," I said.

And then he told me.

"First, you should know that when I was an undergraduate, I was already interested in Gender and Queer Theory. But it was a pretty conservative school, and people just thought I was weird — even my professors," he said.

I could empathize with that. I remembered the paper for my Old English class, which compared the Beowulf poet's use of prevision with Hitchcock's use of foreshadowing to heighten suspense. I got a

B — the lowest grade you can get in graduate school that still counts toward your degree. It was then that I realized that I'd have to choose between film and the Middle Ages.

"I got disheartened by my senior year, and my Grade Point Average fell. It wasn't high enough to get into the graduate schools I wanted. So, I decided to get an MA at Peitho U., and apply at my top choices the following year. When I arrived at Peitho and met Thourelle, it felt like fate. She was really the most brilliant and beautiful woman I'd ever encountered. And so different: the way she dressed, the way she talked, the way she thought. Do you understand?" he asked, looking at me plaintively.

"Of course. If a teacher is compelling, the classroom's like an erotic petri dish," I responded. The only thing I didn't understand was how people could find a woman who looks like a puppet so beautiful.

Hanif continued. "When she seemed to take a particular interest in me, I couldn't believe my luck. She was the first professor who ever took me seriously; who got me. I can't tell you how much that meant to me. I took a reading course with her where she introduced me to the Platonic dialogues. Then she invited me over one evening to discuss the possibility of writing an article together. It took me forever to get dressed."

I smiled to myself. Could he really be straight?

"When I got there, she offered me a drink, and we sat in her living room. I had never been in such a beautifully furnished room before, at least not in a private home. Everything was in white and black. There was a Kagan cloud sofa in white, a Corbusier lounge chair in white and black cowhide, a series of white Nelson lamps suspended together at different heights — you get the idea. I was just getting into design, and it felt like I was in a museum: heady but also intimidating," he said.

Hanif's description made me think ruefully about our faculty club and its mid-century pretensions. "I can see why it would be intimidating. Just the fear of spilling something," I said.

"Which is why I asked for white wine," Hanif replied. He lifted my hand to his lips and kissed it. "I can't believe I'm telling you this. Are you sure you want to know?"

"If you feel OK about telling me," I responded.

He nodded and continued. "When we settled in with our drinks, she told me about the article she thought we should write. I'd written a paper on Greek pederasty for her class. She wanted to analyze how attitudes toward sexuality played into Plato's description of Socrates' relationship with Alcibiades."

"I thought they had a chaste relationship," I said.

"Professor Bell, you're too damned smart," he said with a grin. "Yes, it was a chaste relationship. Alcibiades was young, handsome, and from a famous family; he had it all. First, Socrates approaches Alcibiades as a suitor, but soon the tables are turned and Alciabides is pursuing him. Then Socrates loses interest in Alcibiades — most scholars think because Alcibiades was unsuited for a life of philosophy. That's basically what I thought before that evening. But Sylvia had a different theory altogether. There was a breakdown in the relationship — not because Alcibiades was unsuited to philosophy, but because the erotic relationship between teacher and student failed, and this disrupted the transmission of knowledge. It was Socrates' fault. He desired Alcibiades but settled for the safe distance of what he had convinced himself was the superior chaste love, skipping over the sexual component."

"That sounds a lot like *Passionate Pedagogy*," I said.

"You think so? It gets better," Hanif said in a humorous albeit sarcastic tone. "The next time I went over, we worked together at her dining room table."

"What was the dining room like?" I asked. OK, I know it was an inane question and considering that this was a difficult subject for Hanif, I shouldn't have prolonged it. But I couldn't help being curious. Was Thourelle's entire life an ode to haut fashion and tasteful furnishings?

"All I can remember is that she had the white marble Saarinen table with the matching tulip chairs. Oh yes, she also had the Eames cabinet — the only colorful thing in her entire place," he said.

"Sorry to interrupt. Go on," I said.

"Well, that evening, we were examining the letters of Abelard and Heloise. My job was to work on the series of anonymous love letters that some scholars believe were written by Abelard and Heloise. I was supposed to look for what the letters said about their joint intellectual life for any clues about when the relationship was consummated," he said.

"Did she tell you why?" I asked.

"Sylvia believed that it was only after a completed erotic exchange with Heloise that Abelard achieved his full brilliance," Hanif said.

"Wait a second. Abelard was Heloise's teacher. Isn't she the one who's supposed to get the intellectual charge?" I asked.

"Thourelle believed the intellectual current flowed both ways," he responded.

"Maybe. But it doesn't change the fact that Heloise ended up lonely and bitter in a religious community, where she didn't write anything except letters to Abelard," I objected.

"Even so, the letters were key. It was in the letters that Heloise identified the individual conscience as the ultimate tribunal for good and evil," he said.

"I know where you're going with this. Heloise's 'ethic of pure intention' would later become the central argument in Abelard's treatise, *Ethica*. Hardly an original argument," was my snotty response.

"Well, what did I know? I was just starting out in grad school and was totally mesmerized. Thourelle was the brainy Scheherazade of my dreams. And I was totally turned on. I think I went around with an erection for about three weeks." Hanif was instantly remorseful. "Oh God, I can't believe I said that. Does it bother you?" he said, with a concerned look on his face.

In fact, it was information I didn't need or want, although I did my best to conceal my reaction. Why was it upsetting, you might ask? Well, I'd always been jealous of Thourelle on a professional level. Now, I could be jealous of her erstwhile erotic hold over Hanif. I doubt very much that anyone had ever wandered around with an erection for several weeks on my behalf. But I wanted to reassure him. He was telling this story at my request, after all. So, I said, "I totally get it. I've always believed that there is no sex like no sex. In fact, the ideology of medieval courtly love is that love declines with consummation."

"Well, that's not what I have in mind for us," he responded. Then he quickly added, "I'm sorry, I didn't mean to say that. I shouldn't project. But I'd read all your work before I met you and was already half in love with you when we did finally meet. Does that sound dumb?" he asked.

"Not to a medievalist," I laughed. "A common trope in romance is to love someone 'sight unseen.' It's the ultimate love." Was that the reason for Hanif's co-conspirator look? That he was half in love with me? Anyway, his revelation worked magic on my sexual morale, eclipsing some (but not all) of Thourelle's erectile charm. "But I didn't mean to interrupt you. How many nights did you and Thourelle work on this alleged article?" I asked, hoping the answer wasn't 1001.

"I don't know exactly, maybe four or five. The evenings all blend together," Hanif replied. "Except there was one special night when the research and the relationship finally merged. It was a weekend, and Thourelle invited me to dinner with the understanding that we would work afterward. The subject of feminism came up. I can't remember who introduced it, but it was probably Sylvia. She seemed to have a distinct endgame in mind, and feminism seemed central to where she wanted to go."

"Did you have a sense of this endgame at the time?"

"No. The question of feminism emerged naturally. We were talking about her core beliefs, and Sylvia said that feminism was the closest thing she had to a religion. But she was afraid that contemporary feminism had become too absorbed with power dynamics: the emphasis on the more powerful versus the less powerful party in a relationship. She didn't deny that these dynamics existed but believed that the preoccupation itself could become disempowering. The less powerful were cast as victims — rather than sexual agents, working to fulfill their erotic desires — and the more powerful became abusers. Sylvia was especially sensitive to this bias in a university context and the way it determined the limits of relations between teachers and students," Hanif said.

"But that ship had already sailed," I responded.

"True. Sylvia realized she was swimming against the tide. But she truly believed it was more empowering to accept students as adults with the power of consent," Hanif said.

"I'm not surprised. The erotic connection between teacher and student is essential to her understanding of the learning process," I said.

"Exactly," Hanif replied. "And I guess she wanted to make sure we were on track with the learning process because when she was explaining her theory, she put her hand on my thigh. Quite high up."

Hanif was silent until I eventually prompted: "What did you do?"

"What do you think I did? Here was a gorgeous professor who also happened to be my idol. She was not only critical of the university for discouraging teacher-student relations but also actively hitting on me. This was basically a precis for *Passionate Pedagogy*, but I couldn't have known that. Even if I had known, it wouldn't have made any difference. Of course, I agreed with her that the university's policy was crazy. And the next thing I knew, we were in her bed." Hanif stopped momentarily, looking pensive.

"Hanif, we don't need to talk about this anymore," I said.

"No, I want to tell you, but there isn't much more to tell. It only happened a couple of times and, to be honest, each time was more wonderful than the last. Then she suddenly dropped me. I was frantic. I sent her emails, left phone messages, put little gifts in her mailbox, but she just ignored it all. I was heartbroken, but I was also angry. I felt used. Not just sexually; she'd also been using me as an unpaid Research Assistant. Of course, I only realized this after the fact. She also used a lot of my research on Greek pederasty," he said.

"That sucks," I said sympathetically. Even so, it wasn't an open-and-shut case. I know that in the Sciences there are many student complaints of their work being appropriated by professors. But it is the professor who runs the lab and sets the research agenda, so the graduate students' research arguably belongs to the professor. This was not the case in the Humanities. Even so, Thourelle's determination that he read Plato and her intention to co-author an article had something in common with the scientific model.

"Yes, it did suck. Then I learned about the others," said Hanif.

"What others?" I asked.

"There were twelve of us in her seminar on pedagogy. We were a miscellaneous group, both in terms of gender and orientation. But Sylvia didn't discriminate. Each of us had come to realize that we'd been duped, and then we began to compare notes. At first, we bonded over being exploited by the same person — the way Bernie Madoff's victims must've felt. But when a member of our group took her own life, the rest of us felt obligated to make a Title IX complaint against Thourelle," said Hanif.

Oh God, one of Thourelle's student-lovers had committed suicide. This was a much darker story than I had ever had imagined.

"There was a hearing. Peitho U. doesn't forbid relations between professors and students, provided the professor isn't currently evaluating the student. Sylvia's lawyer argued that the relationships only began once her seminar was over and that we were all well past the age of consent. But our lawyer countered that the students had been deceived in two basic ways. The sex may have seemed consensual, but Sylvia was manipulating us into doing research on her behalf. When challenged about having sexual relations with a number of students, she argued that it was a polyamorous arrangement. But a true polyamorous relationship requires both consent and full disclosure by all partners. That wasn't Sylvia's way: she led each of us to believe that our relationship with her was exclusive," said Hanif.

It was difficult to reconcile Thourelle's alleged promiscuity with her alleged asexuality. "She presents herself as an ace, but it sounds as if she were just a randy bisexual," I said.

"It's more complicated than that," Hanif responded. "Don't get me wrong. I'm not trying to defend her. I think she's dangerous. But asexuality is really a spectrum of orientations."

I remembered what Dr. Owen had said about the Split Attraction Model.

"Do you think she ever cared about you?" I asked.

Hanif was nervously playing with the packets of sugar on the table, making a small white pyramid in front of him.

"I don't really think she could've cared. There's such a thing as a gray-pansexual aromantic: someone potentially attracted to all genders but devoid of any romantic inclinations. Maybe Sylvia is one of them," he said.

"But why so many lovers? Does a real asexual have that kind of libido?" I asked.

"Despite her critique on power, for Sylvia, sex *was* power. You don't need much sexual libido to enjoy power. There were also practical considerations: we not only helped with the research for *Passionate Pedagogy*; we were also her guinea pigs," Hanif said, somewhat ruefully.

"And now she has a fiancé. How does that fit with her sexual profile?" I asked.

"I can only say that I feel sorry for the guy. The short time I was with her, she presented herself as straight and in love with me. I believed her. Probably her fiancé has the same illusions," Hanif responded.

I wondered if Hanif was really over Thourelle. Maybe I was just a surrogate.

"Does it bother you being in the same department as her?" I asked.

"I thought it might. I knew she was here, and I did have one other offer. But this was the better department. And you were here. When I finally did see her, I didn't feel anything," he replied.

A waitress dropped a tray on the other side of the room, and we both jumped. (I also screamed, of course). *Time to go*, I said, and he nodded. We split the check and left the restaurant. Even though it was late October, the weather was strangely balmy. We walked around the perfectly preserved town square, admiring the stucco courthouse with its handsome clock tower, lit up by night. The grass had recently been cut, probably for the last time that year, and the air was filled with that fresh, green smell. There was a bench in front of the courthouse, flanked by two anomalous canons, which, perhaps as a result of some town councilor's dark humor, were both pointing directly at the bench. This did not deter us. We sat down and turned to each other wordlessly. Hanif put his arms around me and drew me close. We kissed for a long time. Sweet, slow, lingering kisses.

Then we went back to his place and made love ... in a bed! There were some bumps along the way, but they were all my fault. I didn't want to take my clothes off and then insisted that he turn off the light. (We compromised: he put a dishtowel over one of the bedside lamps.) In the morning, however, we finally could see each other in our totality. Hanif's body was a thing of beautiful. He used to be on a swim team and still had those wonderful swimmer's shoulders: muscled, but not too much. His torso had the legendary six-pack, which I'd seen in movies but never in bed. I was also struck by his skin quality: so smooth and perfect. By contrast, I'd entered the Nora Ephron *I Feel Bad About My Neck* stage of life, yet here I was sleeping with this Adonis. Hanif's skin had the tautness and elasticity that tend to disappear in the late 30s; early 40s for the lucky. (Jan thinks that male skin has a longer life expectancy, but I think that's just internalized sexism reflecting society's rejection of the aging female body.) I hadn't felt skin like that for 20 years. It brought back memories of early days, early loves. And then there was his smell. It was not just his habitual smell of sandalwood; it was a young smell. Sweat without any pungency; breath that didn't make one recoil in the morning.

Why do we get smellier as we get older?

Is it just women?

Or is it just me?

Beside Hanif, I felt like that statue of Diana of Ephesus. When he told me that I had a beautiful body, I was on the verge of contradicting him, as is my wont. But then I suddenly remembered Dalia and stopped myself. Dalia was one of my older brother's former girlfriends. Her attraction to my brother may have suggested that she was not of sound mind, but her body was magnificent. Hence my brother's proud and frequent comment: *You could crack an egg on that ass!* Then Dalia made the mistake of sharing her own critique of her body with him: that her legs were short and her ankles too thick. He'd never noticed before, and yet, after her disclosure, he confessed to me that he could never see her in quite the same way. In fine, I shut my mouth.

Despite my sense of inadequacy, and continuing sense of disbelief that Hanif could really want me, and fear that maybe someone had put him up to it (think Stephen King's *Carrie*), I left his place aglow with happiness. There was but one thing bothering me: apart from a reversion to the stylish half-beard on his face, the rest of his body was absolutely bald. Back, front, legs, genitals: everything. It looked like he'd been dipped in a jar of Neet. This alarmed me. It was my first experience with a *naked* naked man. As soon as I got home, I spent an hour on Google, only to learn that Hanif had been manscaped.

Chapter 14: Saboteur

Hanif and I spent most of the weekend together at my place. Having him around made me happy. My small post-divorce bungalow had always seemed somewhat tired and rather pokey. Now when I walked into the living room and saw Hanif reading on the couch, I realized that he was just the ornament the house had needed. Would that he stayed on the couch forever. Hanif was hard at work turning his queering animals dissertation into a book, but also had a grant proposal he was working on. It was the first one he'd ever submitted as a faculty member, so he asked if I could look it over. I spent some time editing it (and to be frank, rewriting much of it). He was touchingly grateful.

"Do you think I could use you as a referee?" he asked. I paused, wondering whether anyone assessing the fellowship would know that we were involved. Probably not. It would be too early for word to have gotten around.

"Of course, if you don't want to, I understand," he added, mistaking my pause for reluctance.

"No, it's not that. I'm happy to write. It's OK if you have one colleague write, especially if they're in a related field. But the more people you can muster that aren't colleagues and weren't on your dissertation committee, the better," I said.

"Thanks. You're a doll," he said, flashing me one of his incomparable smiles.

Meanwhile, I was also putting the final touches on my book on medieval pedagogy. I'd been working on this book for years, and now I finally had my page proofs. It was my last tango with the text — a situation that always made me feel ambivalent. It's hard to let go of something that you've struggled with for so long. (I also kept wondering if it was really any good.)

It was Sunday evening, and we'd just finished an early dinner. I was surprised how happy it made me to be cooking for someone again. Hanif had just left when the phone rang. The speaker identified herself as Sylvia; it took me a moment to realize that it was Thourelle. The timing was so strange that for a moment, I wondered if she'd been watching the house. (I glanced nervously outside and jumped when I saw a dark car parked in front before realizing it was mine.) Thourelle said she had something important to talk to me about and wanted to see me as soon as possible. We arranged that she should drop by my office the next day around 3:00 p.m.

I was sitting in my office, trying to work on my page proofs, and unaccountably nervous. Thourelle arrived on the hour, sustaining her new look of tight clothing and heavy makeup. I invited her to sit down.

"I've never been in your office before. It's nice — homey," she said, looking around.

Considering that the office had Edvard Munch's *The Scream* on one wall, Gustav Klimt's *Judith with the Head of Holofernes* on the other, and my demented art therapy pictures over my desk, I figured she might be a bit apprehensive as well. Then her eyes lighted on my page proofs.

"Your pedagogy book?" she asked.

I nodded.

"I can't wait to read it. The medieval schools were so passionate, so filled with eros, don't you think?" she asked.

"From a certain perspective, sure. But I argue that any eroticism in the medieval schools was basically a continuation of Roman pederasty. So, it's innately abusive," I responded. Not very diplomatic, true, but I wasn't prepared to misrepresent my position just to put her at ease. There was an awkward silence. I had come to perceive Thourelle as a commanding presence who takes what she wants, trampling over the weak. Yet, sitting in my office, she seemed small and vulnerable. She kept fiddling with her skirt, smoothing out wrinkles that weren't, in fact, there. I hadn't asked for this meeting and didn't particularly want her in my office. But now that she was here, I didn't want to make the situation more uncomfortable than need be because that would make me uncomfortable. I tried to think of a subject that could dissipate some of the tension. Not henna, I suppose. Since she'd arrived on campus, we seemed to have tacitly agreed to put that argument behind us.

"Those are great boots," I ventured. Indeed, they were: close-fitting, over-the-knee boots made of snakeskin — python or cobra, I thought — and grey, of course. "You really have fabulous footwear." It worked for Lily Briscoe with Mr. Ramsey, so I thought I would give it a try.

She smiled and began to look more relaxed.

"Thank you. It's hard to find decent stores around here, so I've started buying some of my basics online," she replied.

I'd been buying my clothes online for so long that I sometimes forgot there were other ways to shop. Whenever I was procrastinating or got stuck on something I was writing, I automatically went into shopping mode. It was only one disaffected click away. I would never be able to achieve Thourelle's bespoke look.

"I'm sorry we haven't had a chance to spend more time together. But last year, I was getting adjusted to a new school. And this year, with my engagement and all, I don't know where the time's gone," she said.

It was funny to see Thourelle adopt the persona of the harried bride. The image of her coming down the aisle in a slate grey bridal gown popped into my head. I realized, however, that Thourelle wasn't the one who should be apologizing. Not only was I the veteran of this university, but our scholarly interests converged. It'd really been my responsibility to make friendly overtures. I hadn't ignored her entirely, but I'd only done the bare minimum: the mandatory cocktail party when she first arrived; a perfunctory lunch in the faculty club. I think that was it.

"Well, it's never too late. I hope we'll be colleagues for a long time," I said with congenial mendacity. "When is your wedding, by the way?" I was tempted to use the sick-making euphemism "big day."

"Not until the spring, but I've so much to do before then: invitations, caterers, you know," she responded. Was that just a manner of speaking, or was she alluding to my failed marriage? I remember an erstwhile shrink asking me why I didn't just ignore hidden meanings and stay on the surface of a conversation. *Because I can't*, is the answer. My mind works in reverse to the way I assume other minds work: hidden meanings are the ones that seem most obvious.

"We still haven't found a venue," she continued, complaining about the lack of feasible options. The university had a rather grand ballroom, which they'd considered, but who wants to get married at your workplace? I privately agreed. Of course, they could always get married in the bar where they first met.

"The only thing that's been settled is that the graduate students are insisting on throwing us a shower. But they're in control of the guest list. I've no idea who they're inviting," she said, apologizing in advance.

"How thoughtful of them. They're a lively group. I bet it'll be fun," was my response.

Meanwhile, I was conscious of how we were wasting each other's time by making small talk about her wedding and wondered when she would get to the point. Thourelle was clearly thinking along similar lines, because she suddenly changed course.

"I suppose you're curious about why I wanted to see you," she said.

"Well, you don't need an excuse to see me — that's the great thing about collegiality — but it sounded like you had something particular on your mind," I replied.

"Yes, I do," she said, nodding. "I wanted to give you a friendly word of warning and hope you will keep what I'm about to tell you to yourself." She wasn't looking at me but was playing with her engagement ring, turning it this way and that. Then she looked up: "Will you?"

I wasn't sure how to respond, but eventually said: "I'll try to do as you ask, but it really depends on what you're going to tell me." I already had a pretty good idea about the subject matter, if not the specifics.

"Alright, but, again, I hope you'll decide that what I'm about to tell you is best kept to yourself," she said.

I nodded, and she continued. "It's about Hanif Twist." I echoed his name as if I were surprised but was probably unconvincing: I've never been good at faking things.

"You probably know that we knew each other earlier," she said.

"Yes, you were at Peitho U. when he was working on his MA," I said.

"That's right. What you probably don't know is that he became infatuated with me — thought he was in love," she said. Hanif had, of course, told me this already, but I did my best to look like I was hearing it for the first time.

"Oh," I said by way of evasive response.

"Hanif is, as you know, very smart and intellectually lively. He was always dropping by my office to discuss what he'd read or show me something he'd written, always on fire with new ideas. I didn't object; in fact, I encouraged him. I like to see graduate students come alive with a passion for learning. It's really what *Passionate Pedagogy*'s all about. But somehow, the lines got crossed. He got the impression that I was interested in him romantically," Thourelle said.

Leaving aside the question of who was the first to cross which line, thus far, her account seemed credible. I could well imagine Hanif as an ardent graduate student, dropping by a favorite professor's office. I've had irrepressible students like that.

At this point in her narrative, however, there was an ominous pause, suggesting that its tenor was about to change.

"One evening, I was alone in my office when Hanif dropped by, which wasn't that unusual. He said he wanted feedback on a conference paper he'd shown me. This was clearly a pretext because before I even had a chance to fetch the paper, he blurted out that he loved me. I hadn't seen that coming and wasn't sure what to do. I was fond of Hanif, and we had a good intellectual rapport. I didn't want to just reject him and throw him out of my office. So, I asked him to sit down and tried to make it clear to him that I wasn't interested in a romantic relationship. I even revealed that I was an asexual, not seeking that sort of relationship with anyone. I did this as gently as I could, but it was extremely awkward, and I wanted him to leave. When I got up to get his conference paper from the filing cabinet, he blocked my way, attempting to kiss me. I could smell alcohol on his breath. He tried to overpower me sexually — to rape me, in fact. I barely got away," she said. Her eyes widened with what I suppose was a show of retrospective terror.

I was incredulous. It was difficult to reconcile the Hanif I knew with sexual violence. In fact, it was impossible.

"How did you manage to get away?" I asked. This was a very real question. While Hanif was no giant, Thourelle couldn't have weighed more than 105 lbs.

"When I was living in New York, I took a course in self-defense. It turns out that a well-aimed kick to the groin is just as debilitating as I'd been led to believe. I grabbed my purse and ran," said Thourelle.

I had to come up with some sort of response, but wasn't sure what I could say. When a female colleague tells you that she's been the victim of sexual assault, you can't just brush it to one side and say you don't believe her. Yet, she had to be lying. Didn't she?

Eventually, I said, "Sylvia, I feel that I'm in an impossible situation. I can't say that what you're telling me didn't happen, because I wasn't there. But Hanif strikes me as more sensitive than most males, certainly more deferential to women. I just don't see him as a rapist."

This response might seem simple-minded to some. Certain radical feminists considered testosterone to be a kind of rape hormone: scratch the surface of any male, and you'd find a rapist. Yet Hanif appeared to be the type of male whose very existence disproved this grim premise. Of course, millions of people once felt the same way about Bill Cosby.

"I have two questions for you: how well do you really know Hanif, and have you ever seen him angry?" she asked.

I left her questions hanging in the air — perhaps because I didn't have very satisfying answers to either of them. It didn't matter that I'd technically known Hanif for a number of years: I couldn't claim to know him well, and I'd never seen him angry. As a matter of fact, it was even difficult for me to imagine Hanif being angry, let alone exhibiting an out-of-control temper.

"Did you go to the police?" I asked.

"No. I'd managed to escape, and I didn't want to ruin his career. I was hoping it was an isolated episode," she said.

This struck a false note. The responsible thing would've been to report him. Someone who perpetrates sexual violence will do it again. I didn't say any of this out loud. The fact that I didn't comment must've seemed like a tacit expression of my disapproval and probable skepticism. But Thourelle went on to admit that it was a mistake not to report him. Hanif's response to her rejection was vindictive. He slandered her to the other graduate students, claiming that it was Thourelle who pursued him and wouldn't leave him alone. Hanif was popular and persuasive, and the other students had already observed how much time he spent in Thourelle's office. It wasn't difficult for him to recast Thourelle as a voracious cougar.

Eventually a number of the students banded together to lodge a Title IX complaint against Thourelle. Hanif was the ringleader, but it wasn't difficult for him to get others to sign on. Apparently, there were two female graduate students who were clearly besotted with him and would've believed anything he said. There were also several others who'd received mediocre grades in Thourelle's seminar, whom she attempted to discourage from pursuing academic careers. Thourelle was forced to bring a countersuit, primarily for defamation, but also including an account of Hanif's attempted rape.

"It got very ugly," she said with her eyes closed.

I was about to ask her why she was telling me this when she told me, "The reason I'm sharing this is because I've heard that you and Hanif are becoming quite close. I wanted to warn you: if you disappoint him or in some way cross him, there's no telling what he might do — especially if you become involved sexually."

I've heard that you and Hanif are becoming quite close. Who was her informant? Jan and Berenice were the only ones who knew about my feelings for Hanif (Dr. Owen doesn't count), but even they didn't know how far our relations had progressed. Oh damn, maybe she heard about that night at the pool when I was shooting my mouth off about — who knows what? I really can't remember. Yet that didn't seem very likely: the other women were my friends and barely knew Thourelle. I once again thought about how her phone call came right after Hanif left my house yesterday. Maybe I wasn't being paranoid and she had been watching.

"You wouldn't have heard about this lawsuit; the case was settled out of court, and the records were sealed. All parties were sworn to silence," she said.

At least Hanif and Thourelle agreed on that much.

"I'm taking quite a risk by telling you about this incident. I hope you'll keep it to yourself. But I had to tell you. If something happened, it would be on my conscience," she said.

"Well, I want to thank you for your warning, but I assure you it's unnecessary. Hanif and I are just friends." I was trying to keep my voice as even as possible.

"Which is, of course, what I thought about Hanif and myself — at least before that night in my office. He was a graduate student at the time. This meant he was technically more vulnerable, and his accusation of sexual harassment against a faculty member more serious. But it's certainly possible for a junior professor to bring a harassment case against a senior colleague — especially if they're in the same department," she replied.

At that point, I heard a tap on the door. It was Hanif, of course. The timing couldn't have been worse.

"Oh, I see you're busy. Hello Sylvia," Hanif said, forcing her to return a stiff greeting. I had to admire his poise.

"Come by my office later this afternoon if you can," he said to me. "I need a break and thought we could go up to the faculty club." He nodded to us both and was gone.

It was an awkward situation, but Hanif had played it to perfection. His attitude toward me was undeniably familiar, but it would have been appropriate for either a friend or a lover. Even more impressive was his cordial and professional greeting to Thourelle, which betrayed none of the strangeness one might expect of a would-be rapist in the presence of a former victim. In contrast, both Thourelle and I lacked Hanif's aplomb. Thourelle's terse greeting seemed forced, and I'm certain that I looked uncomfortable in the extreme. After Hanif left, the only thing that I could think to say was *Lupus fabula*. Translation: speak of the wolf in the fable. That's what the Romans used to say for our *Speak of the Devil*. Thourelle looked at me as if I were babbling, which made me doubt her much-vaunted competence in classical Latin.

"Well, I've kept you long enough." She got up and went toward the door. But before she left, she turned around. "Please think about what I said."

Who in my situation could've helped but thinking about what she said? There was considerable common ground between Thourelle and Hanif's differing accounts. Both initially presented Hanif as an adoring and appreciative student, and both agreed that there was a rift that resulted from some kind of sexual abuse. Otherwise, the two accounts diverged wildly: the cynical seduction and exploitation of multiple students by a female professor versus the attempted rape of a female professor by a male graduate student who managed to convince his peers that she was the one at fault. Hanif had the advantage of getting out in front of Thourelle with his version of events. But his precipitous revelation could also be construed as suspect: perhaps he was attempting a preemptive strike.

Thourelle's decision to confide in me was prompted by the knowledge that Hanif and I were becoming "close," but this did not necessarily mean she was lying. If she were telling the truth, she would, of course, assume that Hanif would persist in his slanderous lies. Although both were legally bound not to talk about the case, he'd probably confide in a close friend or lover, which might prompt Thourelle to counter with her version of events. But if Hanif were telling the truth, her dramatic tale of sexual assault had been deliberately concocted to trump his story. In the context of the #MeTo movement, female victims of sexual assault had the advantage, at least until their stories were definitively disproved. In contrast, the case of Reitman vs Ronell demonstrated that the complaints of a male student harassed by a female professor were much easier to ignore or dismiss despite the prejudicial power dynamics. Even when Reitman succeeded in proving his case, Ronell was only suspended for a year — a risibly light penalty.

There was no way of getting at what actually happened between Hanif and Thourelle. But I was disturbed and not up to meeting Hanif for a drink. I texted him and told him I wasn't feeling well and had gone home but would see him tomorrow.

Chapter 15: Psycho

By the time I got home that evening, I was distinctly out of sorts. I hadn't done any preparation for the next day's teaching, but instead of working, I sat frozen in front of the TV watching CNN, not hearing a word, drinking scotch. Around ten, my mother called and guilted me about coming home for Thanksgiving until I finally hung up on her. Afterward, I needed to get some air before settling down to work.

Ever since my teens, I've stolidly refused to be afraid of walking around on my own at night. It's not that I'm a courageous person, but I knew that I would require a degree of imperviousness if I ever expected to live and travel independently. Once a woman becomes too focused on the horrible things that could happen to her, she's already become complicit with misogynist efforts to disempower her. She has constructed her own little cage.

And yet, recently, I'd become ill at ease in the evenings — some evenings anyway. This was one of them. When I was half way around the block, I had the sense that someone was following me, at the same time recognizing how unlikely that might be. This was a pretty safe town, after all. I tried to remain relaxed: predators are said to have an uncanny ability to detect fear. I didn't look over my shoulder but continued to walk at a steady pace, careful not to speed up. My keys were in my pocket, and I arranged them between my fingers to form a crude claw, just in case.

Once my nocturnal perambulation was over, I locked the door carefully behind me. Hanif had called while I was out to ask how I was and say goodnight, but I didn't call back. I told myself that it was too late when, in fact, I wasn't sure what to say to him. I worked for several hours before going to bed and then had a difficult time falling asleep. Once I did, my sleep was riddled with disturbing scenes of Hanif and Thourelle in the throes of passion. It reminded me of the hallucinatory scene in *Jacob's Ladder* when Tim Robbins sees his girlfriend having sex with a demon. I woke up in a cold sweat. There was probably nothing stalking me apart from Hanif and Thourelle's vexed history.

I was exhausted the next day, emotionally worn out and numb. I might've once again been tempted to defect from office hours. This time I didn't have a choice, however; I was conscripted by my Chair. I ran into Jan in the hall, looking harried. She immediately collared me and dragged me into her office.

"Look at this," she said, waving a couple of sheets of paper. "I just got this list of next semester's graduate courses from the Director of Graduate Studies."

I shrugged. It was December: hadn't the list been out for over a month?

"Thourelle has changed the topic of her graduate seminar from *Pure Pedagogies* to *The Psychopathology of Everyday Sex*." Jan was irate.

The last thing I wanted to talk about was Thourelle. Even so, I managed to rise to the occasion. "If it means that she's given up on *Pure Pedagogies,* that's probably just as well. It's a lame project that she invented for the job market to balance out *Passionate Pedagogies*. Now that she got the job, she can drop it."

"Well, read the goddam description, and then tell me if you still think it's a good thing," she said, handing me a page.

The Psychopathology of Everyday Sex (Eng 666): Professor Sylvia Thourelle

Contemporary society tends to be self-congratulatory for both its degrees of sexual liberation and sexual tolerance. But, as Freud suggested long ago in his *Psychopathology of Everyday Life,* some degree of sexual repression is a condition for civilized life. This course attempts to explore our own sexual boundaries and emphasize our taboos by focusing on non-normative sexualities and their practice. Some topics — such as transsexualism, asexuality, and polyamorous relations — could be classified as marginal. Others — such as the belief in female ejaculation — are scientifically controversial. But still others — such as pedophilia, zoophilia, and sex trafficking — are illegal. In all instances, special efforts will be taken to comprehend not just the critics of a given sexual practice or lifestyle but also its proponents and practitioners. To this end, the classroom seminar will be complemented by a series of speakers who represent these alternative sexualities.

This course is designed to be disturbing, both by testing the limits of academia's much-vaunted liberalism and by demonstrating the degree to which the margins of society are essential for defining the center.

Tentative Reading List

* David Archard, *Sexual Consent (1997)*

*J. Michael Bailey, *The Man Who Would be Queen: The Science of Gender-Bending and Transsexualism (2003)*

*Julie Sondra Decker, *The Invisible Orientation: An Introduction to Asexuality (2015)*

* Melissa Gira Grant, *Playing the Whore: The Work of Sex Work (2014)*

*Dr. Amy Hammel-Zabin, *Conversations with a Pedophile (2013)*

*R.J. Maratea, "Screwing the Pooch: Legitimizing Accounts in a Zoophilia Community." *Deviant Behavior* 32 (2011): 915-943.

* Dr. Castle, *The Black Pill Theory: Why the Incels are Right and You are Wrong (2019)*

*Deborah Sundahl, *Female Ejaculation and the G-Spot (2014)*

*Elisabeth Sheff, *The Polyamorists Next Door: Inside Multiple-Partner Relationships and Their Families (2014)*

"What do you think?" Jan asked.

"It's an interesting reading list," I responded.

Jan was pacing back and forth. "This course doesn't belong in our department."

"Why not?" I asked.

"How does this have anything to do with English literature? It looks like a course in abnormal psychology," Jan responded.

"Jan, the literary canon's gone. We don't focus on the classics anymore," I said.

"But this isn't even literature!" Jan exclaimed. "And what about these so-called guest speakers?"

"Visiting artists?" I said tentatively.

"Give me a break. It's more like a sexual freak show. Do you know any of these titles?" Jan had a desperate look on her face.

"Not really."

"But you specialize in sex," Jan said in an accusatory tone.

"Medieval sex! Give me a break," I replied.

"I don't want any more trouble with the Dean — especially over Thourelle. And this course is a veritable hornets' nest. Go see if Hanif's around. Tell him it's an emergency." It sounded like an order.

Not only had I not returned Hanif's call last night, but I'd also ignored a text he'd sent me in the morning. I was feeling confused and emotionally unavailable, even to myself, and had no idea what to say to Hanif. I certainly didn't feel like fetching him on Jan's behalf.

"What's Hanif got to do with it?" I asked.

"Hanif's middle name might as well be transgression. He's bound to know something about this list," she replied.

While I walked to Hanif's office, I wondered what Jan meant when she said *Hanif's middle name might as well be transgression*. Had she somehow caught wind of his former relations with Thourelle (and if so, which version)? Or with me? Or was she just alluding to his research? Or all of the above?

Hanif's door was shut. When I knocked, he didn't answer right away. When he opened the door, I saw that he was not alone. There was a beautiful woman with shoulder-length brown hair across from Hanif, who was seated at his desk.

"Hey there," I said, trying to sound casual. "Excuse me for interrupting. You've been summoned by your Chair, and she seems to think it's an emergency."

The woman got up from her chair, hooking her hair behind her ears and adjusting her skirt.

"That's fine. We're just finishing up. Have you met Anna?" asked Hanif.

Finishing up what? I thought. But my more politic, ever-vigilant *döppelganger*-self, said:

"No, I haven't had the pleasure." We both nodded and smiled at one another and then she withdrew.

Hanif drew me into the office and closed the door, gazing at me thoughtfully. "Heather, are we OK?" he asked.

I wasn't sure we were, but I wanted us to be. So, I nodded.

"Then give me a hug," he said.

Unfortunately, I am not good at faking hugs. First Thourelle's revelation and now the brunette beauty in his office. I felt emotionally paralyzed, and I'm sure this was reflected in how stiff and unresponsive I was. But Hanif held me anyway, gently rocking me.

"I'll be OK," I muttered into his chest.

"Is it Thourelle?" he asked.

I didn't answer.

"I was worried when I saw her in your office. Let's talk about it later, OK?" he said.

We agreed to meet for a drink around five o'clock.

Hanif dutifully followed me to Jan's office and was soon holding the objectionable course description and its louche reading list.

"Can you give me a run down on who some of these authors are?" asked Jan.

Hanif scanned the list.

"Sure. I've heard of most of them. Starting at the top: J. Michael Bailey is a professor of psychology at Northwestern. I think he's legit. This particular work was controversial, though, because he was basically arguing that male-to-female sex reassignment is not a question of a female trapped in a male body, which is the way it is usually represented and as is believed to be the case with female-to-male reassignments. He presents male-to-female ones as a question of erotic preference."

I looked over at Jan. She was attempting to look impartial, but couldn't help puckering up her brow.

"Decker on asexuality is basic, but a good intro. I haven't read Mareta's 'Screwing the Pooch,'" Hanif continued.

"But isn't that your field?" Jan asked.

"For Christ's sake, Jan. We've been through this already. 'Queering' in animal studies doesn't mean that Hanif either does it with animals or studies those who do." I made a mental note to warn Hanif that he shouldn't mention his work on bears to Jan.

When Jan apologized, Hanif graciously assured her that no apology was necessary, struggling to suppress a laugh.

"OK. Moving forward, the claims that women have an erogenous zone called the G-spot and that they ejaculate are highly controversial. Sundahl's book argues the case, claiming the denial of experts reflects society's puritanical values."

My God. Aren't we done with that yet? The G-spot was "discovered" in the 40s, but no credible gynecologist or sexologist, then or since, has affirmed its existence. There were ardent advocates, however. I was in a reading group once where the only male member kept offering to "prove" the existence of the G-spot on the rest of us. We kicked him out.

"Sheff is a sociologist who studies what she refers to as 'non-traditional' relationships. She goes through the reasons why someone might identify as polyamorous, the pros and cons. It's one of Thourelle's favorite topics, right up there with asexuality. If you didn't know that already," Hanif said, looking at Jan.

Jan didn't. And I bet she wasn't sure what polyamorous meant either, but after the queering gaffe, she wasn't about to ask.

"Grant is a journalist and former sex worker who believes that prostitution should be decriminalized and mainstreamed into the economy. Judging from the titles, the books on pedophilia and the incel movement present the position of the practitioners," Hanif said.

Hanif then began reading the course description to himself, nodding. "It sounds like an intriguing class," he said, looking up when he had finished.

Jan's anxiety was mounting: I knew this because the catarrh in her throat seemed to be bothering her again. "What do the two of you advise that I do about this?"

Hanif didn't say anything. With his experience of Thourelle's graduate classes, I doubt he was surprised by the list.

"What can you do, Jan? This sounds like a legitimate course. Blocking it denies academic freedom," I said.

"I don't mind the stuff on transsexualism or G-spots, but what about topics like pedophilia and bestiality? Isn't that pushing too far?" Jan asked.

"I think we can assume that Thourelle is examining these issues — not endorsing them. And considering the rise of both child and animal abuse, they deserve attention," I responded.

"Then where are the books on her list denouncing these sick pricks?" Jan was becoming increasingly irate. I knew this because she so rarely indulged in vulgar terms.

Hanif stepped up to field this one: "I know how her seminars work. The students are expected to read these books, and then they dig up scholarship and media responses that present a counterargument."

Just like Abelard's *Sic et Non,* I thought. But I said aloud: "If she's doing what Hanif claims, it's arguably a service to the university." In spite of my conflicted feelings about Thourelle, I could see the integrity in her approach.

"I don't agree, and I doubt that the administration will either. Nor will the parents or the alumni who, I might remind you, come up with some 40% of our yearly operating budget," Jan answered grimly.

"She's sticking her neck out. The rest of us are so afraid of getting sued that we're always second-guessing ourselves. So, we monitor everything we say and scrutinize every reading — ready to cut anything that might offend. Thourelle doesn't," I said, privately reflecting that such risks were even more to her credit since she'd already been sued by students. Whatever might've happened at Peitho U., one would think it would make her leery of putting herself in jeopardy again.

Jan, who knew that I disliked Thourelle, was looking at me with disbelief. Once again, I found myself in the bizarre position of defending a woman who was not only a thorn in my side but one that seemed to be digging itself in more deeply all the time. At this point,

Hanif looked at his watch: he had a meeting with a student and had to run.

After Hanif left, Jan said: "Help me, Heather! How do I stop her? The Dean will be breathing down my neck." She looked panicked. It was frustrating that Jan seemed to care so much about the administration's disapproval.

"Jan, you've got to let this one go. It's not an argument you can win. You need to get on the right side of this." I said this as gently as I could.

"Are you kidding? That bitch is turning the department into a laughingstock," Jan responded once again, lapsing into another uncharacteristic expletive. "And what about our responsibility to the students? They shouldn't be exposed to this."

"Jan, listen to yourself! We're talking about graduate students. They're not children; they don't need to be coddled. They're here to be taught, not just stuffed with facts," I said. Considering how much time they spend on the internet, students were probably more inured to sexual content of all kinds than most members of the faculty would ever be.

"Thourelle's trying to make them think about important social and ethical issues. How many courses do that?" I continued.

Certainly not mine. I was always too concerned that my students be familiar with terms like feudalism or were able to identify passages from Chaucer. Who had time to make them think?

Jan and I continued to argue for another ten minutes or so. When I left her office, she was not in the least bit appeased.

I knew that Hanif would want to know what Thourelle had said about him. I would if I were him. He certainly had a right to know about the alleged assault charges. But if Thourelle were lying, as I kept telling myself she must be, how could he possibly benefit from learning the full extent of her malice? I didn't know the effect such a revelation might have or to what lengths he might go in order to clear his name. He'd certainly become paranoid about what she might've said and to whom. Perhaps he'd even see fit to confront Thourelle. If he were to confront her, however, there was always the danger of her retaliation, spewing her poison still further.

Yet, supposing I was wrong, and Thourelle was telling the truth about Hanif. I could still see no point in confronting him with charges that conflicted so dramatically with his own account of their relationship. He'd be left with no choice but to deny them.

There was a third possibility. Decades ago, I saw a dance performance: a *pas de deux* about a heterosexual date presented from two points of view. First, the dancers portrayed the man's vision of a romantic evening that concluded in rapturous love-making; then, we saw the woman's version, which was basically an evening of manipulation and intimidation that ended in rape. This was years before the problem of date rape emerged on campuses across the country. Still, the performance seemed to anticipate this crisis: a meditation on how delusional a rapist might be. Could Hanif's conviction that Thourelle desired him have precipitated an assault?

Several hours later, Hanif and I were sitting together in the booth of a dimly lit bar. I was of two minds. One part was stewing over what Thourelle had said; the other was wondering what Hanif and that beautiful graduate student were doing behind closed doors. I was duly ashamed of my possessive and jealous proclivities, but shame did nothing to loosen their grip. Even though I eschewed the university policy about leaving your office door open when you were meeting with a student, the fact that Hanif had bothered to close his door irked me. And why hadn't he opened it right away after I'd knocked? What was going on in there? And so, Hanif and I, usually so animated with one another, were like two bodies sharing a single coma — *silence blossoming like tumors on our lips*. I was beginning to think that we might sit there, mute, all evening, when Hanif spoke up.

"Are you going to tell me what she said?" he asked.

It was only then that I made up my mind. "Suffice it to say that Thourelle wanted to warn me about you. Her understanding of certain encounters between the two of you is very different from yours. It's not helpful for me to repeat what she said."

Hanif pondered this for a while. "But you seem so upset. You don't believe her, do you?" he asked.

"No, I don't," I said, trying to sound firm. "But it upset me to hear lies about someone I care about."

"Why won't you tell me what she said?" he persisted.

"Because I don't think there's any point. It sounds like she's hurt you enough already," I replied.

Hanif momentarily put his head in his hands. I couldn't see his face, but I knew he was troubled. But troubled is a nebulous state that can metamorphose in a moment. When he looked up, I realized that he was more than troubled: he was mad.

"You talk about us, but you don't act like there's an us. If you really believed in me, you'd protect me," he said.

"I'm trying to protect you," I protested.

"No, you're not. You've been dodging my calls and avoiding me," he responded.

I didn't say anything.

"What the hell did she tell you?" he continued.

Hanif hadn't raised his voice. We were, after all, in a public place. In fact, the level of his voice had dropped. Even so, it had an unfamiliar quality — a kind of menace. I was reminded of the prequel to a tornado: that dense, jaundiced sky that forced an unnatural quiet upon the world. A scary calm. Then I thought about that faraway place I'd read about in some anthropological work where women were considered irrational and dangerous creatures, and the men felt compelled to address them in wheedling conciliatory tones. That'd always struck me as the world upside down. In my experience, it was men who were the irrational and dangerous creatures — especially when they were angry. I'd learned that from my father. But I'd never discovered the language to tame them. Hanif was angry, and my response to male anger was invariably a retreat into myself.

"Did she tell you that I got violent with her?" he continued.

"How did you know?" I asked.

"Because I was there for the hearing. I'm familiar with her lies," he responded.

I wanted to reassure him, so I forced myself to speak. "Hanif, I already told you that I don't believe her." I reached across the table to take his hand, but he shook me off.

"Whatever," he said with a shrug. He casually took out his phone and began checking his email.

Whatever — the favorite dismissal of contemptuous teens. So, Hanif was dismissing me. I suddenly felt deeply ashamed that I'd ever, even for a moment, believed that he could care for me. I found myself fast-forwarding into the familiar domain of rejection, but this time, I'd try and get ahead of the pain. When a relationship is moving relentlessly downhill, it's always best to jump out while you can.

I'd have a better chance of saving face if I were the first to leave — a shallow consideration, to be sure, but I was feeling so miserable that I wasn't about to reproach myself for any petty triumphs I might accrue. I was picking up my coat and purse when Hanif put his hand on my forearm.

"Don't go. Please. I'm so sorry. I don't want to act this way. But knowing that Thourelle's out there saying whatever she wants about me makes me furious."

"I understand," I said, beginning to thaw out.

He took my hand and kissed it. "Thank you," he said.

Hanif begged me to come back to his place that night, so I did. Perhaps that was a mistake. It was our first disagreement, and we were going to try and fix it by having sex. Yet isn't that the way things work? Aren't such psychic fissures best sutured with flesh? As I was drifting off to sleep in Hanif's arms, I thought about Thourelle's question: *Have you ever seen Hanif angry?* Well, now I had. Because I refused to discuss my conversation with Thourelle, I ended up paying the price: for a few moments, I'd witnessed Hanif's beautiful face drained of all charm.

In the morning, Hanif's momentary anger seemed like a bad dream, and he was his old enchanting self. He brought me blueberry pancakes in bed. I'd magically gotten over my bouts of romantically inflicted inedia and proved this by getting blueberry stains all over his new Egyptian cotton sheets. They were white, so I insisted on taking them home to bleach them. Most of the stains came out, but when the sheets were restored to the bed, his room smelt a bit like a hospital for quite a long time.

I demonstrated an unusual degree of self-discipline when I decided against interrogating Hanif about the fair Anna. I was just insecure and over-imaginative, that's all.

Chapter 16: Sabotage

It was the last week of classes before Winter Break. In addition to *Medieval Sex*, I was teaching a freshmen seminar entitled *Medieval Saints and Sinners*. I delight in first-year students. The best of them remind me of puppies (perhaps the ultimate compliment from me) because they've so much to learn and anticipate it all with such unabashed joy. They're so happy to be at university and finally have a shot at adulthood; so full of interesting questions and not yet obsessed with their Grade Point Average. Freshmen are wonderful until they learn not to be.

This class had been a particular joy to teach. It's usually not hard to get students interested in sinners, and who doesn't love the medieval potty mouth? But this particular group was especially excited by the saints. Did Francis of Assisi really kiss lepers? Did Catherine of Genoa really eat a bowl of lice? Did Thomas Aquinas really levitate while saying Mass? Their general awe of medieval otherness reminded me why I'd fallen in love with the Middle Ages in the first place.

Yes, teaching can be great. It can also be a pain in the ass, especially when it comes to certain graduate students. If the best freshmen are puppies, the worst graduate students are feral dogs: the kind that don't have the courage to look you in the eye and attack but dart out to bite your calves as you're walking away. Where am I going with this, you ask? Obviously, I'm about to give you an update on my *Medieval Sex* class and the redoubtable Dawn Cather. My time working with her was finally drawing to a close, and every day, I became more anxious for it to be over. A semester with her was like a long car ride with a full bladder.

At last, exam week arrived. Final exams were comparatively easy to grade because they weren't returned to the student and so required minimal comments. Even so, you can't just throw them down the stairs and give the higher grades to the ones landing face up, as much as we used to joke about it. After asking Ms. Cather to bring me a sampling of five exams that she'd graded, it became clear that she was an unabashed practitioner of the staircase method. It was the last week that I had to contend with her, and my diplomacy had ebbed accordingly. I made it clear that I wasn't happy with her grading and preferred to complete the exams myself. This was a tactical error. Before the grades were turned in, I received an email from Sally Field that Ms. Cather had launched a series of Title IX complaints against me. Here was Ms. Cather's list:

1. The respondent, Heather Bell, has twice attempted to close the door of her office against Dawn Cather's will, ignoring university policy. Professor Bell's motives were unclear, but considering her teaching and research interests, they were perhaps sexual in nature.

2. The respondent mocked the plaintiff about her name, suggesting that she was a member of some ungodly sect.

3. The respondent tried to manipulate the plaintiff into lecturing in her place, although the Teaching Assistant's contract says explicitly that she is not required to lecture. Bell attempted coercion by claiming that she would write a "better" letter of recommendation if the plaintiff would agree to lecture.

4. The respondent refused to provide trigger warnings: as a result, the plaintiff, a survivor of an abusive marriage who suffers from Post-

Traumatic Stress Disorder, was traumatized by the lecture on marital sex.

5. The respondent assigned obscene readings by perverted medieval monks. The Bureau of Social Equity concurred with this assessment.

6. The respondent would make crude jokes about her subject matter, would frequently use offensive language during lectures, and distributed pastries with disturbing labels on the last day of class, which the plaintiff found both obscene and menacing.

The first three charges were distortions of what had occurred during that first fatal meeting in my office. I wondered why she was taking so many notes. (In the case of Number 2, I was tempted to seek out Ms. Cather to reassure her that I now associated her name with catheter, not Cathar.) Number 4, which concerned my failure to give trigger warnings about marital sex, was technically true, but since that week's topic was announced in the syllabus as marital sex, this struck me as sufficient warning. As for Number 5: I suppose the representation was accurate — if you're a lunatic. The reading in question was none other than Damian's *Book of Gomorrah*. I should've suspected that Ms. Cather was up to something when she shared it with Sally Field. As to Number 6, I invariably make jokes during lectures: medieval sexuality can be a dark subject that needs lightening up. But she was probably alluding to my discussion of Chaucer's Miller's Tale when Nicholas grabbed Alyson by the "queynte," and I pointed out that this was an archaic form for "cunt." As for the pastries: I always bring cupcakes to the last class with distinctive lettering. "Medieval Sex" doesn't fit on a cupcake; MS is an abbreviation for either the word manuscript or a disease; therefore, I settled for the word "Sex" — which has the advantage of capturing half of the course's name.

Only the first charge implied that I may've been guilty of any sexual wrongdoing (apart from my sexually laden speech). But this, in conjunction with Numbers 4, 5, and 6, clearly sought to demonstrate that I'd created a hostile work environment — potentially the most dangerous charge. The American Association of University Professors' review of Title IX cases over the past decade determined that in case after case, what constituted a hostile work environment was becoming less and less objective in favor of whatever the plaintiff thought it was. This seemed to pertain to Ms. Cather's complaints.

I was dismayed but, when I thought about it, not surprised by Ms. Cather's suit. Sometimes, you know when a person is trouble from the moment you meet them, but there's very little you can do about it. It's like the time my car skidded on ice in a parking lot, and I helplessly watched myself moving sideways in slow motion until I collided with a tree. Did Ms. Cather represent the relentless ice or the implacable tree? A bit of both. From our first meeting, I had her pegged as a simmering caldron of slovenly graduate-student resentment. When I insisted on grading the final exams on my own, she probably assumed that I was on the verge of failing her as a Teaching Assistant. (I probably should've, though such an action may well have been unprecedented, and I probably wouldn't have dared. The more usual approach was to point out some of Ms. Cather's shortcomings in a written report, which I eventually did.) If she waited until the grades were posted and she received a (richly deserved) "Fail", it would look like she'd launched the suit in retaliation. In other words, she beat me to the punch, which means she's smarter than I thought.

I had to respond to these charges in person before the Christmas break. Each university develops its own procedures for a Title IX hearing, but they all have certain baleful things in common. It wasn't a traditional courtroom by any stretch of the imagination. The evidentiary standards were much more lax, and the respondent (defendant?) wasn't allowed to bring a lawyer. I was, however, allowed a support person. I chose Jan.

Most of my day had been blighted by the demoralizing process of responding to Ms. Cather's complaints. Afterwards, I sat in front of the computer listlessly, trying to catch up on email. It was time to go home, but I often have trouble transitioning at this time of day. Summoning up the will to propel myself from one setting to the next was especially difficult when the weather was dismal. I could feel myself ossifying. Eventually, I made an effort to get up and put on my coat, which seemed to weigh a ton. It was one of those fake fur jobs that I thought looked cute without interrogating why. Now I know why: I was a dead ringer for Paddington Bear.

When I left the office, it was already dark. Though not technically nighttime, in mid-December, it began to get dark around 4:30 p.m. I've always empathized with people in still more northerly climes whose quotidian light ratio lasts about as long as it takes me to read the editorial page. No wonder they develop drinking problems. So, what's my excuse? As I lumbered toward my car, I noticed that the hood was listing to one side. It turned out that there was a flat tire in the front: completely flat. Maybe it just needed air? I knelt down to have a look. The tire had been slashed. It was then that I saw a piece of paper stuck under the windshield wiper. It contained one word in block letters: *Cougar!*

I didn't have another tire. The spare in my trunk hadn't been repaired since last spring's jaunt over half a block of broken glass, courtesy of some fun-loving pranksters. Even if the spare had been pumped up and ready to go, it would be of limited use since I had no idea how to change a tire. I called the garage, but it was already closed, so I began to walk home. *Cougar,* I thought. When I initially heard a woman referred to as a cougar, I thought it must be a compliment. A cougar was a beautiful beast. Now I know better. The combination of tasteless taunt and tattered tire was like a charivari: a ritual humiliation with "rough music" and insults directed against newlyweds on their wedding night. In the premodern world, it was used to stigmatize age disparity: usually, a nubile woman forced to marry some rich geezer. I'd just fallen prey to the modern equivalent. Whoever slashed my tire not only knew about Hanif and me but was mocking our age difference, presumably because they wanted Hanif. I felt mortified and angry, cursing Anna (or whatever fecund woman was coveting Hanif and damaging my property). She was a *&@R%#$&+!, as they say in the comic books, and I don't mean that lightly. I also had a curse to spare for Ms. Cather.

It was one of those frigid evenings when the streets themselves were sensible enough to be deserted. Yet, once again, I felt as if someone was following me. The tire slasher? That seemed farfetched. Even so, I thought that I could hear footsteps keeping pace with mine along the sidewalk behind me. This sense of being watched or followed had been occurring frequently enough in the last few weeks that I was less afraid of a physical assault than of the possibility that I was going nuts. To distract myself, I began singing Peter Gabriel's "Solsbury Hill," which I had long ago adopted as my walking song. Since there was no one around, apart from me and my bogey (imaginary or not), I was singing rather loudly. When someone came up behind me and laid a hand on my shoulder, I jumped and screamed. Involuntarily choosing fight over flight, I spun around with clenched fists and swung out blindly, knocking Sylvia Thourelle to the ground.

I certainly wasn't expecting that, nor was she. Embarrassed and dismayed, I immediately helped Thourelle to her feet, apologizing profusely. Understandably, she was rather shaken up. We were only half a block from my house, so I insisted she accompany me home. She seemed reluctant at first, but who can blame her? Very soon, she was sitting on my couch, holding an icepack to her eye with one hand and a brandy in the other. It looked like she was going to have one of those classic black eyes.

"Sylvia, I'm so sorry," I said for about the tenth time. "I've always startled easily. I wish you'd called out to me rather than coming up behind me," I said.

"I did call, but you were singing and didn't hear me," she said, taking a sip of brandy.

I felt like an idiot. How many adults sing at the top of their voices when they walk? Of course, I couldn't have known I had an audience.

"You have a nice voice," she added.

"Thank you. I've been taking voice lessons," I said inanely.

Thourelle nodded approvingly. "Here at the music school?"

"Yes. If you're interested, I'll send you my teacher's info. She's Russian."

"I'd appreciate that."

I think we both realized how bizarre the timing of this conversation was. Thourelle clearly had something important to tell me; I'd slowed her down by almost knocking her out, yet here we were chatting about voice lessons. Somewhat abashed, we sat staring at the flames in the gas fireplace in silence, trying to figure out how to get back on track. I wasn't much help because I had no idea which track we were supposed to be on.

"I'm sorry to scare you, but I needed to talk. Then I saw you walking ahead of me and thought this was the perfect opportunity. But you walk so quickly; it was difficult to catch up," Thourelle said.

I surreptitiously glanced at her boots; the heels were at least five inches tall.

"It's not fair to discuss Hanif when he's not here," I said.

I expected her to acknowledge that Hanif was exactly what she wanted to talk about and perhaps even insist that we call him up right away. It turned out, however, that she had no interest in discussing Hanif; she wanted to talk about Jan.

"Jan came to my office to warn me against offering the graduate course I'm proposing. Her manner was so strange. I honestly think she was trying to threaten me. The two of you are such good friends. I thought maybe you could advise me," Thourelle said.

"That doesn't sound like Jan," I said with a frown. "I admit that your course description set off her alarm bells. She thought it was too provocative. But Jan's pretty level-headed: not the threatening kind. What did she say?" I asked.

"She said that the department had experienced 'profligate professors' before and wouldn't tolerate them again. She claimed to take her responsibility to the students very seriously and would do whatever was necessary to keep them from harmful influences. I admit that the threats were oblique, but still, they felt real," Thourelle wound up apologetically.

"Jan was certainly being impolitic, but I don't think her comments are particularly ominous. Besides, the Chair doesn't have the power to veto courses. That's up to the curriculum review committee," I said.

"I don't understand it," said Thourelle, half to herself. "I like Jan, at least I have until now. I've tried to get to know her better, but it's been impossible. It's like there's a wall," Thourelle said.

"Sometimes Jan gets stressed out; she takes her job too seriously. But I promise to talk with her," I responded.

Thourelle thanked me and got up to leave. I was afraid that my stellar blow might have left her feeling unsteady. She wouldn't let me call her a cab, however, saying that she was only a couple of blocks away.

"My car is in the shop, but it turns out that I really enjoy walking. Helps me decompress," she said.

I held my breath as she went down the steps in her treacherous heels. When she reached the bottom, she turned and said: "Do you know, with a little practice, you'd have a great right hook."

After Thourelle left, I was divided between shame and chagrin. On the shame side: I'd given Thourelle a black eye, which I recognized was not very collegial. There seemed to be some kind of monkey's paw wish-fulfilment at work here. Years ago, during the henna wars, I was aching to slug Thourelle. But now that she was my colleague and I no longer wanted to punch her out, my wish was suddenly granted. Of course, it could've been my unconscious lashing out: her very existence seemed to present a threat to the people I cared most about, and I had to protect them.

I needed to talk to Jan right away, so I called a Code Purple. This was a signal we'd established long ago, indicating that one of us was stressed. When a Code Purple was called, both parties had to drop whatever they were doing to engage in some therapeutic activity: sometimes a movie or dinner, but usually a shopping expedition. Why purple? Well, it happened to be my favorite color, but I'd also read that it was the favorite color of schizophrenics, which spoke to the degree of stress associated with the Code. Since we both subscribed to the quasi-biblical adage that we are our sister's keeper, it was also possible to call a Code Purple on behalf of the other, lest that other not realize her degree of danger. That's what I was doing. Assuming that Thourelle was telling the truth, Jan was unusually addled. But since I did not want Jan to know about my conversation with Thourelle, and Jan might well be affronted to be told she was stressed without any concrete evidence, I pretended the Code Purple was entirely for my benefit. Because I secretly believed that Jan drew covert comfort from perceiving me as more fucked up than she was, the fact that I was in need of a Code Purple would be doubly therapeutic.

It was Thursday night, and the stores were open until nine, so there was plenty of time for whatever tacit threats Jan had made to Thourelle to reveal themselves. We both hated the mall and didn't have time for a drive to the city, so we confined our quest to the several women's clothing stores on the square. We had trouble finding parking, a difficulty that was particularly irksome to me. If you live in a crumby little town, one of the few advantages should be the ease with which you can park. Fortunately, Jan was driving, so I was spared my usual white-knuckle parallel parking.

Once parked, there was a decision ahead of us: to go to the expensive and tasteful place on the corner or the purveyor of New Age fashion across the square. I'm pretty sure you can guess which woman habitually gravitated toward which store. Since I was the one who ostensibly called the Code Purple, Jan deferred to me. Yet because it was really Jan having the crisis, I promised myself that our time in the New Age store would be brief. When we opened the door, we were met by the sweet tinkling of bells and the heavy smell of incense. Jan instantly sneezed. The saleswoman, all alone in the store and tricked out like a Hindu goddess, greeted us with a hectic joy, desperately wanting to be of help. I hate hovering salespeople, however, so I cannily told her that we wanted to look at dresses, which were located upstairs. That meant that the over-assiduous saleswoman had to remain downstairs at the cash register, guarding the store.

I was picking out several non-age-appropriate dresses when Jan asked the expected question.

"Why the Code Purple? What's happened?" she asked.

"Oh, it's about Thourelle," I said in all honesty.

"What about Thourelle?" queried Jan.

"An hour or so ago, I punched her and gave her a black eye," I said, keeping my eyes on dresses while systematically moving hangers from left to right.

"Oh my God, I'm so proud of you! That woman's been driving me nuts. First, that obscene course of hers. Now she's complaining that her office has cockroaches. I really wanted to beat her up, but all I did was key her car," Jan exclaimed.

"You what?" I said in shock.

"Keyed her car, but it would've been much more gratifying to punch her," she responded.

I was in the dressing room at the time and couldn't see Jan's face. I could tell by her voice, however, that she was smiling.

"Jan, I hit Thourelle by accident. I heard someone following me; I didn't know it was her," I said.

At that moment, I came out of the dressing room in an Afghani mirrored skirt. Jan shook her head, and I retreated.

"Oh," said Jan, with disappointment in her voice. "So, did you call the Code Purple because you're afraid she might sue you?"

"Precisely," I lied.

"I think you'll be OK if you play up how frightened you were walking home and that you acted out of self-defense," Jan said.

"I was frightened. Someone had just slashed my tires," I said. I didn't mention the *Cougar* inscription.

"That's terrible! Did you call the campus police?" Jan asked with real concern.

"I haven't reported it yet. I will." I said, not at all sure that I would. "But I had to tell someone."

Jan was making sympathetic noises as I was coming out of the dressing room, only to begin vigorously shaking her head the moment she saw the dress I had on.

"I really liked this one. I thought I looked kind of like a Geisha," I said. The dress was basically a loud, not to mention cheap, knock-off of the kind of dress that Thourelle wore when she gave her talk at the retreat.

"If you're really interested in Hanif, take that dress off immediately," Jan said.

Having been dressed down for attempting to dress up, I redressed in my own clothes, trying not to look in the mirror. It seemed like one of those trick mirrors that turn ordinary people into hobbits.

When we returned to the main floor, the saleswoman was so crestfallen that we came downstairs empty-handed that I was on the verge of running upstairs and grabbing the kimono-dress. But Jan pulled me out of the store, and we went across the square to the elegant shop. When we were greeted warmly by the discreet saleswoman, I automatically said, *We're just looking,* which earned me an ocular missile of contempt. The saleswoman's attitude was markedly different with Jan, however, with whom she had long ago established the kind of patron-client relationship frequently found in the late Roman Empire and which posh stores cultivate to make repeat customers feel like patricians. She already knew Jan's size and understood her taste. So, she brought Jan an armful of dresses on hangers, placed them on a large hook in the dressing room, and then retreated to the back of the store. The dressing rooms in this shop were capacious, replete with an armchair, so I went in with Jan to watch the personalized fashion show.

Jan was trying on a variety of close-fitting dresses, most of them too dressy for work. Maybe she had a secret life I didn't know about. She held out a black, shapeless garment to me.

"I think that the saleswoman intended this for you. It's not my style," she said.

"It looks small," I responded doubtfully.

"But it's one size," Jan said. So, I was compelled to strip down and try it on.

"That looks good," said Jan.

"Yeah, but there's no back zipper. Just the little one on the side. It's hard to get on," I said. And it was even harder to get off. My arms got stuck as I pulled the dress over my head. I felt panicked: I couldn't see and was afraid of ripping a $450 dress. When Jan tried to help, my earring got caught, and I yelped.

Eventually, after I disentangled myself and was thankfully restored to my own clothes, I asked, "Jan, why did you key Thourelle's car?"

Jan was trying on an elegant sleeveless dress in navy blue wool. She looked fabulous.

"She deserved it," Jan said with conviction, turning around to examine her back in the three-way-mirror.

"For what?" I asked.

"I asked her to tone down her course just a little, and she flatly refused. Don't worry. Nobody saw me. She was parked on the street," Jan said. The covered garage had a security camera.

"Was this planned or just a spontaneous show of malice?" I asked.

Jan didn't answer. "I'd have to wear this with a strapless bra," she said.

"Yes, definitely a strapless bra. But the dress makes you look like Natalie Wood, so you'd better buy it," I said.

Jan called the saleslady and gave her the dress to wrap up.

Once the saleslady had retreated, I said. "The Chair doesn't have the power to interfere with other people's courses. You know that. The key thing is totally nuts. I'm really worried about you."

"I wasn't *interfering*. I just thought I could get her to see reason," Jan said impatiently. She was now trying on a red silk sheath. Would that I could wear something like that.

"Promise you won't try to mess with Thourelle's course again."

I only got a sullen expression in return.

"Do you promise?" I persisted.

"OK, I promise, provided you give me advance notice the next time you plan to punch Thourelle," she responded.

Jan drove me home, but before I got out of the car, I couldn't help asking, "Jan, if you were angry with me, really angry, you'd tell me, wouldn't you? You'd never key my car, right?"

"Of course not. Do you think I'm deranged?" she asked. "But I might slash your tires," she added with a wink.

Chapter 17: Woman to Woman

The Christmas holidays were upon us. This year, there was a lot of snow — more than usual. The effect on the campus was magical, but I didn't have a garage and digging my car out was no joke. It was a time when most colleagues fled to warmer climes or bigger cities. But I had no

where that I particularly wanted to go. Hanif went home for two weeks to be with his model family in Columbus. We exchanged gifts before he left: I knitted him a scarf and toque the color of his eyes; he gave me an antique water pitcher made from opaline glass.

I spent a turbulent Christmas with my nightmarish family in Chicago. My sister Louise lived with her husband and two kids in one of the burbs, and it was great to see her again. When we were together, however, we couldn't restrain ourselves from ganging up on our mother.

"Do you remember the time she was giving a birthday party for Sister Roseanne?" Louise asked.

"Fifteen voracious nuns about to descend on us, and she goes to communion," I responded.

"I did not," my mother protested.

"You did so," Louise said.

"That's right. When we complained, you said *I have my priorities* and slammed the door," I recounted.

"OK. If I was such a terrible mother, how did the two of you both turn out so well?" she asked.

"We didn't. We're both fucked up!" we'd shout in unison.

I was regressing quickly — like that psychopathologist in Ken Russell's *Altered States,* who devolved into a blob of primordial matter. Blessedly, my visit was cut short by several days for a mission of mercy. Three days before Christmas, Thourelle fell down a flight of stairs at the office. There was something oily on the staircase, and she slipped. A fall down twenty-some stairs is pretty serious stuff. (Scarlett O'Hara fell down twenty-three, and they were carpeted. There was a staggering one hundred and ninety-two in the Odessa Steps sequence. Even with landings between the steps, that run-away-pram probably met with a terrible end.)

So, I suppose you could say that Thourelle got off easy with a cracked cheek bone, a broken arm, a badly sprained ankle, and deep bruises all over. Tommy and Thourelle had planned to visit his parents in Miami and were scheduled to leave on the 26th. It would've been the first meet-the-parents for Thourelle, which made me wonder if her accident was caused by potential trepidation. Freud says there are no mistakes. I certainly wouldn't be looking forward to a holiday if I was the same age as the parents of my under-age lover. (Or so I told myself when Hanif didn't invite me to meet his family: too soon, right?) It would've been even more of a challenge for Thourelle since Tommy was all but twenty-one, and she was pushing-forty. Thourelle encouraged Tommy to go without her, but this would've left her very much on her own.

I learned of Thourelle's predicament when Tommy phoned. I don't know whose idea it was to call me. It certainly was a peculiar one because Thourelle and I could hardly be described as close — though clearly, mutual animosities do foster a unique intimacy. Look at

Grendel and Beowulf: they always seemed to be grabbing one another's thighs. Then it occurred to me that, next to Tommy, I may be the nearest thing to a friend or confidante that Thourelle had. (I'm not counting the graduate students, most of whom had already dispersed for the holidays.) When Tommy, naturally worried, asked if I could look out for Thourelle, it was hard to refuse. In fact, I was happy to be of help. The first time I dropped by with groceries, I was shocked at how terrible her face looked. She still had the black eye I had given her on one side (morphed into a full spectrum of color) and the damaged cheek, with a dramatic dressing, on the other. For much of the time I was looking in on her, she was asleep — probably the result of shock and industrial pain-killers. On a couple of occasions, however, she asked me to run a bath for her. (She was afraid that the shower would wreak havoc with her elaborate bandaging.) I unwound and later rewound the elastic bandage on her ankle, helped her in and out of the bath — careful to keep the plaster cast on her arm elevated — and toweled her down. She was grateful. I could see it in her tired smiles. But she didn't speak much.

My last visit was during the day preceding New Year's Eve. Tommy was returning in the evening, so I'd bought a bottle of prosecco, put it in the fridge and left some smoked salmon, camembert, caviar (lumpfish, not sturgeon), and a baguette on the counter. Thourelle seemed to be in pretty good spirits, and was more talkative.

"Poor Tommy. Everyone's going to think that he beat me up," Thourelle said, examining herself in a hand mirror with a grimace. She'd been allowed to remove the dressing from her cheek, but the results were disconcerting.

"To tell you the truth, I was afraid of that when I gave you the black eye," I responded.

"Yeah, I know. I told anyone who asked that I got it mud wrestling, but I don't know if they believed me," she said.

I automatically began to apologize again for socking her (after I'd stopped laughing), but she raised her hand to shut me up.

"It's OK," she said. "Now I know better than to come up behind you. Exaggerated Startle Response, right?" she said.

"Probably. It's never been diagnosed," I said.

"Did you know that it's a common side-effect of trauma?" she asked.

In fact, I didn't know. Was this side-effect restricted to upper-case Trauma, or did it accommodate lower-case trauma as well?

"Well, you've experienced enough traumas lately that you might develop Exaggerated Startle Response as well," I said.

"I've certainly had my share. But these things come in cycles. The black eye, the hacking, the orgies, the fake news, and now the fall: maybe my cycle of bad luck is over," Thourelle said.

"Hacking, orgies, and fake news?" I exclaimed. "Are you serious?"

"Someone hacked into my email and sent naked pictures, photoshopped with the faces from my undergraduate class. They were sent to just about everyone in my address book. I'm surprised you didn't get one," she said.

"For Christ's sake, who'd do something like that?" I asked.

"I suspect one of the students. A couple of them kept griping about their grades. And they're all so good with computers; they could easily cover their tracks," she said.

"And the orgies?" I prompted.

"The Dean called me because he'd received an anonymous tip claiming that I was conducting orgies in my office, which is supposedly how I came by all those naked pictures. Somebody clearly told the janitorial staff as well, and they won't even go into my office, so it never gets cleaned. That's probably why I got cockroaches. I had to put those little cardboard glue boxes everywhere," she said glumly.

"That's disgusting. I'm so sorry," and I really was! But dwelling on Thourelle's string of bad luck wouldn't help, so I changed the subject.

"I've got a little present for you. Maybe it'll cheer you up."

I'd decided to commemorate my last mission of mercy with one of those small Asian cast iron teapots and an assortment of teas. She opened the package with a big smile on her face.

"It's beautiful. I love that color blue. How'd you know that I'm a huge tea-drinker?" she asked.

"By snooping around your kitchen. Besides, I figured that's what people are supposed to drink when they're convalescing."

"I've something for you as well," Thourelle said. "I couldn't go anywhere, so it's improvised. But I think you'll find it useful." She handed me a box wrapped in grey (of course) fabric. "The wrapping is part of the present but not the best part," she said.

The cloth exterior turned out to be an elegant scarf in patterned silk. It was a narrow rectangle of dramatic scope that was wound around some object multiple times like a mummy's wrappings. Inside was a package of Egyptian henna.

"In case you ever run out," she said coyly.

"Is this the same one that I sent you?" I asked, incredulous.

"Of course. I figure it's an important historical artifact," she responded.

We both burst out laughing. I leaned over and gave her a gingerly hug, attempting to avoid her ankle, arm, and cheek, as well as her myriad of bruises. Later at my home, Thourelle's gift turned out to be even funnier than I initially thought because, on inspection, the pattern on the scarf was formed by a series of tarantulas dancing in circles. Was this an allusion to our former relations as a kind of tarantella? Or did Thourelle somehow know that I hate spiders? Either way, I loved the scarf and wear it to this day. I have yet to see a spider while wearing it, convincing me of its powerful apotropaic powers.

Jan, Berenice, and I spent New Year's together, once again at Berenice's house. Does anyone remember that really gross Franco-Italian film, *La Grande bouffe,* where Marcello Mastroianni and his cronies go to a villa in the countryside with the intent of committing suicide by gormandizing themselves to death? Our evening was a little like that. Fortunately, we started quite early. For appetizers, Berenice made a series of those fabulous Scandinavian open-faced sandwiches: pickled herring, shrimp, smoked salmon and trout, caviar, egg salad, and some weird cheese that reminded me of clotted cream. These delicacies were served on several different kinds of rye bread, and we washed them down with shots of aquavit. I would've been happy to continue eating them all night, but there were plenty of other options to follow: I'd made a linguine pesto course, Berenice made her fabulous *brodetto di pesce,* and we all brought dessert.

By the time midnight rolled around, we'd drunk so much that I'm sure we would've been contenders for alcohol poisoning if we hadn't been careful to drink gallons of water. Our toasts were especially stellar — I say this because each would've required a special alphabet to spell them out, so I'm not going to bother. We'd decided ahead of time that the three of us would each come up with three New Year's resolutions, and the other two would determine whether said resolutions were plausible and potentially achievable. (Both Jan and Berenice rejected my first two: to lose fifteen pounds by spring and to stop drinking. My third, which was to watch Hitchcock's surviving silent films over the course of the year, passed.) When it was Jan's turn, however, she didn't bother rehearsing her resolutions. Instead, she entered upon her recent grievances as Chair, which included a lengthy tirade against Thourelle: her unfitness as a teacher, her general debauchery, and a special gloat over her recent accident.

"It just goes to show that there is such a thing as cosmic justice. Too bad it wasn't worse," Jan wound up.

"Jan, I know you don't mean that," said Berenice.

"Are you serious? I'd light candles to ensure that Thourelle retires prematurely from brain damage if I thought it'd help," Jan responded.

I was glad that I had kept my several visits to Thourelle a secret.

But Jan was not the only one who misspoke that night. In my inebriated state, I'd forgotten all about my pre-New Year's resolution not to tell them about Hanif. I wish I'd kept my mouth shut, but libidinous exuberance won out.

"But there's a Title IX proceeding against you. How does it look if you, a Full Professor, are involved with a much younger Assistant Professor?" Jan exclaimed.

"It might help. If someone as attractive as Hanif were to testify that he was, in fact, humping me, wouldn't that undercut the contention that I'd rigged my office door to seduce Ms. Cather?" I responded.

"It could just speak to your indiscriminate promiscuity," Jan replied.

"Indiscriminate promiscuity, my foot. I haven't been laid in at least four years," I said.

Despite Jan's concerns, I believe that both she and Berenice were rather impressed that I managed to get someone as good-looking as Hanif to sleep with me (so was I), though they would never say so. There were a few inevitable questions, however.

"OK, he's not gay, clearly, but is he bi?" Berenice asked.

"I don't know," I said.

"Did you ask?" Berenice persisted.

"No. It just didn't seem important," I said. And that was true.

Then it was Jan's turn.

"Of course, if he's bi, his technique might be twice as good. Was it great?" she asked.

To which I responded: "I think so, but I can't be sure. It's been so long that my points of reference are dim," which was also true.

They both thought that this degree of amnesia made me an honorary virgin, and we had another toast.

I picked Hanif up at the airport the next afternoon. He was wearing my toque and scarf and his brightest smile. We hugged and kissed with people milling all around us. It was our first public embrace (though I have to admit that I scanned the crowd in advance as scrupulously as that cyborg in *The Terminator,* lest any of my colleagues were present). We were standing at the carousel waiting for Hanif's baggage when he told me that he loved me. I was taken by surprise and had no idea how to respond. But that was OK because Hanif almost immediately pressed a finger against my lips and told me that I didn't have to say anything. He could wait. On the way home, we discussed what I suppose you would call our public presence.

"Are we still a secret?" Hanif asked. "I mean, apart from the few hundred strangers at the airport."

"Not exactly. I told Jan and Berenice, but they won't tell anybody," I said.

"What did they say?" he asked.

"They told me to be careful and take it slowly." This made him laugh. I didn't mention their preoccupation with his orientation, however, which probably would not have made him laugh.

"What about you? Did you tell anybody?" I was expecting him to say no because he was a guy, after all. A guy doesn't need to write a girl's name all over his binder (though he might, on occasion, manfully deface a tree with a pocket knife). A guy doesn't need to talk about his girlfriend all the time because he can restrain himself. And a guy doesn't need a confidant because he is self-sufficient. Or so I thought. But Hanif blithely replied:

"I told my mom."

"Your mom?" I said in disbelief.

"Sure, she's my best friend," Hanif replied.

I never understood that about people Hanif's age, who count their parents as their best friends. How does that work? I considered my parents antagonists rather than friends. If there was an afterlife, I always figured that my parents were my "get out of purgatory free" card.

"What did your mom say?" I really didn't want to know, but since he'd asked me about my friends, I felt obliged to exhibit a similar interest. I was afraid of what I would hear, however. I knew that Hanif's parents were quite young when Hanif was born (I don't suppose there was much else to do in Columbus back then), which meant that his mother was uncomfortably close to my age. If I were her, I'd throw a fit, insisting that Hanif break up with Mrs. Robinson immediately. Otherwise, I'd threaten to kill either myself, his antediluvian lover, or both.

"She was more or less cool with it," Hanif said.

"Tell me about the 'less cool' part," I responded.

"Well, she wants grandchildren," he said.

"She does know that we just started going out, right?" I asked.

"Of course. But she's the type who likes to plan ahead."

Children. I knew this was an issue for January-May marriages in cases where the man was the older party. The younger woman, who generally had never been married before, often conditioned for at least one child. This was not an insurmountable problem: many men could still obey the biblical mandate to be fruitful and multiply at surprisingly advanced ages. Just look at Abraham! Yet it was not as easy a proposition if the tables were turned and the woman was the older of the two. My fellow-crone Sara, for example, needed divine assistance in the opening of her womb. How could a postmenopausal woman like me possibly come across with the goods without a miracle? (The upside: the pregnancy of a post-menopausal woman would make her an excellent candidate for founding a religion, which had always been one of my dreams.) In any event, I was surprised that I hadn't considered the children conundrum before.

Hanif had, however. "I told Mom that we'd adopt, and then she was fine with it," he said complacently. "She's really looking forward to meeting you."

In *All about Eve*, when the famous actress, Margot Channing (Bette Davis), is stalled in the car with her friend, Karen, one of her more memorable lines is: "Funny business, a woman's career. The things you drop on your way up the ladder so you can move faster. You forget you'll need them again when you get back to being a woman." Hanif seemed to be assuming that I was *that* kind of professional woman — the kind who'd missed out on having children on her way up the career ladder. But I wasn't. I knew from an early age that I never wanted children. Marcel, who already had two children at the time we met, was relieved to learn this.

For the rest of the way home, Hanif did most of the talking: I just grunted my assent or dissent to whatever he said. But he knew I was hungover, so probably didn't find that particularly strange. We decided that we would no longer conceal our relationship but would continue to be discreet. For the time being, we would eschew the so-called PDAs. (Public Displays of Affection: I learned the acronym from a class of freshmen who exhibited a heightened disgust for such behavior.) In other words, without any PDAs, it would be possible for people to assume that Hanif and I were "just friends." I thought to myself privately that this stance was especially useful in case things were to go wrong.

Chapter 18: It Takes A Thief

Hanif said he loved me, which was wonderful, but also intimated that he wanted kids, which wasn't. Of course, it was his mom's anxious anticipation that led to the precocious question of kids; Hanif didn't raise it himself. I hoped we could avoid the subject — indefinitely. But there were also other topics that were better avoided, like how I'd taken care of Thourelle over the holidays.

By the time classes started, Thourelle still had a very bruised face, but her black eye was almost gone, and she no longer needed crutches. The cast on her arm was scheduled for removal in a couple of weeks. Even so, her life continued to be troubled. Someone impersonating Thourelle submitted an article to the student newspaper denouncing Title IX and maintaining that professors should be allowed to sleep with their students, provided they were of legal age. Fortunately, a member of the editorial staff called Thourelle with a few questions before the article went to press. When Thourelle denied ever having written any such article, demanding to speak to the editor-in-chief, the editor proved skeptical. He insisted that Thourelle come over to the newspaper's headquarters and show some form of identification before he would agree to kill the story. Naturally, the entire editorial staff was bitterly disappointed that such a scoop could slip through their fingers. They'd all heard about the orgies in Thourelle's office and privately believed that she had, in fact, written the article but had subsequently changed her mind about making her views public. In no time, their opinions became so widely known that the article may as well have been published.

Meanwhile, as soon as Thourelle's cockroach situation had abated, a new problem sprang to prominence like the head of a hydra. She began to hear voices speaking in German through her office walls. This was an odd state of affairs: most of the English faculty were confirmed monoglots, and the German Department was two floors below. Thourelle asked around to see if anyone was trying to up their game by listening to German radio in their office, but no one admitted to this. Eventually, she pressured Jan into getting the physical plant and IT to check out the situation, but neither of them heard anything or discovered any reasonable explanation. I felt sorry for Thourelle. Because I have the attention span of a newt, I never would've been able to stand that kind of background noise while I worked. A couple of departmental members observed that this was the closest thing to a preternatural phenomenon that the department had ever experienced and attempted to reach out to experts in paranormal psychology. But Jan, who was still apoplectic over Thourelle's impact on the department, was devoid of interest and sympathy.

"OK, so she hears voices. So what? Joan of Arc learned to live with it," Jan said caustically.

Meanwhile, April and I became increasingly friendly and lunched together regularly. She clearly suspected that there was something between Hanif and me, continuing to send out probes, which I managed to deflect. But there were plenty of other things to talk about. She'd always arrive at our lunches with a list of questions about the university that she'd been puzzling over. Here is a sampling. Why was our office building airconditioned, except for the upper floors where the faculty offices were located? What about the faculty carrels in the library? The walls, which were made of tin, stopped about 4 feet short of the ceiling and two feet short of the floor. Was this a fire regulation, an effort to economize, an effort to forestall conversation, or in case the lock malfunctioned and someone needed to wriggle out? What was the balance of power between the president, chancellor and provost? Are the campus police a real police force? It felt like a game of institutional *Jeopardy*.

The graduate students' Jack and Jill shower for Thourelle and Tommy was looming, but none of the faculty was invited. Probably just as well. One of my dissertators showed me her invite, and I could see that the shower promised to be a highly idiosyncratic event. It was designated a *kinky* Jack and Jill, which meant that the guests were supposed to shower the couple with a useful array of sex implements. Some (but not all) of the grads may have been at a loss as to where such things could be procured in a small college town (and would've been embarrassed purchasing them had they known), so the invitations thoughtfully provided helpful URLs to several specialized websites. There was also a link to a site where a guest could register what they bought, presumably so the couple wouldn't be burdened with several identical dildos. (It was also likely that the vendors of product lines of this sort discouraged returns or exchanges.)

Or course, my colleagues also learned about the shower. Some were outraged by the theme, proclaiming that, had they been invited, they'd have had no intention of attending. Others seemed wistful, remembering earlier days when there was hardly anywhere to go in town, and the department partied together. One of my senior colleagues reminisced about how, in antediluvian times, before people knew the deleterious effects of alcohol on a fetus, he and his wife threw a baby shower for a colleague whose pregnancy was quite advanced. She got so drunk that she fell down his front stairs backwards.

But if the prospect of the shower made some colleagues nostalgic, it made Jan irate.

"It's disgusting; obscene, in fact. Thourelle could get us sued," Jan snapped.

"But why? The kinky part was the graduate students' idea," I said.

"That doesn't matter. Thourelle should never have sanctioned it," she retorted.

"Well, if she really is an ace, she might need a lot of erotic paraphernalia to help her consummate the marriage," I responded.

"Ace, my foot," said Jan, rolling her eyes. "Talk to the janitorial staff about what goes on in her office." She suggestively lifted her eyebrows.

In the days leading up to the shower, Jan was as tightly coiled as a spring. On the day itself, she was generating enough nervous energy to illuminate the entire town. A few hours before the shower started, Jan took it upon herself to survey the venue and insisted that I accompany her. There wasn't much to see. The event was being held at the Graduate Student Association's headquarters — a large clapboard structure with peeling paint and creaking floorboards. It was usually crammed with flop house furniture, but that had been emptied out to make room for dancing. Under the window facing the road, there was a table made of boards on trestles, with bottles of jug wine at one end and chips and pretzels at the other. There was a keg of beer on the floor, with two in reserve. I admired that kind of foresight; it's a terrible thing to run out of alcohol at a party. Jesus agrees: the prospect of having to sit through a dry wedding prompted his first miracle.

Jan grabbed my sleeve, dragged me over to the back wall, and gesticulated toward a series of film posters. The place was dimly lit, so I hadn't noticed them before. Most of them were for porn classics like *Deepthroat* or *The Devil and Miss Jones* and seemed tame by contemporary standards. So, I simply shrugged.

"What do you think that's for?" Jan said, gesturing toward a stage that'd been erected against the wall to the right of the door.

"I have no idea. Maybe it's like American Bandstand, where the best dancers strut their stuff on stage," I responded.

Meanwhile, the several students responsible for setting up were starting to look at us with undisguised dismay, wondering why we were there and when we'd leave. I kept tugging at Jan, telling her in *sotto voce* tones that we should go. I sighed with relief when, at last, she agreed.

I was on my own that night. Although it was Saturday, Hanif begged off because he was still responding to the first reader's report on his book manuscript. We'd already put in an entire day framing his response, but he still wasn't satisfied. But I did have other options for the evening. Daniel showed up unannounced, begging me to come and protest outside the bookstore where Temple Grandin was doing a book signing.

"But isn't she an animal rights activist?" I asked.

"Heather, for heaven's sake! She figured out how to murder cattle more efficiently. She's like Walter Dejaco," he insisted.

"Who's that?"

"The guy who invented the gas chamber at Auschwitz!"

"But when Clare Danes played her, she identified with the animals," I said.

"How can you identify with animals and still eat them?" was his response.

I had to admit, he had me there. He was carrying a sign with a picture of Ms. Grandin holding a fork and knife with blood dripping down her chin.

"Did you make a sign for me?" I asked.

"No, I've only got one. We can share it," he said.

"I want my own sign," I said, feigning petulance. When he offered to run home and make one, I had to come clean.

"Sorry, Daniel. I'm just not up to it."

Daniel left defeated, but not before soliciting fifty dollars toward the campaign urging the ASPCA to censure Temple Grandin.

In no mood to cook, I went to the Hongui Palace to get some Chinese takeout. I was waiting in the front alcove, reading an old *New Yorker* that was lying on the bench, when I heard Hanif's voice. He was at the cash register paying the bill, soon joined by a young woman with long denim-clad legs. When she turned toward the door, I saw it was Anna. The two of them made a striking couple and looked like they belonged together. I ducked my head down, hoping they wouldn't notice me. I was seated at an angle from them, so it was perfectly possible that they didn't. I watched them glide off together into the night. Of course, it was also plausible that Hanif had seen me, but thought it perfectly possible that I couldn't see them.

So, Hanif was in a restaurant with the same graduate student who'd been closeted with him in his office. Should I be upset? The rational part of me said no. The fact that they were in a public place belied the fact that something salacious was going on. The insecure part of me (approximately fifty percent on a good day; seventy-five percent on a bad) couldn't help but note that, although a favorite hangout for graduate students, this restaurant was something of a dive and not much frequented by the faculty. Was this intentional?

It was after eleven, and I was brooding about Hanif's potential perfidy. My mind was going in circles: either he had nothing to hide, or he thought it was more strategic to hide in the open, so it looked like he had nothing to hide. Think Poe's *Purloined Letter*. I had to distract myself, so I turned on the TV. The movie *Gladiator* was on, which was good. But the character of Lucilla (Connie Nielsen), a stunning brunette, looked a bit like the fair Anna. (Despite such apparent cause for distress, I still couldn't stop myself from wondering for the umpteenth time where Lucilla got her earrings from.) The doorbell rang, which made me scream and levitate about three feet off the couch. I went to the door, half expecting to find Hanif: should I admit that I saw him in the restaurant or keep quiet? Instead, there was Jan, shivering on my stoop, but not from the cold; she was literally shaking with rage.

"Jan, what is it?" I said. She had followed me into the kitchen and was watching while I poured each of us a liberal tumbler of scotch.

"That goddam shower," she said.

"You went back?" I asked, aghast.

"You bet I did. And it was just as I feared. Like Sodom and Gomorrah."

Since theologians hadn't determined what the actual sin of Sodom and Gomorrah was until well into the Middle Ages, I naturally asked for clarification.

"At first, it was just a lot of noise, drinking, and dancing, and I felt relieved. But when the presents began to be unwrapped, things really got out of hand. There was a spotlight on the stage and a creepy impresario dressed like a devil — a devil with breasts AND a penis! Seriously, you couldn't tell if it was a man or a woman," Jan said with repugnance.

I winced: sometimes Jan sounded just like a fundamentalist.

"There was a mic, so I could hear every word and see everything. Everything, I tell you," Jan repeated for emphasis. She nodded her head in a satisfied, self-congratulatory manner as she took a drink.

"What does 'out of hand mean' mean?" I asked apprehensively.

"I mean that when the impresario opened the curtains on the stage, there was Thourelle and Tommy under a strange cubist-looking tree. They were totally nude!" Jan said.

"Really?" I was somewhat incredulous.

"Well, virtually. I mean, I thought they were naked at first. They appeared as if they were," Jan said rather defensively. "But when I looked through my binoculars..."

"Binoculars? Jan, really!" I said in dismay.

"Thank God I brought them," she snapped. "That's how I know they were wearing flesh-colored body suits. Otherwise, I would've called the police. Anyway, the impresario went on to explain that Tommy and Thourelle were really Adam and Eve and still innocent. They didn't know what sin was or how to sin. This is where the guests came in. They were there to teach them," Jan said contemptuously.

"Interesting premise," was all I could think of to say. "Teach them how?"

"People were expected to get up on stage when their gift was unwrapped. You should've seen these gifts: there were vibrating panties, butt plugs, and more kinds of dildos and vibrators than you can possibly imagine. Each person was to demonstrate how their gift worked," Jan said with distaste.

"Seems rather unsanitary," I observed.

"Well, not literally," Jan responded with some impatience. "More of a pantomime. But the performances were very graphic."

"Actually, it sounds hilarious," I said, imagining how one might demonstrate vibrating panties.

"I thought that you'd say something like that," Jan snapped. "But you'd think differently if you'd been there for the last demonstration. That was really over the top!"

Apparently, the last gift was presented by a lithe and sinewy woman with large breasts, who came forward in a green sequined costume resembling a snakeskin. With the accompaniment of seductive Arabic music and a pulsing strobe light, she undulated toward the immobile Eve and attached two rings to her nipples. Eve opened her eyes and came to life. The two women danced together in a sensuous belly dance *like a couple of nymphos* (Jan's words). Then Eve went over to the tree, plucked one of its square fruits, and brought it to Adam, who opened his eyes and began to move. Adam and Eve embraced each other and began to writhe together. Soon, the snake lady joined in.

"It looked just like they were having sex. I couldn't take it anymore," Jan said. "I marched in and told them that the party was over and that everyone had to leave."

I knew that Jan had made a mistake by disrupting the shower. Its erotic premise had been announced ahead of time. If she felt compelled to intervene, she should've done it earlier — not spy on the students and then send them to bed early like bad children. Worse still, it wasn't just the graduate students she was chastising; there was also Thourelle, the colleague for whom this celebration had been staged. The final dance sequence was the tipping point for Jan, but even in her description, it didn't sound like a spontaneous eruption of orgiastic excess. The dance was meticulously choreographed and didactic in nature. The cubist tree was obviously the tree of knowledge, and the square fruits were books. The performance simulated the erotic exchange between teacher and student advanced in *Passionate Pedagogy*.

It was well after midnight when Jan left, but I couldn't sleep. Instead, I lay on the couch watching *All About Eve*, figuring that could count as sleep. I was once again at the scene where Margot and Karen were stuck in the car, and Margot was reflecting upon her relationship with Bill, her beloved director-lover, who happened to be her junior. The age discrepancy was a constant source of insecurity for the aging actress. Karen attempted to reassure Margot, exclaiming: "Bill is all of eight years younger than you!" But Margot responded: "Those years stretch as the years go on; I've seen it happen too often."

I'd forgotten about that exchange, and it hit me with all the éclat of an oracle.

Hanif hadn't dropped by that night, nor did he phone.

Chapter 19: Frenzy

Hanif called the next day to tell me that he'd finished his response to the reader's report and felt like taking a break. Did I want to go to a movie? My initial impulse was to say no in order to punish him, though it would probably punish me more. But instead, I concealed my chagrin and said that I'd love to see a movie. I was profoundly hurt that he'd gone out the night before without telling me on what appeared to be something of a date, yet I was struggling to find the high ground. Admittedly, my sense of direction has always been rather hit-and-miss in questions of the heart: is my high truly high, or is it low masquerading as high? Either way, it seemed as if I was confronted by two basic choices with several attitudinal subsets:

1). Keep quiet about seeing Hanif and Anna and either:

    a) trust him

    b) or interpret his shifty behavior as a warning

2). Admit that I saw him, and

    a) believe whatever he says

    b) or listen attentively and appear to accept his explanation, all the while remaining skeptical

It turned out that the movie was one of those modernizations of a Jane Austen classic and a real travesty. Why can't they leave that poor woman alone? Afterward, Hanif came back to my place. Over a glass of white wine, I said:

"By the way, I think that I saw you last night at Hunghui Palace."

He didn't miss a beat. "Why didn't you come over? You've met Anna before," he said.

"I was waiting for takeout. When I noticed you, you were already out the door." I paused. Then I asked: "Is Anna going to work with you?"

"Possibly. Right now, Jan is directing Anna's dissertation. But I think Anna's almost decided to dump Jan and work with me. If she does, she'd be my first graduate student ever," he said proudly.

Poor Jan. She always took losing a student so personally.

"Why dump Jan?" I asked.

"I'm not exactly certain. All I know is that Anna finds Jan erratic, and it makes her uncomfortable," he said.

Since Anna was an English student, I wondered why she wasn't at Thourelle's shower. I presume she thought dinner with Hanif the better option. Of course, the shower began around eight. She may well have gone there after dinner. Or not.

"Anyway, I happened to run into her at the grocery. She was clearly upset about something and needed to talk. Rather than foraging at home, I suggested we grab a quick bite at Hunghui."

This all sounded perfectly plausible. So, instead of asking any follow-up questions, I decided to cease and desist. And continue brooding.

Besides, I had other things to worry about. You may remember that ridiculous series of Title IX complaints that Ms. Cather brought against me. According to the guidelines handily posted on the Bureau of Equity website, if the respondent (me) had any reason to think that the plaintiff was biased against them, they were supposed to make this clear at the outset. Hence, when Jan and I went to see Sally Field in order to respond to the complaints, I shared my theory that Ms.

Cather's complaints were tactical in anticipation of my failing her as a Teaching Assistant. But Sally Field didn't seem to understand the point I was making and kept saying, "But she brought the complaint *before* you submitted the grade!" This refrain eventually changed to the still more discouraging, "Is it possible that you were planning to give Ms. Cather a failing grade because you knew she was about to file Title IX complaints against you?"

This happened just after I ran into Hanif and Anna, and was feeling pretty hopeless. Nevertheless, I got lucky. The university hired an outside investigator for my case, who turned out to be very reasonable. He understood what I was saying about Ms. Cather's preemptive move. I told him that I had to grade all the finals because she was incompetent and produced the exams so he could see that all the grading was in my hand. (It turned out to be a blessing that we're supposed to keep those bluebooks around for a year; otherwise, I might've pitched them.) He then gave me the opportunity to produce whatever evidence I had at hand to respond to the charges. And so:

1). I took the investigator to my office so he could see that there was something wrong with the door, and it always rolled shut.

2). I showed him an article that I had written a couple of years earlier on rumors concerning the Cathars as recorded by the English courtier, Walter Map, and he found it entirely plausible that I could be genuinely interested in Ms. Cather's last name, and that I brought it up as an icebreaker when we first met. In other words, I was not attempting to insult her.

3). I produced three other graduate students, who had all at some point taught with me, to testify that I routinely gave them the opportunity to lecture (and they all perceived it as a privilege, not abuse).

4). I showed him where it was clearly stated on my syllabus that there would be a lecture on marital sex. I also shared my lecture notes with him. (I don't think he found them particularly interesting.)

5). I explained to him the significance of Peter Damian's treatise in its eleventh-century context.

6). OK, I didn't do as well on the obscenity charge. I told him about Chaucer's "queynte" (which he found very interesting), but I also acknowledged the possibility that I might've forgotten myself on occasion and used some kind of a mild expletive during a lecture. Since Ms. Cather did not provide explicit details (neither the words used, the context, nor the dates), that complaint was dismissed. I did get tripped up by the cupcakes, however. To have "Sex" printed so boldly on a pastry might be shocking, even obscene, to individuals of delicate sensibilities, such as Ms. Cather. My penalty was that I couldn't teach *Medieval Sex* for two years, and, if I were to bring end-of-the-term pastries for the class, they must be entirely without graphics!

I got my exoneration by email and was elated. Finally, my woes with Ms. Cather, Title IX, and Sally Field were at an end. So it is little wonder that I was subsequently deflated by the next email, however, which happened to be from Thourelle.

Sylvia Thourelle <Via@fmale.com>
Wednesday 2/2/22; 2:03 p.m.
To: Heather Bell
Subject: Ongoing Persecution
Dear Heather:

I apologize for inconveniencing you yet again. I get the sense that you must have already spoken to our Chair about her attempts to interfere with my course because this seems to have stopped. Thank you for that. I have recently learned, however, that she has been interviewing English department students in the hope of discovering material that could be used to disparage me. As a result, I have little choice but to begin proceedings for a Title IX case against Jan for producing a hostile work environment and possibly for sexual harassment. You have been very kind to me, so I didn't want to do anything behind your back. I hope that this does not affect our relationship. Sylvia

The email gave me chills. I was terrified that Thourelle knew that, in addition to trying to dig up dirt on her, Jan had actually keyed her car. I picked up the phone and called Thourelle's office. I was in luck because she picked up. It was after four o'clock, so I asked her to join me in the faculty club for a drink, and she agreed. I got there first and was waiting with two glasses of white wine (it seemed a little early for scotch). When she walked through the door, I waved her over. She sat down in the other Barcelona chair knockoff, picked up her glass and raised it in my general direction:

"Cheers," she said.

"Although things aren't very cheery," I responded.

She shrugged: "A least I have my cast off. That's cheery enough for me."

"Sylvia, have you already made a Title IX complaint against Jan?" I asked, looking around to make sure there was no one within ear shot.

Thourelle sighed and shook her head, "Not yet. I was just about to submit it when you called," she said.

"Thank God," I sighed.

"What slowed me down was that I couldn't decide whether to call Louise or Sally Field. They both strike me as dopes, and I was trying to figure out which one of them was least dumb," she said.

She was serious, but it was still funny. "It's a tough call," I agreed. "But I'm so relieved that you haven't done anything…"

Thourelle interrupted me, "I know you're going to try and talk me out of it, but I really have to do something, if only out of self-defense. I am virtually certain that Jan keyed my car."

My heart leapt into my throat as I raised my eyebrows in feigned surprise.

"Really? I doubt that very much. Someone slashed one of my tires recently. Hazing frats; vandals: it could've been anyone," I reasoned.

"It could've been," she agreed, but she was looking at me very pointedly, and I could feel my skin begin to flush. Did she suspect me? "But the timing makes me suspect Jan. I can't be sure because I didn't notice it right away, but I think it happened just after our argument over my course. This kind of uncontrolled anger is dangerous: for Jan and for me," she continued.

If she finds out the truth, the case against Jan would be more than a Title IX complaint: there would also be a civil suit.

"Sylvia, I know you don't owe me any favors. I've always publicly disagreed with you, and I gave you a black eye," I said.

"True. But you were very kind to me after my accident. So let's say we're even," she said.

"OK, then. Would you please hold off filing the complaint for a couple of days? Let me talk with Jan first," I pleaded.

Thourelle thought about it for a while and eventually agreed. "But I'm only postponing for your sake," she said.

Hanif and I were going to play pool that night. I had tried to play a few years ago but was so terrible that I was warned off by the bar's manager, who feared I would rip the felt on the table. But Hanif had actually taken a course in pool as an undergraduate (!) and wanted to show off. He insisted that I would like it. I had been planning to drop in at Jan's house ahead of time and try to reason with her, but Jan came to my office first in what I initially mistook for a contrite state of mind. She told me about her aborted attempts to launch a Title IX case against Thourelle.

"Why, Jan?" I asked, bemused. "You promised not to interfere with her course," I said.

"It's not about her course. We're under a legal obligation to report any instances of sexual misconduct by members of the university community, either on campus or off," she said.

"I know that. But what are you complaining about and why?" I asked.

Jan went on to tell me that she believed Thourelle was sexually exploiting her graduate students. Even if Jan were right, and considering Hanif's experience, it certainly couldn't be ruled out, I thought that she would be hard-pressed to prove this charge and said as much.

"I told you about the act with the serpent woman," she said with disdain.

"Jan, that was a piece of performance art and a pretty tame one at that. There was no nudity or explicit sexual acts, apart from a bit of groping. No obscenity laws were violated."

"You don't need any of those things in order to prove abuse," Jan responded.

"True, but you do need a plaintiff. Who was being abused?" I asked.

"Well, that serpent-woman who ended up in a ménage-a-trois, for one," said Jan.

"But Jan, if she was a graduate student, she's clearly of age. And didn't you tell me that she initiated the make-believe sexual activity? She was the serpent tempting Eve."

Jan, who was sitting on a chair beside my desk, put her head in her hands. "Help me out here. How do we get rid of her? Do you think that I could personally launch a complaint?"

"But how did Thourelle abuse you, exactly? If you were still with Marty, and she slept with him, maybe you could argue hostile work environment, but that strikes me as a stretch." I suddenly wondered if, in this capricious political climate, I could've launched a Title IX suit against Marcel and his graduate student-lover. Maybe. But what would be the point besides vindictiveness?

"Can't I say that she was creating a hostile work environment with that shower?" Jan asked.

"But was she? You're the Chair of the department, after all, so from an administrative standpoint, you outrank her. You weren't invited to the shower. Even so, you went and spied on it. And the graduate students were the ones who threw the shower, not Thourelle. Besides, her graduate students adore her and would never support such a complaint."

Jan admitted that this was, indeed, the case. She'd been working the graduate students ever since the shower, asking them to come forward and testify against Thourelle either as a plaintiff or a witness, but none was forthcoming. In the meantime, Thourelle had doubtless been tipped off by her loyal graduate student retainers.

"I feel that Thourelle is a real threat to everything we stand for as teachers," Jan said through angry tears. "So, I privately consulted a law firm which specializes in Title IX cases. I told them about Thourelle's course, the shower, even how she had posed as an ace for the purpose of seducing students. But they're no help. In fact, they warned me that, if I persisted, Thourelle would be within her rights to bring a case against me for creating a hostile work environment."

After we'd circled around these issues for over an hour, Jan was finally prepared to admit defeat and promised that she would stop attempting to accrue evidence against Thourelle. I didn't think it necessary to apprise Jan that she was in danger of a Title IX complaint being brought against her by Thourelle. Before meeting Hanif, I called Thourelle and gave her an expurgated account of my conversation with Jan, begging her not to pursue the Title IX route. She agreed reluctantly. Her agreement was contingent upon Jan's good behavior, however.

But Jan's concession was too late. Her behavior had placed her in the crosshairs of the disgruntled graduate students who were unhappy about how their Jack and Jill shower had been disrupted. Their griping soon took a litigious turn. The head of the English Graduate Affairs Committee, along with the erstwhile master of ceremonies at the shower, began by consulting with the departmental Title IX liaison. Louise had it in for Jan. She'd been livid when the department selected

Jan as Chair over her, and was convinced that this misfire of justice could only have been achieved through Jan's evil machinations. In short, rather than attempting a diplomatic solution, calming the students down and proposing some kind of rapprochement, Louise pursued the more militant option. She made an appointment with Sally Field on behalf of the restive students in order to launch a Title IX investigation against Jan and was there to support them throughout the interview. Jan was given a redacted summary of the complaints. There were three.

1). Professor Westlock was not invited to the shower for Professor Thourelle but secretly attended, concealing herself outside. In addition to spying on said students, she disrupted the performance of an honest and in no way obscene depiction of polyamorous bisexual love, hence discriminating against sexual minorities who self-identify as bisexual, polyamorous, or both. In so doing, she has created a hostile work environment, not just for those minorities but the graduate students at large.

2). Professor Westlock engaged in a persecutory follow up in which she tried to pressure graduate students into testifying against Professor Thourelle for her participation in the dance-drama discussed above. In other words, she was using her position as Chair of English coercively, asking graduate students to perjure themselves in order to support her persecutory ends.

3). Professor Westlock has launched a vendetta against Professor Thourelle for her educational efforts to represent alternative sexualities in the course *The Psychopathology of Everyday Sex*. After failing to block the course from being offered, she tried to dissuade graduate students from enrolling. She has also raised objections to the projected extra-curricular presentations associated with the course. These actions contravene both academic freedom and freedom of speech.

This list of complaints was less fatuous and, hence, more ominous than Ms. Cather's parallel list. The question was if Jan could convince whomever was assigned to investigate the case of the efficacy of her position. She retained legal representation in anticipation of a formal hearing. Meanwhile, Jan went to the Bureau of Social Equity to respond to these allegations, and I went as her support person. Then we waited.

Jan became increasingly despondent. In a matter of weeks, she had metamorphosed from a departmental Chair who simply disliked Thourelle for her effect on the department's reputation to a woman driven by an implacable hatred for a personal enemy. Jan was also convinced that Thourelle was the hidden force directing the graduate students' Title IX case, despite my best efforts to assure her otherwise.

Chapter 20: Stage Fright

I'd decided to go for the high road: the dinner between Hanif and the beguiling Anna was perfectly innocent. Hanif and I were in love, and when Valentine's Day rolled around, this required special commemoration. A romantic card was, of course, mandatory, so I went to a specialty card shop in the mall to study the options. I was struck by how many of the cards alluded to food: *Love is always the answer. And chocolate… lots and lots of chocolate*; *All I really need is love, but a little chocolate now and then doesn't hurt!*; *Besides pizza, you're my favorite*; *Donut you know I like you a hole bunch*; *I'm bananas over you*; *Lettuce be lovers*; *Life is butter with you in it*. My personal favorite, however, had less to do with the food itself and more to do with the result of food: *I love you with all my butt. I would say heart, but my butt is bigger*. But (ha, ha) I wasn't sure if it struck the right note.

Eventually, I went for a more traditional offering: *Ours is my favorite love story*, replete with a rainbow in the background. But the most challenging part of my V-Day preparations still lay ahead. I'd determined to go to Victoria's Secret to get some amorous underthings. I was poking around the camisoles, wondering which of these would best conceal my midriff, when I sensed the presence of someone behind me. I turned to discover Thourelle's fiancé, Tommy.

He recognized me and immediately began thanking me for the care I'd taken of Thourelle over the Christmas Break.

"And thanks for the prosecco and appetizers. I was in such a hurry to reach Sylvia that I'd forgotten about New Year's Eve and hadn't brought anything. But you made it festive," he said.

While I listened to Tommy as patiently as I could, I was extremely conscious of the assorted garments in my hand. It was almost as bad as buying condoms. The fact that it was Tommy, student-lover to a woman with whom my lover, Hanif, had (maybe) been a former student-lover, made me feel especially self-conscious. Maybe it was a reflexive consanguinity thing: the medievals believed that marriage made husband and wife one flesh but that fornication could do the job just as well (albeit more sinfully). This would make me tacitly related not only to everyone that I'd ever slept with but to everyone with whom my sexual partners had ever slept as well, and so on. The mind boggles. Of course, Tommy wouldn't have known about Hanif and Thourelle, or would he? Didn't Hanif tell me his version of the legal altercation with Thourelle, even though he wasn't supposed to speak about it to anyone? Then I caught myself. "His version" implied that there were two equally viable versions of their relationship: not just Hanif's truth versus Thourelle's fabrications.

Tommy must've felt awkward too. He was, after all, in a Victoria's Secret shop, presumably in search of something capable of catalyzing the libido of a self-proclaimed ace. I left him to it, said goodbye, and began walking to the cash register. I stood in line, meditating upon my selection: a Spandex camisole with matching high-waisted briefs. I might as well have ordered something from Knix. I was on the verge of returning them to the appropriate rack and beginning again when suddenly Thourelle appeared, doubtless looking for Tommy. It was an awkward place to encounter any colleague, especially this one, and we greeted each other with circumspection. There was an awkward pause as we cast around for something to say, both aware of the need to sidestep the issues of Jan and Title IX altogether. Eventually, it occurred to me to ask if she'd gotten in touch with my voice teacher. She had.

"I like the Russian accent, but her shouting scares me," Thourelle said.

"It's nothing personal. Russians are passionate about music, that's all," I said.

I noticed that Thourelle was cradling her arm.

"Hasn't the break healed yet?" I asked, indicating her arm.

"Oh, yes. This is something else. I was in the line at the liquor store about an hour ago and suddenly felt a twinge in my arm. I'm afraid that it was a spider, or something, that had been hiding in my coat sleeve," she said.

"God, I hope not," I murmured. I was on the verge of blurting out that the brown recluse spider was endemic to the state and tended to crawl indoors in the cold weather, but then shut my mouth. Thourelle had enough problems without my arachnophobe interventions.

"I shook my coat out, and I didn't see anything, so it's probably nothing," she continued.

At this point, Thourelle glanced at the garments in my hand, smiled and raised her eyebrows in what, retrospectively, was probably only friendly curiosity. But I panicked and began to babble explanations (*This is for a friend who thinks her husband's having an affair with his dental hygienist*). When the lady at the cash register began to put my ensemble in a pink transparent bag, I insisted that she try and locate a brown paper bag in the stock room — like I was buying a mickey of vodka to drink in the park.

When I got home, I looked at the card. It really was rather dreadful, so I set about making my own. I had limited means at my disposal: I have no talent for drawing; my penmanship sucks; so I cut letters out of the newspaper and glued them to a piece of cardboard packaging from a pair of pantyhose. *BE MINE OR SUFFER THE CONSEQUENCES*, it read, accompanied by the shapes of a heart and a dagger, which I cut out of the editorial page. Admittedly, it looked more like an anonymous death threat than a testimonial of love, but it felt more authentic than the card. I stuck it in a brown paper self-seal envelope and glued the letters "HT" on the front. I'd also bought him a giant-size box of animal crackers and an illustrated children's book called *Saints and Their Animals*. (It had a picture of St. Jerome and the lion who befriended him after the saint removed the thorn from his paw.) I wrapped these gifts more conventionally, in red paper with pink ribbon.

Hanif wanted to make me a romantic Valentine's dinner. Up until now, he'd been frantically working on his book manuscript, so I'd usually done the cooking (apart from the eventful blueberry pancakes), or we'd gone out. In other words, this was something of a first. Hanif greeted me at the door in a deep cherry red shirt and a white chef's apron, grinning from ear to ear. The house was full of evocative cooking smells that I tried to distinguish between: garlic, for sure, and ginger. *Curry?* I asked aloud. *In the soup*, he responded.

I looked around his living room. It wasn't the first time I'd been to his place, but it was the first time that I'd really paid attention. When I was an Assistant Professor who couldn't drive, I'd lived in a real dive within walking distance of campus. It was a bungalow that had one of those basements with dirt floors, accessed from the outside through a set of metal doors. (Think Auntie Em calling Dorothy.) It turned out that this very basement harbored an extended family of possums. When I had them removed by an animal shelter, however, the house remained infested by fleas, and I became covered with bites. I'm a medievalist, after all, so I was all too aware that *Yersinia pestis* (the plague bacillus) was transmitted by the flea *Xenopsylla cheopsis*, which was carried by the black rat. Yet there were a number of animals (marmots, certainly; squirrels and gophers, possibly) that could act as hosts for the infected flea. In fact, there were permanent reservoirs of plague-carrying rodents throughout the US. Could the possum be one of the potential carriers, even though it was a marsupial? The whole scenario made me nervous, but not nervous enough to move.

My point is that, as a fledgling faculty member, I was still living the half-life of a graduate student, or worse. Hanif's living room displayed none of this self-punishing myopia. While I had once tacked posters to the wall, Hanif had purchased an attractive set of abstract prints from an emerging artist. In the center of the room was a stylish rust-orange couch that picked up the colors in the hand-knotted rug, which, in the words of the Big Lebowski, tied the room together. The windows were adorned with a handsome set of off-white Roman blinds.

We sat in the living room, eating *maoutabbai* (an eggplant-yogurt concoction) and *za'atar man'ouche* (spiced flat bread), the way Hanif's mother made it. Maybe Hanif's superior culinary skills, taste, and style should count as equalizing factors that reduced my seniority.

"How did you learn to cook?"

"My mom. I always used to follow her around in the kitchen mixing things for her, licking the spoons, you know." Actually, I didn't. My mother rarely cooked and invariably burned anything she tried to cook, presumably to manage familial expectations.

"What about your dad?"

Hanif shook his head. "Didn't like cooking."

"I don't mean that. What was he like? You hardly ever talk about him," I said.

"Yes, I do! I told you about the beautiful desk he made me and about the time he helped me reel in the 25-pound bass. He's great, but we're way different. I still remember the look on his face when we were visiting Santa at the department store one Christmas, and I asked for a doll," he said.

I understood. I have a cousin, a sweet man, who loved dolls. As children, we'd play dolls whenever we got together. He was sensitive like Hanif and became a gifted cellist. Of course, my cousin also turned out to be gay.

"Actually, it's you who never talks about your father," Hanif said.

Of course, Hanif was right. I remembered Dr. Owen's parting words of advice were not to repress thoughts about my father — advice which I'd managed to repress.

At this point, my eyes wandered to the mantle, where a Valentine's card was prominently displayed. Following my gaze, Hanif said. "From my mother." Then he jumped up. "Dinner's ready," he said, taking my arm and propelling me toward the table.

Hanif was not only a good cook, he was a confident cook. His approach to food was daringly syncretic. Case in point: the menu for this evening was a delicious lentil and squash soup (*also Mom's recipe*, he said), sake-ginger glazed salmon with celery risotto and a shaved fennel salad with arugula and pomegranate seeds. Hanif was in especially good spirits because he'd recently received the second reader's report on his book.

"Wait, I'll get it for you. You have to see it to believe it!" he said, leaping up. When he returned to the table, he was suddenly self-conscious. "I suppose it's not very cool for me to be blowing my own horn," he said.

"Don't be silly! Blow as much as you can. Academia is a tough business," I responded.

The report was, indeed, glowing — so much so that the press insisted on giving Hanif a contract even before he responded to the reader's very mild (and totally optional) suggestions. The book was called *Sad Tails: Animals We Use and Abuse*. I especially liked the chapter Hanif had added (at my suggestion) on the medieval sheep-meat-wool-cloth trade between England and the Low Countries entitled "The Silence of the Lambs."

For dessert, there was a lemon soufflé.

"I'd never make a dessert like this," I said.

"Don't you like it?" Hanif asked with concern.

"It's delicious. I wouldn't make it because it would never turn out this good." I said this while examining the perfect little cavity inside my slice, with its soft pillow of lemon curd. How does the lemon get in there without leaking into the dough?

"Heather, I have something important to ask you," Hanif said.

I looked up expectantly: he had suddenly slipped down onto one knee.

"Will you marry me?" he said, looking deeply into my eyes.

I swallowed wrong and had a fit of coughing. Hanif quickly stood up and began to slap my back.

"What brought this on?" I eventually managed.

"Heather, you're the coolest, funniest, sexiest woman I know, and I love you. We're a great match. I know we'd be happy together," he said.

I must've looked extremely skeptical because he went on to say:

"Come on! I'm proposing to you, not infecting you with Corona Virus!"

My heart was beating very fast. Who wouldn't leap at the chance to marry such an attractive, intelligent, sensitive person? Even so, I hadn't expected this and was on my guard.

"But why the hurry?" I asked.

"We love each other, so why wait? We've only been going out for a few months, but we've known each other for years. My book has been accepted, which means I'll probably get tenure. So, marry me! We could become one of those power couples that everyone's afraid of," Hanif responded, smiling.

Marry me! That sounded great. But the remainder — *We could become one of those power couples that everyone's afraid of* — gave me pause. I knew he was being facetious, but even so, I didn't like being projected into a power couple framework. It smacked of ambitious elitism while also reminding me that I wasn't the first older female academic that Hanif had (perhaps) been involved with. It also foregrounded Hanif's very real preoccupation with self-presentation on every level. He was constantly checking in with me to ask how his different interventions were going over in department meetings. Hanif wanted our colleagues to perceive him as a mover and a shaker. He didn't seem to realize that he was asking the wrong person about how to achieve this end.

Yet, forget these mental reservations. Every pore of my infatuated carnal self was begging me to say yes. But before I could, there was an important issue that needed clarification.

"Hanif, I don't think I want children," I said. In fact, I knew that I didn't want children, so even this was a lie. But coward that I am, I chose to relay this sentiment in such a way that it sounded as if the subject of kids was still up for negotiation.

There was a pause. I could see that I'd taken him by surprise. Yet he eventually said: "That's cool. We don't have to have kids."

"But I thought you wanted children," I said.

"No, it was my mother who wanted grandchildren. Hardly the same thing," Hanif said. "All I want is you." He turned his wondrous smile on me, and my heart began to beat faster.

"Anyway, maybe you'll reconsider," he said, which, of course, sounded ominous to me. If I were in Hanif's position and wanted to have children, I would never have chosen a reluctant mother for my partner. It was like planning a sequel to *Mommy Dearest*.

Hanif's proposal had, strangely enough, knocked some of the romantic wind out of our sails. Valentine's Day had fallen on a Sunday this year, and, since Hanif taught early Monday morning and had to prepare for class, we'd agreed ahead of time that I wouldn't spend the night. I thought there might be the opportunity for me to tantalize Hanif with my new undies, but it was just as well there wasn't. They made me feel cramped, slightly smelly, and overall uncomely. Plus, I needed to do some soul-searching: perhaps I would discover a hitherto unknown recess that harbored my maternal instincts. When I was about to leave, Hanif took me in his arms and held me. I put my head on his shoulder and closed my eyes.

"You're more important to me than having children," he whispered in my ear. For the moment, I felt as if I were truly loved.

I returned home in a state of confusion. Of course, Hanif's unexpected proposal may've been reason enough, but there was something else that was bothering me — something I couldn't put my finger on. Although I prefer to take showers, and quick ones at that, I decided to indulge in one of my rare baths in the hopes that it would relax me. (I use Mr. Bubble, which, though hard on the skin, never fails to provide a rich cloud cover.) I lay there in the tub for over an hour, letting out the tepid water and refilling it with hot water, aimlessly watching my fingers begin to prune. Then it came to me. At the end of our long embrace, when I opened my eyes, I was facing the mantle where Hanif's sole Valentine's card had been on display — the one from his mother. The card was gone. I was almost certain. Hanif must've removed it when he went to get the reader's report. But why? I could think of two possibilities. Either the Valentine from his mother contained something he didn't want me to see (presumably a negative comment about our relationship), or the card wasn't from his mother. Was it from Anna or perhaps some other woman that I didn't know about? Was it just a student's quirky gratitude, a harmless flirtation, or was Hanif involved with someone else?

When I finally dragged myself to bed, I fell into a restless sleep. It was no surprise when the dream that I'd come to think of as my "anxiety dream" recurred. I was in the cab again on my way home from the coffee house. I got out of the cab and walked up the steps. It'd been snowing and was very cold. I took my key out of my pocket to open the front door. The key turned, the door opened a few inches and then stopped. Somebody had put the safety chain on the door. I rang the bell again and again, but no one came to the door. I went underneath my parents' window and called. No answer. I started to cry. I had nowhere to go.

I woke up in tears. I finally remembered the experience that prompted the dream. I was out with friends and had no way of getting home. It was late: too late to phone, and the El had stopped running. Someone lent me money for a cab, but by the time I got home, my father had locked me out to teach me a lesson. It was the middle of winter. The next morning, my mother found me in the garage, wrapped in an old paint tarp. She kept saying, *I'm so sorry*, over and over. She'd heard me at the door but hadn't let me in because she was afraid of my dad — we all were. I tried to tell her that it wasn't her fault, but I could only mumble: I couldn't form words. I was rushed to the hospital with hypothermia, which then developed into double pneumonia. I spent two weeks in the hospital but was out of school for at least two months. I was forced to go to summer school, so I wouldn't have to repeat the year.

I was sixteen at the time. The incident occurred during that hazy period in my teenage years that Dr. Owen had identified — the period that I remembered so little about. Other memories from my teens began to return: how I won a poetry award, played the first voice in a performance of *Under Milkwood*, had the role of Eve in a dance drama about the creation of the world, took a silent film course where I fell in love with Lillian Gish, and had a painful crush on a boy named Jeff who wore a red sash with his jeans instead of a belt. He was sensitive and beautiful and reminded me of Hanif.

How had I forgotten all this?

Chapter 21: The Skin Game

Thourelle's course, *The Psychopathology of Everyday Sex,* was extraordinarily successful. It filled up quickly, and there was an extensive waiting list in the event that anyone dropped. (Nobody did.) Because it was a graduate seminar, it was capped at 15 students. These students were expected to read, discuss, and find scholarly critiques and discussions in the media for the inflammatory readings on the syllabus.

As the Title IX suit against Jan had noted, there was also an extra-curricular component to the course, which students in the class were not obligated to attend but invariably did. Every Wednesday at 4:00 p.m., various groups were invited to give presentations on topics related to the class. These sessions were open to the public and widely attended, raising both the visibility and the notoriety of Thourelle's course. The extra-curricular forum was so popular that Thourelle had to move venues from an ordinary amphitheater-style classroom to one of the university's auditoriums, which seated 500 people and was usually full.

Some of the presentations were scholarly and informative. There were two male-to-female transgender speakers who contested the claims of Bailey's *The Man Who Would Be Queen*. The speakers happened to be sociologists who conducted their own study to refute Bailey (admittedly with a sample that was suspiciously small), ascertaining that individuals who sought male-to-female sex reassignment were every bit as conflicted about their birth sex as was the case with female-to-male reassignments.

But other presentations seemed to vie with one another in degree of offensiveness. I had no idea that there could be so many perverted miscreants in a sleepy college town. Thourelle managed to find a zoophile to speak about the joys and trials of inter-species love. (The speaker wore a mask because zoophilia is, after all, illegal.) Daniel organized a large group of protesters to picket the event. He had also alerted the ASPCA, who attempted to seize the handsome chocolate-colored lab which accompanied the speaker. Both the dog and his owner resisted valiantly. Later, the zoophile swore to the audience that the dog was a service animal and that they were just friends.

The presentation that turned out to be the most volatile was the one that sought to prove the existence of the G-Spot and the reality of female ejaculation. There were two individuals committed to this position, a man and a woman. The man was a medical doctor. Usually, the stage was set up with a table and chairs for panelists. But in this case, there was only a large armchair in the middle of the stage, which seemed a bit odd. As soon as the presenters had been introduced, the woman stripped from the waist down while the man took a long piece of machinery out of a canvas case.

"Hello. I'm Dr. Smith, a trained gynecologist. The woman you see here is my working partner, who goes by the pseudonym of Regina Canal. We live in a puritanical, sex-negative society that condemns sexual pleasure. Women are particular sufferers. Modern-day science has done what it could to keep women ignorant about their own bodies by denying the existence of both the G-Spot and its role in female ejaculation. We're here to prove them wrong." He paused dramatically. The audience, not sure what was expected of them, decided that they should applaud.

Dr. Smith seemed gratified and continued. "I'm holding what I refer to as a love-saw — an ordinary reciprocating saw where the blade has been replaced by a dildo. Its powerful thrust and vibrations stimulate a woman's G-Spot, causing multiple orgasms attended by ejaculation in a matter of seconds."

He approached the woman, who was sitting in the armchair. When he asked if she was ready, she answered by opening her legs. Then Dr. Smith carefully inserted the love-saw into Regina's vagina and turned it on. The love-saw was rather noisy, but you could still hear Regina's moaning above the din. Because I was seated to one side of the auditorium, however, I could only see Dr. Smith, and not Ms. Canal, for which I was grateful. The demonstration went on for somewhere between 5 and 10 minutes. When it was over, Regina Canal stood up, a little shaky at first, and slowly walked toward the mic, still half-naked.

"Thank you, Dr. Smith. You and your love-saw have changed my life," Regina said with sincerity, giving a sated smile. They shook hands and nodded: two professionals commending one another over a job well done.

"Do I have any volunteers? Anybody want a go with the love-saw?" Dr. Smith asked. "I have some disinfectant wipes, so it's all perfectly sanitary," he added.

"You won't regret it," Regina chimed in. "My best friend didn't want to try it, but once she did, she begged her husband to upgrade his saw for Mother's Day."

Despite this compelling testimonial, the entire audience, even Thourelle's most outré graduate students, were not only silent but absolutely still, lest the good doctor mistakenly call upon them. Thourelle got up and thanked the performers, who then took questions. Most of the questions seemed to revolve around the love-saw itself: Does it hurt? Is it hard to make one? Does it take batteries, or is it rechargeable? How many times better is the love-saw than a dildo or an actual penis? Does it work for anal sex?

I'd been planning to challenge the speakers on the politics of female ejaculation, which I saw as a dangerously retrograde position. Back in the Middle Ages, when the male body was the gold standard, women were regarded as deformed men. Because of insufficient heat at conception, their genitalia had never emerged properly but remained on the inside. As inverted males, it was assumed that women, like men, achieved orgasm by releasing their seed through ejaculation. For the medieval courts, this meant that if a woman was raped and got pregnant, she must've enjoyed it, implying that she was asking for it. A few years ago, it became clear that the Missouri congressman, Todd Akin, still subscribed to this view. But by now, such physiological contentions had been eclipsed by the love-saw, so I held my peace.

The last question was posed by a man in his late 20s from outside of the university community. He stood up and, with a leer, asked for Regina Canal's phone number. He clearly thought this was a setting in which anything goes because his hand was inside his fly, and he appeared to be playing with himself. (I heard later that he had been masturbating throughout the demonstration.) He was apprehended by two campus security guards positioned at the front of the auditorium. Apparently, they'd been there for all the extracurricular performances, but no one had ever noticed them before. Once the leering masturbator had been disposed of, Thourelle once again thanked her guests and brought the session to a close.

There was considerable fallout after the love-saw incident. At the beginning of each of these extracurricular performances, Thourelle would say expressly that all photographs or videos were forbidden. Even so, someone had videoed the entire session and posted it online. Before the university could have it removed, a well-wisher had sent the link to Regina Canal's husband, who happened to be an evangelical pastor. (His church was one of the ones I used to pass en route to my sessions with Dr. Owen.) The irate pastor attempted to have his wife committed to an asylum for nymphomania and, when that failed, filed for a divorce.

Meanwhile, a number of female faculty members were upset that Dr. Smith, that indefatigable pioneer of female pleasure, happened to be their personal gynecologist. There was one large OBGYN clinic that served most of the town. Within a week, all of Dr. Smith's patients had migrated over to other members of the practice. I later heard that Dr. Smith was forced to retrain as a podiatrist.

The media went wild over the event, describing it as an instance of liberal lenience out of control and condemning the decadent permissiveness of institutions of higher learning. Jan was furious and renewed efforts to interfere with the course. She tried to pressure the Dean, and ultimately the President of the university, into censuring Thourelle and forbidding these extra-curricular presentations. The administration wasn't sure how to respond. The President, who privately agreed with Jan, did not want to appear to oppose academic freedom. He appealed to the Faculty Senate (which he generally regarded as a nuisance) to make a statement condemning such flagrant exhibitionism. But the senators would make no such statement, clearly appreciating that any attempt to interfere with someone else's classroom could backfire against them. Attendance was, after all, optional, and considering the "sexplosion" of porn on the internet, not to mention the growing number of porn addicts that allegedly existed among millennials and Generation Z, the senators were confident that students had seen worse. When confronted with this degree of nonchalance, the President decided that this exhibition provided him with an excellent opportunity to uphold academic freedom, and this was the position he ultimately took with the media, even writing an editorial in a prominent paper. Thourelle thus emerged from the incident as something of a hero, while *The Psychopathology of Everyday Sex* became the stuff of legend.

Chapter 22: Murder!

Life in a small to mid-size university town was sometimes dull, so you had to get your thrills wherever you could. The change of seasons was a predictable source of excitement — especially the transition from winter to spring. I mentioned earlier that an early spring was one of our main strengths in recruitment, a phenomenon which was impossible to oversell. In Chicago, spring barely happened: you were catapulted from winter into summer. But because we were quite far south, the promise of spring was already perceptible in early February. I would rush out every morning to my garden to make sure I didn't miss the very first snowdrops pressing through the snow. Then came the small eruptions of yet-to-be-determined green things: the shape of things to come. Now, it was March. The snow was completely gone, and the crocuses were beginning to show their faces. The yellow ones always came first, then the purple. Soon, the daffodils and forsythia would be up. When the trees began to sprout leaves, I was always filled with a residual sense of relief. When I was very young and first learned that dead people were buried in the ground, I developed the theory that naked trees were really giants who'd been buried upside down with their legs in the air. The leaves helped disguise their awkward predicament and preserve their post-mortem modesty.

Sometimes, when the winters were especially severe, I was afraid that the cold had killed everything once and for all. That's what made the spring's rhythm of little rebirths so reassuring. Things that look dead, like shrubs and trees, suddenly spring to life, just like Lazarus. I hoped that Hanif and I could be reborn as well. Not that our relationship had died. But since Hanif's proposal, there was a distance between us. Maybe it was my fault. There seemed to be too many mysteries: Thourelle, Anna, not to mention the disappearing Valentine's card. Was I just being paranoid, or were these legitimate concerns? It also seemed odd that Hanif didn't press me on the marriage issue or even bring it up again. I suppose that, because I'd suggested that Hanif was rushing things with his proposal, his subsequent silence could be construed as considerate. But with the kinds of doubts that were filtering through my mind, I would've been grateful for some importunate behavior on his behalf. It would've been reassuring to know that this exquisite man still wanted to marry me.

While I was wondering if Hanif's proposal was a passing whim, I did some cursory research on adoption. The results were sobering. There just weren't enough babies to go around — even for the most eligible couples. And I can't imagine that we looked particularly eligible: a prospective mother who hadn't bothered to have children in her first (failed) marriage but wanted them now that she was post-menopausal and married to a man 15 years her junior. Even if we were lucky enough to get a baby, there was no guaranteed happy ending. Children can develop detachment disorders before the age of one, which means that they lack the ability to cultivate emotional bonds with others (and are also more inclined to psychopathy). And those adopted from other countries frequently turn into special-needs children owing to nutritional or sensory deprivation in their first few months of life.

Older children were an even riskier proposition. At least 10% of adopted children between 6 and 10 "disrupt," which means they failed to adjust to their new environment and were returned to wherever they came from. A notorious instance of disruption occurred in 2010 when a Tennessee family adopted a seven-year-old boy from Russia. After six months, they sent him back to Russia unaccompanied, with a note saying that they'd been misled by the adoption agency: the child had severe psychological problems and was putting the rest of the family at risk. Apparently, the last straw was when he started threatening his adoptive family, drawing pictures of their house burning down. Even so, people who really want children, biological or adopted, were prepared to take the required leap of faith and move forward. I wasn't.

I didn't tell anyone about Hanif's proposal. This kind of reticence was rather unusual for me: I tended to live up to my reputation for indiscretion, not keeping anything about myself to myself. I was probably afraid that whomever I told might try and weigh in on the children issue. I'm pretty sure that Berenice and Jan would've shouted *don't do it!* in unison. Of course, it was up to Hanif if he wanted to tell his mother that he'd proposed, even though this would probably force some sort of referendum on me. I assumed that she'd advise him to break off the relationship, and maybe he wasn't ready for that. I certainly wasn't. Thus, Hanif and I carried on, but I couldn't help but think that the relationship had taken a turn for the worse on Valentine's Day.

While gentle alarms were going off in my head over Hanif, I was becoming progressively worried about Jan. She'd become taciturn, was losing an alarming amount of weight, and looked profoundly miserable. Jan's fiftieth birthday was coming up. When Berenice and I tried to make plans to celebrate, Jan refused, claiming too much work. But a good friend's fiftieth birthday was not really something you could ignore, or so Berenice and I thought. We were determined to ambush Jan at her home with a birthday dinner. Berenice decided on Indian food because it travels easily and reheats well: she made a shrimp vindaloo and aloo gobi, and I brought a carrot cake (replete with appropriate lettering and candles), a bottle of Oban, and a couple of bottles of prosecco. I got to Jan's house first. When she didn't answer the door, I used my key. I figured we could get set up in the kitchen and surprise her when she got home. But it turned out that Jan was there after all, and not the least bit glad to see me.

"Can't you leave me alone?" she asked, her voice devoid of humor or warmth.

"Most days, yes. But not on your fiftieth birthday," I said, moving past her into the kitchen. Jan seemed to be cooking something already, however. A pot of beans. Maybe she was on some fad diet, which might explain the weight loss. When I asked her what she was cooking, she literally screamed at me to get away from the pot.

"OK, fine," I said.

"Now, will you just go?"

"Not until we have a birthday toast. Berenice will be here any minute," I replied. I opened up the Oban. Jan reluctantly sat down at the kitchen table.

There was an assortment of books on Jan's kitchen able. The first one to catch my eye was *Marginal Comment* — a memoir by the British classicist, Sir Kenneth Dover. Why would an Americanist who specializes in the likes of Fitzgerald and Melville be interested in the reminiscences of an Oxford don, best known for his work on Greek homosexuality? Admittedly, the book had created quite a stir when it was first published in the 90s — mostly because Dover confessed that when he was President of Corpus Christi College, Oxford, he wanted to kill Trevor Aston, a senior fellow at the college, and tried to figure out how to get away with the crime without being caught. Aston was bipolar and so troublesome that he was tearing the college apart. At least, that was Dover's justification. He consulted a lawyer about whether he'd be culpable if Aston phoned him and threatened suicide, as he had done on several occasions, but Dover did nothing to interfere. The lawyer said yes: a crime of omission is still a crime. So, Dover gave up on the scheme, or so he said. Yet very soon after, Aston commits suicide by a drug overdose. It was such convenient timing that one couldn't help but wonder whether Dover had played a role after all. The story stuck in my mind because Aston was a medievalist, as was his ex-wife, who also came to a bad end — drowning herself in the family moat.

The other books were mysteries — equally odd since Jan despised the genre. But at least she'd picked some good ones. There was one of my favorites, Dorothy L. Sayers' *Unnatural Death*, in which the murderer uses a large empty hypodermic needle in order to cause an air embolism and stop the heart. She also had Agatha Christie's *The House of Lurking Death* and Francis Iles's *Before the Fact*, both of which turned on murder by an untraceable poison. Then, there was a bunch of news articles printed off the web. One was about Georgi Markev, the journalist who was stabbed by a poisoned umbrella under Waterloo Bridge in 1978; the other concerned the more recent case of Alexei Navalny — Putin's unfortunate rival.

A switch in my brain was suddenly thrown, and I jumped up and ran to the stove.

"What's in the pot, Jan?"

"Stay away from that," she warned.

"Are those castor bean seeds?" I asked.

Castor bean seeds were the source of the deadly poison, ricin, which was as near to an untraceable poison as existed. Anyone who'd watched *Breaking Bad* knew that all you needed to do was boil the seeds from the castor bean plant to soften them, mash them up, and then extract the ricin through easily available solvents. There was no antidote.

"Is this for Thourelle?" I asked in horror.

"She deserves it!" Jan screamed before breaking down into hysterical sobs.

Jan may've wanted to kill Thourelle, but now that I knew what she was up to, she would have had to kill me as well, which must have struck her as a lot of work. I put on some rubber gloves and carefully walked the pot into the bathroom and, just as carefully, flushed it down the toilet. The stuff was so lethal that I put the pot itself, and all the surrounding implements, in the dishwasher and turned it on the *Pots and Pans* cycle. I then scrubbed down all the surfaces in the kitchen, including the floor.

"Jan, where are the rest of the beans?"

She pointed to a drawer, with a defeated look on her face, and I pocketed them.

At this point, Berenice arrived. I didn't tell her about the ricin. All she knew was that Jan had some sort of breakdown and was in a bad way. We made her eat a little of the curry (which I insisted on microwaving rather than heating up on the stove) and tucked her into bed. I put the cake in the freezer. Maybe we could bring it out when there was something to celebrate. I again glanced at the mysteries on the kitchen table. *Before the Fact* was the book that Hitchcock based his movie *Suspicion* on — the second movie playing that night I went to the drive-in with Hanif, though we left before it started. For some reason, this omission made me really sad. I don't know why. I had my own DVD of *Suspicion,* so we were free to watch it whenever we wanted. Nevertheless, thoughts of the drive-in made me nostalgic for simpler times, when the greatest obstacle to our relationship was my preoccupation with my age and weight.

We couldn't leave Jan alone in the state she was in, so Berenice and I both decided to sleep at her house. I called Hanif to tell him that I wouldn't be coming over later that night after all. I got the impression that he didn't particularly mind. Paranoid or perceptive?

Let the reader decide. I made Berenice take the bed in the guest room, while I slept on the couch.

Fortunately, Spring Break was coming up in two weeks. We insisted that Jan stay home for the next week (the last week of classes before exam week) and told the office that she'd come down with the flu. One of the perks that Jan got as Chair was a reduced teaching load. She was only teaching one course this semester, and it was a survey in American Literature. I got one of her graduate students to step in for the last week of classes, which were largely review sessions. Meanwhile, Berenice was scouring the web, trying to find a cheap package deal for somewhere warm during Spring Break. We would buy Jan the trip as a birthday present, splitting the cost, and Berenice would go with her. It was a challenge to find any openings because, at this time of year, most destinations in tropical zones were booked solid months in advance. In addition, Berenice would have to cancel or move her patients' appointments for that week.

Berenice called me when she found a package to a small island off Cuba. It sounded perfect. The only downside was that, due to the skullduggery of American politics, they'd have to go through Toronto, where there was a substantial layover.

"That's OK. I was there last year. They've just redone the international terminal, and there are some fabulous restaurants and stores. Jan can shop. That always makes her happy," I said.

Berenice agreed. "I'm pushing *Pay now*," she said.

Chapter 23: Suspicion

For the first few days of Spring Break, Hanif was attending a conference that Daniel had helped organize entitled *Animals and Cannibals*, which focused on the evils of animal protein writ large. I called him a couple of times, but he never picked up, which was disconcerting. I knew from experience, however, that Hanif took his conferences seriously and was doing some strenuous networking. That was to be expected at this point in his career. Even so, I began to wonder if he was alright.

One evening, I texted, "R U OK?" and didn't hear from him. But now that I thought about it, the substitution of letters for words might have seemed cryptic. What if he thought *RUOK* was one word? It might look like a verbal butt call. So, I called the front desk at the conference hotel, and they put me through to his room. I was alarmed when a woman picked up and was on the verge of hanging up. But I managed to compose myself and asked for Hanif. When she told me that I had the wrong room, I wanted to protest that I'd been connected by the front desk. Instead, I just apologized and hung up. I didn't try to call again.

When Hanif returned, I learned that he'd forgotten the cord for recharging his phone, hence the silence. We spent the rest of Spring

Break together, doing some work by day and cooking elaborate meals by night. We were also working our way through a Hitchcock Fest that I had cobbled together. It was beautifully curated, if I do say so myself. We watched *Sabotage* (1936), not to be confused with *Secret Agent* (also 1936) or *Saboteur* (1942). As much as I dote on Robert Cummings in *Saboteur*, *Sabotage* was especially interesting for Hitchcock fans because the master of suspense would later acknowledge in an interview with Truffaut that he'd committed a fatal error in the film: he should never have allowed the female lead's kid brother, Stevie, to be blown up by the time bomb concealed in the birdcage he was carrying. Hitchcock had since realized that you shouldn't kill children — ever.

Although Hitchcock never made the same mistake again, he did redouble his commitment to torturing the women and children as much as possible — a practice essential to his craft. This policy was exemplified in *The Man Who Knew Too Much*, which revolved around the kidnapping of a child seen through the lens of the mother's anxiety. We compared both the 1934 and the 1956 versions. I preferred the earlier version because anything with Peter Lorre is always great, and I've never been much of a Doris Day fan. Hanif, however, who likes Jimmy Stewart, preferred the later one. This was but another testimonial to Hanif's good taste because it was the later version that both Hitchcock and Truffaut preferred as well.

Hanif was either riveted by my efforts to introduce him to Hitchcock, or he made a good show of it. Up until then, his knowledge of Hitchcock was mostly derived from the Slovenian literary theorist Slavoj Žižek, who used Hitchcock to illustrate his Lacanian readings of just about everything. Hanif was still devoted to Žižek, but I had stopped reading him when he came out in favor of Trump over Hillary Clinton.

Over a candlelit dinner of tuna cassoulet and heirloom tomatoes, I finally got the courage to ask Hanif something that had bothered me since I first knew him.

"Hanif, can I ask you something? It's something I've wanted to ask you for a long time."

"Sure. You can ask me anything." Of course, people always say that. Then they get totally pissed off if you in some way overstep. This might be the case with Hanif, so I took a deep breath.

"Are you bisexual?" I asked.

"No," he responded, laughing.

"Then why do you sometimes behave as if you're gay?"

"Because I am. Next question?"

He must have seen the stricken look on my face because he immediately said: "It's a joke! I'm not gay. Why ever do you think I seem gay?"

And then, I had to trot out my so-called "evidence." His interventions at conferences, his intellectual queering of this and that, his manscaped body, his remarkably good taste in clothing. Hanif countered by assessing my evidence as pathetic and challenging my ability to marshal a scholarly argument. Then I asked him about his relationship with Paolo.

"Paolo and I are close. And his sexuality is very fluid: he always goes for the person that he finds the most beautiful at the moment. I've seen him with an array of beautiful men and women."

"Did you ever sleep with him?"

"No."

"Have you ever slept with a man?" I asked.

"Once: a professor at my college when I was an undergrad. I told you how weird I seemed to everyone. He was the only person who I felt got me. He encouraged me to go onto grad school and even pulled strings to get me into Peitho," he said. So, Thourelle wasn't the first professor he'd been involved with.

"Were you in love with him?" I asked.

"For a time, I thought I was. But it didn't last long. It was more of an experiment with my sexual boundaries than who I really am. I've never been with a man since. I guess I'm primarily straight after all."

"Primarily straight?"

"I just don't believe that anybody is entirely one thing. Desire is much more complex than that. Don't you think?"

"I agree, in theory. But I almost felt you were trying to make a point with Paolo. You were both so touchy-feely," I said.

"Come on. If we'd been two women, nobody would even have noticed."

This may be true. In our culture, women get to touch each other more, right? It's one of the perks of being the second sex.

"Look, I know that Paolo likes to flirt with me in public. But I don't care. It's what he does. I told him after the departmental party that I thought I was in love with you."

"What did he say?" I asked.

"He congratulated me. He loves older women and thought you looked like my mom." Hanif took one look at my face and started laughing. "I'm kidding."

"That's funny; the boy is funny," I said, turning to my imaginary TV audience.

"Is there anything else you want to know?" he asked.

"Yes. I sometimes think that the way you position yourself at conferences encourages people to think you're gay. Are you aware of that?" I asked.

"No. Who thinks I'm gay?" he asked. He was getting rattled.

"I did, for one," I said.

"Because I work on Queer Theory? It's like asking me if I'm a zoophile or just pose as one. You've been hanging out with Jan too much," he said. There was a pause during which, I presume, Hanif mused about how he was perceived. "Why would I have asked you to marry me if I was gay?"

"I've wondered," I said. I was, of course, half serious, but Hanif thought I was joking, laughed, and nuzzled my ear.

That night, we finally watched *Suspicion* together, happily lying in bed, sharing a pint of coffee-flavored Häagen Dazs.

"That's not the story's original ending," I said when it was over.

"How was it supposed to end?" Hanif asked.

"The husband kills the wife; she even helps him. In the book, Lina can see that Johnnie is ambivalent about killing her. She loves him and is afraid that he'll screw up and get caught. So, she takes the poisoned milk off the tray that Johnnie brought to her bedside and purposefully drinks it," I said.

Hitchcock should never have changed the ending. It's the one thing that doesn't work in an otherwise perfect film.

"Why did Hitchcock change the ending?" Hanif asked.

"He claims that the studio insisted that no audience wanted Cary Grant cast as a murderer. But Hitchcock's letters suggest that he was the one responsible. He wrote that he'd always wanted to do a movie about a woman's fantasy life, and this seemed like a good opportunity," I responded.

"So, rather than Johnnie planning to kill Lina for her insurance money, it became Lina's demented fantasy that Johnnie was planning to kill her for her insurance money, right?" Hanif asked.

I nodded.

"Well, why doesn't that work? The scene with Johnnie walking up the stairs holding a glass of milk is totally surreal. It looks delusional," he continued.

"You're right. Hitchcock put a light bulb in the glass to give it that weird glow so it would seem like part of a sick fantasy. But the ending still doesn't work. Johnnie Aysgarth's amorality is too well-established: stealing from his cousin's estate; betting on horses; allowing Beaky to drink brandy, even though he knew it'd probably kill him. The only ending that makes sense is for Johnnie to kill Lina," I insisted. Hanif soon conceded.

Apart from Hanif's allusion to his proposal as evidence that he was straight, we didn't discuss the topic of marriage during Spring Break. As the Valentine's Day proposal receded in time, I almost began to believe that I was delusional and that it'd never happened. In *The Art of Courtly Love,* Andreas Capellanus insists that love is always either waxing or waning; it never stays still. If Hanif's marriage proposal was no longer on the table, that would be a sure sign that we were on a downward trajectory. A more courageous woman would've asked Hanif directly how he felt, but I was afraid.

Chapter 24: Vertigo

Spring Break was over, and the university was back in session. Now began the mad dash from April through to the first week of May, when exam week ended and the academic year would draw to a close. Nature was erupting everywhere, making it a difficult time to concentrate. The red buds painted the sky like Japanese brushstrokes; the dogwood blossoms crept out of their bark; and the magnolias were unfolding in amorous array. Both Hanif and I agreed the magnolia flowers were intensely erotic but for different reasons. I thought that they gestured toward the way human genitals looked before the Fall and as they would appear once again at the end of time, after we'd attained our glorified bodies. (Augustine said that we kept our genitals in the Afterlife; we just don't use them.) Hanif was reminded of the lurid colors of the male baboon's ass when he was ready to mate.

It was hard to rein the students in at this time of year. The river that runs through campus swelled with the thaw, and they would fling themselves on innertubes to ride the current. (It looked dangerous: I figured that these were probably the same daredevils who wore shorts and sandals in February.) All the students gazed longingly out the classroom windows, begging to have their classes outside. I wasn't falling for that one again. The great outdoors was too distracting. The looney preachers, standing on wooden crates and prognosticating the apocalypse, were out in droves; frisbees put everyone at risk; and enticing sidewalk cafes were springing up all over. Besides, the only time I agreed to take a class outside, half of my students disappeared, eventually reappearing with huge bottles of Coke. Apparently, there were some sleazebags lying in wait who gave these fiscally naïve undergraduates free magnums of Coke, provided they signed up for credit cards. To this day, I feel certain that at least half of them ended up in debtors' prison.

When Jan came back from Cuba, tanned with sun-streaked hair, she seemed like a different person or, at the very least, a person I hadn't seen for years. Not only was she much more tranquil, but she exuded the kind of deep-down happiness that reveals itself the moment a person enters the room. If you will excuse me for lapsing into New Age lingo, Jan seemed centered, and I sensed the difference right away.

Although Jan and Berenice were already friends before Cuba, it was a friendship that was primarily based on dinners and drinks, with some exercise thrown in. They'd never spent an extended period together, let alone travelled. I was afraid that there might be friction between them: that Jan would lapse into her imperious mode and that Berenice would adopt her *you're being childish, so I'm going to ignore you until you behave* stance. Thankfully, my fears were groundless. The trip was a delight, and Jan touted Berenice as the perfect traveling companion. Berenice didn't care about who got which bed, or who showered first; she would rise earlier in the morning but always wait to have breakfast with Jan. She gave Jan all the hangers, claiming she didn't need them, shoving her own clothes into drawers. In the face of a crisis, like running out of toilet paper, Berenice didn't panic: she just rang the front desk. In short, Berenice was infinitely accommodating — someone who was there when you needed her but disappeared when you didn't want her around.

Yet, as if sensitivity, tactfulness, and flexibility were insufficient, Berenice was allegedly endowed with other qualities that far exceeded the common mean. I already knew that she had a riotous sense of humor. What I didn't know was that she could survive on practically no sleep and proved to be something of a sensation on the dance floor night after night. Finally, Jan had found someone who could teach her how to salsa! Jan was also amazed at how Berenice, clearly enabled by her experience as a therapist, could talk to just about anybody. There'd been a couple of female architects who'd been vacationing on the island for years: Jan disliked them immediately, thinking that they were stuck up and acted as if they owned the place. But on the third day of their vacation, Jan came down for breakfast to find Berenice and the architects as thick as thieves and that they'd made plans to hire a boat. It turned out that the architects were fabulous people — the best. They promised to come and visit in the Fall. Jan brought me back some 100-proof rum, guaranteeing that with just one shot, I'd forget that I didn't like rum. Even though the Title IX case against Jan, which had been suspended during Spring Break, was about to start gearing up, Jan remained strangely serene.

I was sitting in my office when there was a tap on my door. Despite the fact that it was my office hours and that my office door was partially open, I nevertheless jumped and screamed, as per usual. I heard a laugh, and Thourelle popped her head in the door.

"I see your Exaggerated Startle Response is still going strong," she said.

"Sorry. No time to find an exorcist," I responded. Thourelle came in without being asked and sat at the chair beside my desk.

"What's up?" I asked.

I must've looked apprehensive. After all, Thourelle's appearance had hitherto augured disturbing news. She seemed to be aware of my apprehension because she immediately reassured me.

"Don't worry, I come in peace. Besides, I don't need an excuse, right? Isn't that the great thing about collegiality?" Thourelle asked wryly.

Yes, I had said that to her. And now she was giving it back to me, just like the henna. Thourelle really was quite funny.

"Exactly," I responded with a smile. "And so, colleague mine, tell me what you're working on now."

And she did. Apparently, she was returning to the Platonic dialogues to try and get a better handle on the relationship between Socrates and Alcibiades.

"I'm especially interested in the way Socrates posed as a suitor for Alcibiades but really wanted something else," she said.

"It happens," I responded, wondering if that descriptor applied to Hanif.

"Too true," she said. Then she looked at me at length, "Are you OK? Seriously. You look rather morose."

The question caught me off guard. Nobody had really bothered to ask me how I was feeling for some time. And I wasn't *OK*. The situation with Hanif was making me unsure of him, which made me unsure of myself. The more I thought about it, the more miserable I became. So when Thourelle asked if I was OK, for a horrible moment, I was afraid I was going to cry. Thourelle must've sensed my distress because she leaned across the desk to pat my hand. Somehow, that worked, and the tears were averted.

I smiled at Thourelle, and she smiled back.

"Heather, I'm here to ask you for a favor," she said. I must've looked apprehensive because she held up her hand and said: "There's no hidden agenda. I just wanted to introduce you to a graduate student. Are you free for dinner sometime this weekend?" she asked.

This gave me pause — not because I didn't want to accommodate Thourelle, because I did. Despite our latent rivalry, her past entanglement with Hanif, and the potentially explosive situation with

Jan, I'd found my way to liking her. It all began when I popped her in the eye. Seriously. I was impressed by her response: no outrage, just a wry acceptance of life's comedic nature. But the true leaven for our relationship was her Christmas convalescence — her grateful helplessness, her intelligent conversation, and her sardonic regifting of the henna. My former image of Thourelle as a strident self-aggrandizing shrew wasn't exactly off base, but it was beside the point. Whatever else Thourelle might be, I recognized that she was an original and valued her for that.

No, the reason that I hesitated over Thourelle's invitation was that I had yet to make plans with Hanif for the weekend. In other words, I was trapped by that self-induced paralysis which preys upon women: waiting for the man to make his move. Please don't judge me. You really don't need to because I'm already so ashamed. Hanif still said he loved me but was no longer taking up as much space in my life as last month — or even last week. It was understandable. I knew that Hanif was working very hard on an article based on his paper at the fetish conference. He'd gotten a "revise and resubmit" from the journal, which is almost a shoo-in acceptance, provided you revise according to the readers' recommendations. And Hanif was happy to comply. I'd read several drafts of the revised article, and it was going to be great. But Hanif wasn't satisfied yet, and it was taking up most of his time. Whenever I tried to see him, I felt like a humble petitioner. That was on my good days. On the bad ones, I didn't even try. I'm beginning to believe that all relationships have the power dynamics of a seesaw. If each of you takes turns being the one up and the one down, it was fun. But if one person is always up and the other always down, it's no fun at all. Hanif and I were stuck in our respective positions. He'd been up, and I'd been down for too long, and it felt wretched. But I hoped things would change.

Anyway, anti-feminist feminist that I am, I brandished what seemed to be my least desirable night to Thourelle, just in case Hanif came through for one (or even both) of the other nights.

"I'm free Friday. Would that work?" I asked.

"Beautifully." Thourelle was beaming. "You're a pescatarian, right?" I bobbed my head in acknowledgement. "Except octopus," I remembered. I had watched *My Octopus Teacher* on Netflix and had wept from beginning to end.

"Right. I saw it too," she said, apparently reading my mind with ease. "Anyway, I've finally discovered a place in town to buy seafood products that won't put our lives at risk."

Early Friday evening, I was in the liquor store taking an inordinate amount of time to choose an appropriate wine that complements seafood. Usually, I would've grabbed just any old bottle of white that was over twenty dollars. This time, however, I was reading the descriptions and taking note of the various accolades bestowed on a given vintage. Clearly, I cared a lot about what Thourelle thought of me; in fact, I'd spent almost as long getting dressed for her as I once had for Hanif. And just as I was reflecting on this interesting parallel, who should sidle up beside me but the man himself?

"Hey gorgeous," he said, giving me a kiss on the cheek.

"Hello, stranger," I responded. "What've you been up to?" I instantly started kicking myself in the psychic butt. Had that sounded like a reproach from a spurned lover? Because, in truth, it probably was, but I'd be damned if I wanted to be perceived as such. Hanif, however, didn't notice or acted as if he didn't. I'd frequently observed that he was something of an adept at interpreting every utterance in the manner that a former therapist had recommended: he knew how to stay on the surface if it suited him.

"I was thinking of calling you up to see if you'd like to go out for dinner tonight," he said.

Did *thinking of calling you up* imply that he had yet to make up his mind, or was he on the verge of doing so when he ran into me?

"Oh, that would've been great," I said. "Unfortunately, I have plans."

OK, *I have plans* is not very forthcoming. Was I being coy, or was I attempting to conceal the nature of these plans? Even I didn't know the answer to that one.

Whatever my intentions, Hanif seemed to bristle when he heard I had plans — or so I interpreted the ever-so-slight spasm that seemed to cross his face. But this was almost instantly succeeded by a look of benign jocularity.

"Where are you off to? Or should I ask, with whom? Do I need to call someone out?" he asked.

"No. It's purely collegial. I'm having dinner at Thourelle's."

The jocular expression flickered; underneath, I detected a backdrop of consternation.

"Oh, I see. A girls' night of confessions and massage. Since when have the two of you been so chummy?" He was clearly attempting a light tone. For the last few months, Thourelle was a topic we scrupulously avoided. He still didn't know about her Christmas convalescence. Nor did Jan, for that matter.

"She wants to introduce me to a graduate student," I explained, correcting his assumption while ignoring his question. But this parrying was frustrating and, I couldn't help feeling, beneath us. So, I ended up grabbing the first bottle of white wine in my line of vision.

"Got to run, or I'll be late. I'll give you a call," I said, looking over my shoulder as I progressed to the cash register.

I congratulated myself on my smooth getaway, only to begin wondering what I was getting away from. Was I attempting to avoid: a). more questions about Thourelle? b). possible reproaches for seeing her socially? Or, c). Was I afraid that Hanif, having ascertained that I was busy that evening, would make no effort to engage me at some other point over the course of the weekend? The C's have it. And since I was the one who'd said *I'll give you a call,* the ball was technically in my court. Oh fuck. I hate this defective detective method of analysis. My little grey cells were beginning to hurt.

"I'm so glad you could make it," said Thourelle, taking my coat. "This is Lisle."

Lisle and I shook hands. She was tall and athletic, with very striking eyes: large, almond-shaped, and sea-water grey. They were accented by beautifully expressive eyebrows. Her cheekbones were high, and she also had a high sculpted forehead. Her hair was long and black, with French braiding along the temples. But the color was a heavy, toneless black that made me think it must have been dyed. Maybe she was going through a Goth phase. Because her complexion was so fair, I suspected her original color was some variation of blonde. That would make sense since her name implied Germanic descent.

"Professor Bell, I'm so happy to meet you. I've read some of your articles on medieval pedagogy, and they're fabulous." Lisle had a slight accent, making me think that she was, in fact, German. I've never taken compliments well. My automatic reaction is to deflect them by detailing all the deficiencies in my work. But a colleague once told me (not very gently) to cut the crap because this only confuses people — especially graduate students. Thus, I forced myself to sit still and be gracious:

"Thank you."

"Your work was recommended to me by Professor Thourelle," she said, glancing at our hostess. "She couldn't say enough good things about it."

Thourelle and I exchanged smiles. I'd given her a copy of my book on pedagogy when it first appeared, but I always assumed that she hadn't read it. I've never considered Thourelle much of a fan.

Over a dinner of Italian Branzino and caper butter, I learned that Lisle was writing a dissertation on the instruction of girls in premodern Sussex and wanted me to be on her dissertation committee.

"In fact, I hope you'll agree to direct it. I know I haven't taken a course with you. I wanted to, but you were on leave during the second year of my coursework. I'd be happy to do a reading course or whatever you suggest so you can get to know me better," she said.

"If Professor Thourelle's already on your committee, I don't see why you need me, frankly," I said.

But at that point, Thourelle broke in. "Heather, it hasn't been formally announced, but I'm going to be leaving the university."

"Why?" I asked, feeling not just surprise but also some degree of distress. "I know you've had a run of bad luck, but it'll get better," I said. How do you reassure someone that the Chair of her department has stopped actively persecuting her?

Thourelle shook her head. "It's nothing like that. Tommy has been accepted for graduate school at Suadela U. Perhaps you didn't know, but I interviewed with them before I accepted the job offer here. After I withdrew from the search, it folded. So, before Tommy accepted the offer, I contacted a friend on the search committee, just in case they were interested. They were."

"Well, congratulations to you and Tommy. That's a great job and a great graduate program," I said, and I meant it.

Lisle had to leave relatively early because she was on a rowing team that met on Saturday mornings practically at dawn. She promised to send me her dissertation prospectus, and related pieces of writing, so I had a clearer sense of what she was doing.

"But, just so you won't be in suspense, I'll probably say yes," I added. She smiled gratefully.

After Lisle had left, Thourelle said: "I hope you don't have to rush off. There are a couple of things I wanted to talk to you about."

"I'm in no hurry," I responded. Once we were settled in the living room with our brandies, Thourelle said, "It's about Jan." When I opened my mouth to speak, Thourelle raised her hand to silence me. It was just as well. I had no idea what I might've said anyway.

"Please hear me out. I wanted to talk about the graduate students' Title IX against Jan. You've heard about it I take it?" Thourelle asked.

"Of course," I replied.

"Well, I feel dreadful about it. I'm going to try and make the students drop the suit," she said.

"If you could only do that, Jan would be eternally grateful, as would I."

Thourelle smiled. With her broad mouth and marionette-like chin, she looked like a coquettish cat. The impression was intensified by the way she was curled up in her Saarinen womb chair.

"Well, you're the one who should be eternally grateful because I'm doing it for you," she said.

"Doing it for me?" I asked.

"Jan's a neurotic bitch, if you don't mind my saying say. She's been gunning for me from the get-go. But you're a loyal friend to her, and I have to admire that. You're like Olivier to her Roland. I could use a friend like you," Thourelle said.

"Yet, you're going — now that we're finally becoming friends," I replied.

"So, you feel it too. We are finally becoming friends. And that's my main regret about leaving," she said, holding my gaze and smiling. "Why did it take so long? Why didn't we become friends right away?" she asked, shaking her head with frustration.

"Probably my fault. I'm envious and competitive," I responded.

"No more than I am," she said.

"OK, let's not compete about who's the most competitive," I entreated, which made us both laugh.

For the first time ever, I was beginning to feel comfortable around Thourelle. The evidence was that I was quite content sitting with her in silence, sipping brandy.

Then Thourelle asked abruptly: "Do you smoke dope?"

"Not since college," I responded.

"Do you want to?" she asked.

"Maybe. But I have to warn you that I get very silly when I'm stoned. I also become convinced that all my ideas are brilliant," I said.

"I can deal." She lit a joint and inhaled deeply. Then she walked across the room to where I was sitting on the edge of her authentic Barcelona day bed and handed it to me. I took a drag, held it, and then said: "Let the craziness begin!"

And crazy it was. Thourelle and I needed to be stoned to get over our carefully cultivated mistrust of one another. And then we had a blast. After playing Scrabble in Latin for an hour or so (it turned out she was pretty good), we discovered that we both loved dancing to Golden Oldies of all description.

"After we're married, I hope Tommy will teach me more about the contemporary music scene, but now I'm happy to wallow in the past," she said.

Thourelle hooked her computer up to a pair of tiny speakers, and we danced to the panoply of things that YouTube had on offer. Here's our playlist, at least as far as I can reconstruct. You can try it on your own. I've also included sound bites from our very stoned conversation, which, as I now remember from college, always seemed meaningful and portentous at the time but, on review, was idiotic.

As the guest, I was given first choice.

Heather's Choice: Eurythmics, *Thorn in My Side*

T: I love this song.

H: Really? It reminds me of you.

T: Why?

T: Can't remember.

Thourelle's Choice:* Buddy Holly, *Every day

T: Buddy Holly, Richie Valens, the Big Bopper. Can you believe that all that talent got swallowed up in a moment?

H: I think the world was being punished for something.

T: Punished? You medievalists pretend to be intellectuals, but I think you're all secretly religious fanatics.

H: Little Peggy March, *I Will Follow Him*

H: OK, here's some religion for you. I think that Peggy March was in a convent school when she wrote it. It's really about God.

T: That's crazy. I think this song has more in common with Tammy Wynette's "Stand By Your Man."

H: That's probably about God, too.

T: Jay and the Americans, *Come a Little Bit Closer*

T: I should get a turn to lead. You're only a couple of inches taller.

H: OK.

H: Gary Puckett and the Union Gap, *Young Girl*

H: Does it worry you?

T: Does what worry me?

H: That Tommy is so much younger than you?

T: Nah!

H: You're a good lead!

T: I know.

[Then the music got slower]

T: Lee Hazleton and Nancy Sinatra, *Some Velvet Morning*

H: What's this song about? Who the hell is Phaedra?

T: I used to wonder whether he said, "I'm going to open up your "gait" as in a horse's gait, or "gate" like a garden gate.

H: Well, which is it?

T: In the video, Hazleton's riding a horse. So, I guess it's a double entendre.

H: But that means he's singing the entire song to his horse.

T: Like William IX of Aquitaine.

H: The first troubadour. What about him?

T: Didn't he write a poem to his horse?

H: I can't believe you knew that.

H. Neil Young, *Wrecking Ball*

H: I never used to like slow dancing.

T: Why not?

H: In high school, guys were always pressing their boners against my thigh.

T: Good reason to dance with women.

H: Yes, sirree Bob!

T: I like Emmy Lou's version better.

H: Neil's pain is more authentic. *[Pause]* I'm really stoned.

T: Don't worry. You can stay here.

T:* Leonard Cohen, *Hallelujah

T: Two Canadians in a row.

H: All that cold makes them so soulful. Afraid of dying of hypothermia.

T: But neither Neil Young nor Leonard Cohen can sing.

H: So what?

H: Bobby Gentry, *Ode to Billie Joe*

T: Wow, that's a real blast from the past.

H: I figure this is about infanticide. Or do you think late-term abortion?

T: Not sure. Don't tell the evangelicals. They'll appropriate it.

H: We should all honor Bobby. She was one of the first women to produce her own songs.

T:* REM, *Everybody Hurts

T: What's the matter?

H: Turn it off. Please. That song upsets me.

Thourelle didn't ask why the song upset me or why I was sobbing. She just crossed the room to where her computer was perched on the credenza and turned the music off. Then she returned to me and took me in her arms, rocking me gently. I eventually stopped crying, and Thourelle led me to the daybed. I lay down and let the night's silence engulf me. When I awoke early in the morning, she was curled up beside me — happily nestled in my armpit. I usually thought about her as Thourelle, not Sylvia. The name Sylvia was so sweet, so lilting, so elven that it didn't seem to fit someone that formidable. But right now, she looked like a Sylvia: a fragile, sylvan creature who'd crept out of the forest into my arms. I looked at her for a long time, trying to recognize in this diminutive creature, who resembled a sleeping child of indeterminate sex, my erstwhile foe. My enemy was sleeping. My enemy had disappeared.

I slowly got up, kissed the top of her head, and tiptoed out.

As I was unlocking my car, I was accosted by Hanif. How long had he been out there — waiting for me and watching? Neither Thourelle nor I had thought to draw the living room blinds.

"What on earth are you doing here?" I asked.

"I might ask you the same thing," he said. His voice was quiet enough, but it was the kind of quiet that vibrated with barely suppressed anger. The only other time I'd seen Hanif angry was also over my contact with Thourelle.

"You knew I was coming here for dinner," I said.

"Yeah, but I didn't know you were planning to stay the night and fuck your brains out," he answered.

I was stunned that Hanif was speaking to me that way. He said other hateful things, but I can't remember exactly what. Once upon a time, when I had a summer job as a cocktail waitress, an angry customer swore at me, calling me a whore, and much worse. The world began to spin, and I almost fainted. That's how it felt this time. What was strange about Hanif's outburst was that it didn't seem to come from a place of possessiveness or jealousy. As unseemly as such emotional alley cats may have been, they were nevertheless familiar. But this anger was different and more primal: it seemed closely linked with fear. I wasn't sure what sparked Hanif's fear but could only imagine that it was associated with what Thourelle might've told me about him, along with the attendant concern that I believed what she said.

I started to get into my car, but Hanif grabbed my arm to hold me back. When I managed to wrench it free and clamber into the driver's seat, he took ahold of the handle and wouldn't let me close the door.

"Hanif, where's this coming from? Do you really want me to call the police?" I asked, more frightened than I was letting on. Wordlessly, he closed the door, and I drove off.

When I got home, I was still feeling dizzy. The first thing I did was turn my cell phone off. I didn't want to speak to Hanif; I didn't want to know how many times he tried to call me; I didn't want to listen to ferocious voice messages or apologetic texts. And I especially didn't want to know if he didn't try to contact me. Even so, I knew that such self-imposed measures of isolation were only temporary. Hanif and I had gotten close enough and gone in deep enough that we couldn't just end our relationship with all these ragged edges. Besides, I couldn't get rid of the foolish notion that there was a reasonable explanation for Hanif's behavior and that all would be well. This misplaced optimism wasn't exactly accessible to me; it was lurking somewhere deep in my psyche like a hunted animal. I knew that when I found it, I'd do my best to kill it.

Chapter 24: Spellbound

It was a cinematic dream. I was watching myself from the outside, like a character in a movie. There was background noise but no dialogue — only a voice that resonated inside my head. First, I saw myself in my father's hospital room, sitting on a chair beside his bed. He looked emaciated; his skin had assumed a yellow pallor. His hands rested on top of the blankets, painfully thin with prominent veins. A needle from an IV was stuck in his left hand. I watched him sleep for a long time until it was time to leave. There was somewhere else I had to be. As I leaned over to kiss him goodbye, he opened his eyes. I was wearing a pair of black onyx earrings framed by marquisettes, which seemed to have caught his eye. He reached up with his free hand, gently touching one of the earrings, and smiled. *Everybody hurts,* the voice said. And I realized that my father must've hurt a lot and that, whether he'd ever managed to love me or not, he'd done the best he could.

Suddenly the scene changed, and I saw myself as I must've once appeared in my early twenties when, long ago, I was trekking in Nepal. I was following the ancient caravan route from the valley of Pokhara to the heights of Muktinath, nestled in the shadow of Annapurna. I could only see myself from behind, ascending the stone steps: the black T-shirt, the purple cotton shorts, my long auburn hair caught up in a ponytail, and the backs of my Lady Gorilla hiking boots. I'd entered a forest with towering rhododendron trees and a fast-moving river. The light filtering through the trees flashed different hues of green as it illuminated leaves, lichens, moss, and water. All the while, a voice was repeating the names of the villages I'd passed through along the way over and over again: *Phedi, Naya Pul, Ghorapani, Tatopani, Tukuche, Marpha, Jomosom.*

When I was nearing the top of the stairs, I saw Marcel standing above me. He was gazing at me in a compassionate and infinitely loving way — the way he used to look at me when we were still in love. I passed Marcel and kept ascending the stairs until I met Hanif. The sun was behind him, creating a halo effect around his head, making it look as though he were on fire. I stopped walking. At first, Hanif appeared sad. His face was downcast, and he wouldn't meet my eyes. But then he looked at me directly, nodded to himself, and waved me on.

Eventually, the steps ended. I'd arrived at the shrine of Muktinath, where an eternal flame burns on top of the water. The voice said: *You don't need any of them.* And I was filled with a sense of utter contentment.

The phone woke me up.

"Heather, did I wake you?" It was Berenice.

I looked over at the clock and started. It was 9:30 a.m. I must've slept in! Then I remembered it was Saturday.

"I have to get up anyway," I said as I swung my legs over the side of the bed.

"Are you free for dinner tonight?" and before I could answer, she added: "Just you."

"Yes, I'm free and, no, I won't bring anyone," I said.

"Not this time anyway, if that's alright with you," Berenice said apologetically.

It was quite all right. Chances are that I had no one to bring anyway. The plan was that Jan and I would come over to Berenice's around 7:00 p.m.

The weather was warming up, so I decided that it was time to do some tequila shots and swung by the liquor store. When I got to Berenice's place, Jan's car was already there. It was Jan who opened the door, and I could see right away that she was in a festive mood. She handed me a glass of prosecco, and we sauntered into the kitchen to watch Berenice make a seafood paella.

Over dinner, I found out why Jan was in such high spirits.

"Thourelle intervened and got the students to drop the Title IX suit," Jan said gleefully, raising her glass.

"But how? I thought that once a case was opened, it was pursued to the bitter end, no matter what," I asked.

"Usually, yes. But this case was different. Thourelle told Sally Field that the graduate students had misinterpreted what they saw at the shower," said Jan.

"Misinterpreted how?"

"They didn't understand that the dance drama was intended as one of the extracurricular events attached to Thourelle's course. This one was about polyamory, and I was part of the event. My role was Lilith, Adam's first wife, who didn't know about the polyamorous situation between the three figures on stage. The purpose was to underline the importance of being ethical about polyamorous relations: a poly has to get the consent of their sexual partners before engaging with others. Lilith had been kept in the dark and was understandably perturbed. And that was the Original Sin: a breakdown in trust," said Jan proudly.

"How very theological!" I responded, laughing. "And the other charges? "

"Gone!" Jan was almost singing the word. "My efforts to get people to testify about the Jack and Jill simply reflected my determination to stay in role," she said.

This seemed like an ingenious alibi: Daniel Day-Lewis had stomped around like Lincoln for a couple of months in preparation for playing the role. Jan was more scrupulous still, allegedly staying in character for weeks after the performance was over — for unspecified reasons of great psychological depth.

Jan's alleged efforts to have Thourelle disciplined for the presentation involving the love-saw were also dismissed. Apparently, Thourelle confessed that she herself had not been properly forewarned as to the exact nature of the performance enacted by Dr. Smith and Regina Canal. She was stunned when the President didn't come down on her like a ton of bricks and thought that it would've been, arguably, justifiable had he done so — not necessarily for the nudity or explicit sexual content, but because she hadn't been in command of the class material, which was pedagogically irresponsible.

"Aren't you glad you let her live?" asked Berenice.

Jan grinned and gave her the finger.

"I've got to show Heather the list," Berenice said, looking at Jan with a broad grin on her face.

"Please don't!" Jan pleaded, shaking her head.

"Come on, Jan. It's fabulous. It's not fair to keep it to ourselves," Berenice responded, jumping up from the table.

"What list?" I asked.

Berenice had already disappeared into her study before Jan could stop her. She returned with two sheets of paper and handed one of them to me. I read:

10 Ways to get rid of Sylvia Thourelle
1. denounce her to the Dean for corrupting her students

2. push her down the stairs or hire someone to push her down the stairs

3. generate invidious gossip so that she feels so uncomfortable in her work environment that she resigns

4. write an Op-ed in the student newspaper in her name attacking Title IX and claiming that students and professors should be allowed to sleep together

5. send photoshopped nudes of undergraduates to everyone

6. tell the cleaning staff she has orgies in her office, so they won't the clean

7. release cockroaches in her office (like Michael Keaton in *Pacific Heights*)

8. hide speakers in her office so she hears voices in foreign languages

9. shove an empty hypodermic needle in her arm so that the air causes a heart embolism

10. administer an untraceable poison

"Such an amazing fantasy life. Jan, you're a therapist's dream!" Berenice said, laughing with glee.

I looked over at Jan, whose eyes were suddenly glued to the window. Berenice stopped laughing when she noticed how quiet we were.

"What's going on?" Berenice demanded, looking first at Jan and then at me.

Neither Jan nor I answered. I got up from the couch and walked around the room before turning to look at Jan.

"Only it's not fantasy, is it, Jan?" I asked in a low voice.

Jan, who continued to look out the window, didn't respond.

"I recognize them," I said, looking down at the list. "The denunciation to the Dean; the gossip; the Op-Ed; the photoshopped nudes; the orgies; the cockroaches. And then, of course, there's the untraceable poison. Right, Jan?"

Berenice's smile had faded. The room had become so quiet that I could hear the kitchen faucet dripping. Eventually, Jan turned away from the window and met my gaze.

"You've missed a few. I planted hidden speakers in her office, which played one of Hitler's speeches in a loop. IT never found the speakers because I removed them before they checked." Jan spoke in measured tones.

"What else?" I asked.

"Number 2. I didn't push Thourelle down the stairs, nor did I hire anyone to push her. But I did put oil on the steps," Jan responded.

"But what if someone else fell?" I was outraged.

"Very unlikely. It was just before Christmas. The janitorial staff were on holiday, and Thourelle was the only one still using her office. I also happen to know that it's only Thourelle and I that take the stairs, anyway," Jan said.

"What else did I miss?" I demanded.

"The hypodermic needle," Jan acknowledged sheepishly.

I suddenly remembered Thourelle holding her arm with the presumption of a spider

bite. "When she was in line at the liquor store?" I asked. Jan nodded.

While we were speaking, Berenice sat there in a state of shock. Then she said: "Jan, I had no idea. I'm sorry."

"Well, you must be one hell of an indiscreet therapist," Jan snapped.

Silence. Then, eventually, Jan said, in more conciliatory tones: "Bernie, I didn't mean it. I'm the one who should be apologizing. I'm so much better now because of you."

"Where did this list come from?" I wondered aloud.

"It was supposed to be a therapeutic assignment," answered Berenice. "When we first got to Cuba, Jan was so sullen and brooding — a real drag to be around. She couldn't stop talking about Thourelle.

So, I gave her a two-part exercise. First, I asked her to express her aggression toward Thourelle in writing; then she had to draw it."

"I'm so sorry," said Jan, looking at Berenice.

Berenice sighed. "Well, I'm sorry too. I just didn't realize that you were so unwell." I was impressed at how Berenice managed to avoid words like "sick" or "nuts."

Jan began to cry, and Berenice went over to sit beside her on the couch to comfort her. Yet, as dire as the situation had been, it was finally over and in the past. Jan had not succeeded; Thourelle was still with us (admittedly, slightly the worse for wear), and Berenice's therapeutic exercises were hilarious. When I burst out laughing, however, the others looked as shocked as if I'd been chortling at a funeral.

"Come on! Don't keep me in suspense. I want to see the drawing," I said.

Berenice looked over at Jan.

"Well, there's no point in hiding it now," Jan said.

So, Berenice handed me the second sheet of paper. "That's Thourelle in the center." She pointed to a stick figure with a red-haired brush cut and a grey triangle of a dress. "These smaller pictures are the different methods of annihilation."

There was a series of circles surrounding the red-haired figure. Each contained a small picture: a staircase, a hypodermic needle, a cockroach, a bottle of poison, etc.

"What's this one?" I asked, pointing to three stick figures, which appeared to have snakes emerging from their mouths.

Jan looked over my shoulder. "That's Number 3: invidious gossip." She pointed at the snakes.

Apparently, Jan was even more artistically challenged than I was.

"Thank God, I'm better now. Please, please try and forget that I was ever so crazy. Do you both forgive me?" Jan asked earnestly.

"Of course," Berenice and I said simultaneously.

We watched as Jan burned the incriminating list and its companion illustration in the fireplace. I was sorry to see the picture go. It would've looked great in my therapeutic art collection.

"It's over now, and time to move on. Besides, we have things to celebrate. Your Title IX woes are over, and Sylvia Thourelle is still alive," I exclaimed.

Jan had already unthawed the carrot cake from her aborted birthday party and brought it over to Berenice's. We lit the candles, sang Happy Birthday after the fact, and insisted that she make a wish. I'd been with Jan through many birthdays and, when it came to blowing out candles, she tended to be one of those people who thought about what she should wish for such a long time that everyone started complaining about how the wax was ruining the cake. This time, she clearly knew what she wanted because she unhesitatingly blew the candles out in one puff.

We were putting dishes in the dishwasher when I remembered that I'd left the tequila in my car. I don't think that either Jan or Berenice heard me return, but I could hear them.

"You should've told me," Berenice said.

"I know, but I'm a coward. I couldn't risk losing you," Jan responded.

Silence ensued. When I entered the kitchen, I interrupted the two of them in the midst of a passionate embrace. Though startled, they did not spring apart but stood together, with their arms still around each other, smiling at me.

"I guess this is the other piece of good news?" I asked, smiling back.

"We were planning to tell you after dinner," Berenice said.

They continued to beam at one another, holding hands. I was surprised but not surprised. Jan and Berenice had taken to each other so quickly that I can only think, retrospectively, that there may've been deeper forces at work. Anyway, it made me glow inside just to look at them together. At the same time, I couldn't help but feel a pang of envy.

"It happened in Cuba," Berenice said. Images of Clark Gable and Claudette Colbert in pajamas flashed through my mind.

"Don't worry. Nothing changes for the three of us," Jan reassured me.

I privately observed, however, that one thing had already changed: Jan's catarrh seemed to have disappeared.

"Of course, nothing will change," said Berenice. "We're a triptych. You brought us together, so you're the center panel."

The three of us embraced in a group hug. But I knew things had to change. After all, my two best friends had fallen in love. They were set on a new trajectory that couldn't possibly include me, nor should it.

"OK, I have a question. I knew both of you first. Why didn't either of you ever hit on me?" I asked.

"Maybe because of your weight ... Ouch," Jan complained, as I punched her arm.

I produced the tequila, and Berenice went to get shot glasses and limes. You probably can guess what comes next, if not the particulars. *Biba, Terviseks, Proost,* we shouted at the top of our voices.

Berenice's phone call that morning had made me forget the dream from the night before temporarily. But over the course of the day, it came flooding back, and I began to untangle what Freud had referred to as "the work of the dream." The dream had taken me back to my father's hospital room, where I saw, maybe for the first time, how he was only another frail human, like the rest of us. When he reached up and touched my earring, he was, in his own way, expressing appreciation, maybe even love, and I forgave him. Afterward, I saw myself trekking in Nepal decades ago. It was a period when I'd felt independent and whole — a time which I'd almost forgotten about. I needed to return to that time in order to rediscover what I'd once known, however briefly: *You don't need any of them*, the voice had said. And I didn't. I would be fine by myself without a man. Not just now but always.

I left Berenice's house around 11:00 p.m., hoping that Hanif was still awake. When I drove to his place, his lights were on, so I rang the bell. It took him a long time to open the door, but when he did, I noticed three things in quick succession: there were two wine glasses on the table, April's shoes were by the door (I never forget a woman's shoes), and Cary Grant's voice was coming from the bedroom. An awkward scenario, to be sure, but in the end of all, it didn't matter. I knew what I was here to do.

Hanif put both his hands on my shoulders and looked deeply into my eyes: "Heather, thank God. I've been trying to reach you. I was worried. Then I fell asleep watching a movie," he said.

I didn't say anything.

"My behavior was completely out of line at Thourelle's. Will you forgive me?"

I didn't say anything.

"Heather, please say something," he entreated.

I forced myself to respond. "I do forgive you. I'd already forgiven you. But are you really going to leave April stuck in the bedroom like that?" I asked.

Hanif was clearly taken aback, wondering how I could've discerned her presence. Meanwhile, April, like an actress waiting in the wings, emerged from the bedroom, a bit disheveled. Somehow, she managed to look ashamed and triumphant at the same time.

"April and I were both at loose ends tonight. So, she came over. We were watching *Suspicion*. She'd never seen it," he said, looking over at April for support. But April already had her shoes and coat on and was gliding out the door.

April had left the movie running. I could hear Lina screaming as Johnnie appeared to be pushing her out of the car into a deep ravine. Lina was an idiot. Hanif must think I'm an idiot, too.

"Did Thourelle tell you anything?" he asked.

I didn't say anything.

"I've got a right to defend myself," he insisted.

I didn't say anything.

"It was just a fling. April doesn't mean anything to me," he maintained.

I didn't say anything.

"Heather, give me another chance. When you seemed unsure of me, I suddenly became unsure of you," he said plaintively, tears springing to his eyes.

I didn't say anything.

"Will you give me a chance to explain?" he asked.

But explanations were the last thing I wanted. I didn't want to know if he was involved with Sylvia, Paolo, Anna, April or anybody else. I didn't care.

"Please say something. Get angry, at least," he implored.

"I'm not angry. I understand," I said. And that was true.

"Let's start over. I know we can fix things," he responded.

I just shook my head.

"Heather, please don't go. I love you. I still want to marry you."

Marriage. The card that always trumped the lonely-hearted. Maybe Hanif was sincere or thought he was being sincere, in which case he was as sincere as he was capable of being. I don't know. In fact, I've come to accept that there's a lot I'll never know about Hanif. He was beautiful, original, quick-minded: already a prodigy as a graduate student. And academics of every orientation fawned over him. Who could blame him for coming to believe in his own legend? The many sexual opportunities that presented themselves were on a continuum with the other kinds of recognition that were lavished upon him. Why should he resist them? If this was who Hanif really was, his sins were but venial, although he would only bring misery to anyone who looked to him for stability. Hanif was but another version of Marcel.

I'd twice caught a glimpse of a darker Hanif, however. This one was something of a chameleon who had, at times, made himself sexually available to academic mentors in a position to help him. That wasn't so bad, I suppose. But this more craven Hanif bore a disturbing resemblance to the person Thourelle had warned against: someone who couldn't stand to be thwarted; someone susceptible to wrath, perhaps even violence; someone who could all too easily become Johnnie Aysgarth to his masochistic Lina.

"Goodbye Hanif. Please don't call me."

I started moving toward the door, looking back at the remarkable man I was leaving behind. A man with enough panache to dress himself and the rest of the world with style. A man so poignantly young, so compelling, so promising, and yet so disappointing.

"I'm so sorry if I've made you unhappy," he said as I stepped over the threshold.

"Never mind. Žižek says happiness is for wimps," was my answer as I shut the door behind me.

Chapter 25: Bon Voyage

About a week after our sad night of leave-taking, Hanif put my copy of *Suspicion* in my office mailbox. There was no note, but he also left a copy of Engel's novel, *Bear*, and this made me laugh. I read it that very night only to discover that a love affair between a woman and a bear could be not only gripping but extremely erotic. Critics were divided over its merit: on the one hand, it was beautifully written, totally unique, and won the Governor General's Award — the highest literary award in Canada. On the other hand, it read like high-end porn for women, the only problem being that the male lead was a bear. The book probably had a heightened impact, given my newly wrought singleness. I identified with Lou: a woman, alone with her books, who felt so isolated that she turned to the animal world for solace. Yet this bizarre liaison led to her spiritual rebirth.

Maybe I should get a pet.

I'm joking! The book was undeniably disturbing, but at least I didn't find myself worrying that I was a zoophile. In fact, I was becoming more appreciative of the infinite ranges of sexual expression and the complexity of orientation. Look at Jan and Berenice: they'd both had a series of heterosexual relationships, neither of them had ever been involved with a woman before and yet they fell passionately in love with one another in midlife. Both Hanif and Thourelle had a sexual fluidity that I had once found disconcerting but now seemed like no big deal.

It was the beginning of May and about three weeks since Hanif and I had parted ways. The only times I'd seen him during those weeks were at the last couple of departmental meetings of the year. It turns out that it's relatively easy not to run into someone, even if your offices are in the same building, as long as you're on different floors. Jan and Berenice knew that Hanif and I weren't seeing one another anymore, but not the details. They felt sorry for me, of course, but I think they were also secretly relieved.

Thourelle and Tommy were to be married at the beginning of June and would be leaving immediately afterward. Both Jan and I were invited to the wedding. Jan was almost superstitiously afraid to attend, fearing some kind of psycho relapse. I thought I might go, but hadn't yet decided. It's tough going to weddings on your own. If I did go, at least I could be assured that there was little chance of running into Hanif there.

For much of my career, I'd regarded Thourelle as both a rival and an amoral siren. But now I was sorry to see her leave. Not only had she become a friend, but also someone that I fervently admired. She reminded me that a truly successful pedagogue teaches students how to think. Learning new ways of thinking is always disturbing and, from this perspective, a real classroom could never be a "safe place" for the student. That's where passion enters the mix: the pedagogue's passion should ignite the student and breathe life into scholarly discourse. Passion is diffuse. It's not limited to the intellectual plane but manifests itself on emotional and carnal planes as well. Thourelle epitomized the unruly side of pedagogy. Like Socrates, she was a gadfly. The citizens of Athens had forced Socrates to drink hemlock for corrupting their youth; the Chair of the English Department had been on the verge of poisoning Thourelle for similar reasons.

Thourelle's last extracurricular seminar was on asexuality. It was a panel discussion involving four individuals, two women and two men, who all identified as aces. They began by discussing what asexuality was and the prejudices against the category itself. There was opposition from the medical world: while a greater range of sexual orientations was recognized by doctors and psychologists than ever before, asexuality was not among them. There was even dissension in the asexual community about whether asexuality was a sexual orientation in and of itself or a lack of orientation, and the members of the panel were split down the middle over this question.

Even so, they were all comfortable being included in the "Queer" category. The panelists also experienced their asexuality differently. One panelist, a heavily made-up woman in her early forties, had never felt either sexual attraction or romantic attraction to anyone and was still a virgin. Another panelist, a man in his twenties who was good-looking in a fraternity-boy kind of way, described himself as a gynesexual gray-biromantic, which meant that he was occasionally attracted to women or individuals who presented themselves as women but could occasionally feel a romantic attraction to more than one gender.

Thourelle and Tommy were also members of the panel. Thourelle described herself as a gray-pansexual aromantic. This meant that, though periodically attracted to others of all genders, she felt no romantic connection. (Hanif's diagnosis had been spot on.) Tommy, on the other hand, was a gray-pansexual panromantic, who was not sexually attracted to anyone, but could feel romantic attachments. This made me wonder if Thourelle's newly eroticized mode of dress was assumed in the hopes that Tommy's libido was not altogether absent but only dormant. Perhaps she was trying to stimulate it.

Tommy and Thourelle had first discovered one another online on an asexuality website several years ago.

"I was already an undergraduate here. We'd been chatting online for almost a year before we decided that Sylvia should fly into town to meet me," said Tommy.

"Our first official date was in Darby's, where we played pool. I had a beer, but poor Tommy wasn't old enough to drink yet." Thourelle exchanged a look with Tommy, and they both laughed.

In short, the rumor mill had it only half right. Thourelle may have slept with Tommy (or not) when he was an undergraduate, but he wasn't an undergraduate at any institution at which she was employed when they first became involved. They were already a couple before she accepted our job offer. In fact, the reason that Thourelle accepted the offer in the first place was because Tommy was here.

"Admittedly, sex is not always smooth going," Thourelle admitted, giving Tommy another salient look.

"Well, practice makes perfect," said Tommy with a smile.

"But as aces, we obviously didn't come together expecting your average heterosexual relationship, if there is such a thing. What brought us together is that we were two aces who both wanted children. That's also what made us decide to get married," said Thourelle.

If it all worked out, their children would be beautiful —especially if they took after Tommy.

Before the session broke up, Thourelle noted that this would be her last professional appearance at the university and that she wanted to thank her colleagues in the English Department for two wonderful years. As we applauded her (and her graduate students whooped and cheered), I wondered if her thanks were heartfelt. I'd asked Daniel to accompany me to the seminar for moral support in case I ran into Hanif. Despite his antipathy for Thourelle, Hanif made a point of attending these presentations. They were edgy and topical, so how could he resist? I spotted him a few rows in front of us, sitting beside a woman whom I initially assumed was April. Their heads were together and they were whispering to one another, just as one would expect of new lovers. But then the woman moved her head and I caught a glimpse of her in profile. It wasn't April after all: it was an attractive cultural historian from the History Department. She was around my age and, yes, being a petty person, I was jealous. But the fact that I was so easy to replace mitigated my jealousy. Poor April clearly wasn't in the running because she was still lacking in intellectual *gravitas*. Maybe Hanif and his cultural historian were destined to become that intellectual power couple that was the stuff of his dreams.

As I was exiting the auditorium, chatting with Daniel, there was a surprise waiting for me at the door. It was Dr. Owen.

"Good heavens, what are you doing here?" I asked.

That doesn't sound very gracious in retrospect. Dr. Owen was looking good. His hair had grown a little longer, he was slightly tanned, and he appeared to have lost weight. He didn't look like a Republican anymore. I glanced around for Daniel, but he seemed to have drifted discreetly away.

"Well, the talks are open to the public, after all, and they've been making quite a stir. I was curious and wanted to see for myself," he responded.

Dr. Owen had read all about the love-saw in the newspapers and was rather sorry to have missed that one. I nodded sympathetically as we moved away from the auditorium and walked over to the quad. The flowering crab trees were in full bloom, scattering petals like confetti on the people underneath.

"I thought there'd be a good chance of seeing you here, considering your interest in asexuality," said Dr. Owen.

He asked if I was free to go for a drink. I was surprised at the invitation but didn't see any reason to refuse. My social life had taken a huge hit over these past weeks, after all. It wasn't just that my relationship with Hanif had ended. Jan and Berenice, as determined as they were to include me in their lives, were still in the first flush of love and naturally needed some time to themselves.

Once Dr. Owen and I were established in a booth with drinks in front of us, we talked about the extra-curricular presentation we'd just watched. I also told him a little about Thourelle and Tommy.

"I wish them well. But if they're correct in how they characterize their orientations, it isn't going to be easy for them. There's also a sizeable age difference," he said, flushing ever so slightly. "I'm sorry. I'm afraid that must seem rather insensitive. I forgot that you were contemplating a relationship with someone quite a bit younger."

"That's over," is all I said.

I purposely left it vague so that he wouldn't know whether the relationship ended at my initiative. I hoped he wouldn't ask. I was still feeling rather raw and didn't want to go into details — especially with my former shrink, who hadn't anticipated a good outcome. I changed the subject, asking him a question that I'd been wondering about for the last few weeks.

"Dr. Owen, can EMDR keep working after you've stopped having sessions?" I was thinking both about my repetitive "anxiety dream" and my final dream that segued from my father to trekking. Both dreams seemed on a continuum with a process that had begun in Dr. Owen's office.

"I'm certain it does," he said, nodding. "Once the practice is underway, the patient continues the dream work."

I told him about my last dream, and this seemed to make him very happy.

"Yes! That's exactly right. You don't need any of them. And now you know you don't. It was always my hope for you," he said, beaming at me.

In fact, he looked so happy and approving that it was my turn to flush. His fervent approbation was too much for me. It was all I could do to stop blurting out, *Dr. Owen, stop! I'm still really fucked up.* But I didn't — partially because it seemed ungracious. He had, after all, helped me. Besides, such an abrasive rejoinder would only have led to more talk about me. Frankly, I was sick of me: thinking about me, talking about me. Me, me, me; always about me. As my sister might've said, I was a woman with an "I" problem. *So, let's talk about him*, I thought. I really didn't know much about Dr. Owen. Yet, somehow, it felt weird to try and elicit personal information from one's former psychiatrist. Then I remembered something I could ask.

"Dr. Owen, do you ever swim in that pond off your driveway?"

A slow smile spread over his face. It was a wistful smile, as if he were remembering something that was pleasant and painful at the same time. "You know, I used to swim, but I haven't for a long time."

I had no follow-up questions, but that didn't seem to matter. The silence that followed wasn't the least bit awkward. But eventually, I noticed that our glasses were almost empty, and he'd already paid the check. Our companionable silence couldn't last: as a chronically insecure person, I'm always afraid of overstaying. The pond was my one great conversational sally, and now it was time to go.

I started to say, "This has been nice," as I gathered up my things when he stopped me.

"Heather, I know that this might seem rather out of the blue. But would you consider going out to dinner with me sometime?"

I must've looked puzzled because he immediately added: "It's been over six months since your last appointment, and you're no longer my patient."

I now remembered that Berenice had checked to see if six months had elapsed before she would agree to have a drink with me.

"Has it really been six months?" I asked. It seemed like only a few weeks since my last appointment.

"Six months almost to the day. Your last appointment was just before Halloween. And so, what do you say?"

"Dr. Owen, just to be clear: are you asking me on a date?" I was not being coy; I really wasn't sure. Maybe he was doing some kind of follow-up study with former patients.

He laughed in a pleasant, self-deprecating manner. "Yes, I'm asking you on a date. But if you agree to go out with me, do you think you could call me something other than Dr. Owen?"

"Do you mean I should call you by your first name?" I asked.

He nodded.

"But I don't know your first name," I continued.

"It's Brian."

"Then yes, Brian. I'd like to have dinner with you."

Acknowledgements

I would like to thank Dori Elliott, Grant Faulkner, Susan Gubar, Laura Hein, Ruth Mazo Karras, Lee Macdougall, Sarah Maza, Jerome Singerman, Paul Strohm, and Gail Vanstone for their help with the manuscript. I am also indebted to my husband, Rick Valicenti, for the dynamic cover.

This is a work of fiction. Any resemblance to individuals, living or dead, is purely coincidental.

Made in the USA
Middletown, DE
17 June 2024